May 2017

LARKFIELD nR.

Books should be returned or renewed by the last
date above. Renew by phone **03000 41 31 31** or
online *www.kent.gov.uk/libs*

AF

4/16

Libraries Registration & Archives

CUSTOMER
SERVICE
EXCELLENCE

CSE

Kent
County
Council
kent.gov.uk

THE MYSTERY AT STOWE

THE DETECTIVE STORY CLUB

LIST OF TITLES

FURTHER TITLES IN PREPARATION

THE MYSTERY AT STOWE

A STORY OF CRIME BY
VERNON LODER

WITH AN INTRODUCTION BY
NIGEL MOSS

COLLINS
CRIME
CLUB

COLLINS CRIME CLUB

An imprint of HarperCollins*Publishers*
1 London Bridge Street
London SE1 9GF
www.harpercollins.co.uk

This edition 2016

First published by Wm Collins Sons & Co. Ltd 1928
Published by The Detective Story Club Ltd 1929

Introduction © Nigel Moss 2016

A catalogue record for this book is
available from the British Library

ISBN 978-0-00-813748-9

Printed and bound in Great Britain by
Clays Ltd, St Ives plc

MIX
Paper from
responsible sources
FSC™ C007454

FSC™ is a non-profit international organisation established to promote
the responsible management of the world's forests. Products carrying the
FSC label are independently certified to assure consumers that they come
from forests that are managed to meet the social, economic and
ecological needs of present and future generations,
and other controlled sources.

Find out more about HarperCollins and the environment at
www.harpercollins.co.uk/green

INTRODUCTION

THE Golden Age of detective fiction is enjoying a renaissance in popularity, demonstrated by the success of various publishing ventures. The British Library Classic Crime series has reissued works by obscure Golden Age authors, such as John Bude, J. Jefferson Farjeon and Alan Melville, with Farjeon's *Mystery in White* the surprise best-selling paperback of Christmas 2014. HarperCollins' major non-fiction study *The Golden Age of Murder* by Martin Edwards (May 2015) sold out its first printing within a few months, and their new editions of titles from the Detective Story Club, which first flourished back in 1929, are reintroducing a range of once hugely popular crime authors. Along with a number of small independent publishers, notably Black Heath, Coachwhip, Dean Street, Faber, Ostara and The Murder Room, coupled with the rapid growth in modestly priced e-books, these initiatives have led to the emergence of a new and appreciative modern audience for little-known and neglected Golden Age authors who have long been out of print.

The period between the two World Wars, which Robert Graves called 'the long week-end', loosely delineates the boundaries of the Golden Age. From 1919 to 1939, detective novels were published in an ever-increasing tide to keep up with a growing public demand for 'whodunits'. They were a reflection of the atmosphere and culture prevailing during that period. There was a strong desire to sublimate the horrors and devastating impact of the First World War, which had been followed by the Spanish flu pandemic, economic hardship (including the Great Depression), and later by an increasing international turbulence and prospect of yet further conflict. In response, people turned more and more to entertainment and escapism, and the new form of detective novel fitted the bill. Human activity, including murder, was described and analysed as a form of play or game—an artificial entertainment existing in a cosy, stylised world, removed from normal routine life. This literary game devised its own distinctive rules and conventions aimed at ensuring fair play between writer and reader. The focus was predominantly on producing stimulating intellectual puzzles and plots: clues and evidence were presented to the reader, with a challenge to solve the mystery before the *denouement* and the detective's masterful unveiling of the guilty party. It offered a welcome form of inward escape.

Typically, the atmosphere of these novels was brisk and business-like, the method of murder often bizarre. Characterisation was subordinate to the plot. Readers were not required to think too deeply or moralise, and psychology was largely absent. The actual commission of murder, with its violence and revulsion, was usually excluded from the narration. But this was not reality, rather an intellectual recreation. Margery Allingham commented on the form: 'a Killing, a Mystery, an Enquiry and a Conclusion with an element of satisfaction in it.' It was claimed these novels, with their rationalistic plots and cleverly crafted puzzles, helped to 'improve the mind'. A surprisingly high proportion of professional people and academics were among the readers, including British Prime Minister Stanley Baldwin and US President Franklin D. Roosevelt. Detective fiction of this era attained a high degree of respectability amongst the reading public on both sides of the Atlantic, and by 1939 detective novels accounted for 25 per cent of all new fiction published in English.

The distractions and pressures of today's world, with extreme violence and hardship forming commonplace daily images in both mainstream and social media, along with the persistent *noir* psychological themes and human depravity depicted in modern crime novels, have perhaps helped to rekindle the public's affection and enthusiasm for the Golden Age fictional world of intellectual plots and puzzles. Now, as then, at heart they offer light entertainment—an enduring appeal of solidity blended with facetious frivolity.

Vernon Loder was among the early wave of Golden Age writers. A popular and prolific author, he wrote 22 titles during the decade immediately preceding the Second World War. *The Mystery at Stowe* was Loder's first work, initially published in 1928 by Collins as a full-priced novel, and reissued the following year in their popular and eye-catching new sixpenny crime list, The Detective Story Club.

In the original Preface to this reissue of *The Mystery at Stowe*, the Club's editor, F. T. (Fred) Smith described Vernon Loder as 'one of the most promising recruits to the ranks of detective story writers'. While Loder was a firm believer that the task of the detective fiction writer was not only to mystify but to entertain, he realised that the key essential for success was brilliant detective work and made this the chief feature of the story. The setting is a traditional country house party, favoured by Golden Age writers and one to which Loder returned in several later novels. The action features a diverse group of party guests, and takes place mostly within Stowe House and its grounds. One of the guests is found dead in her bedroom at dawn, lying beside an open window. She had been killed by a small poisoned dart, found lodged in her upper back. Amateur sleuth Jim Carton is in the mould of the new breed of 'hero' detectives, arguably first modelled by E. C. Bentley's creation Philip Trent—intelligent and engaging, yet modest, sensitive and fallible. He brings the added expertise of having once been an Assistant Commissioner in West Africa, where he had investigated numerous criminal cases, and gained knowledge of the natives' subtle use of little-known poisons in committing murder using a blow-pipe and poisoned darts.

Whereas Loder's murder method had also featured a couple of years earlier in Edgar Wallace's *The Three Just Men* (1926), his mystery is intriguingly plotted and seemingly impenetrable, and red herrings and blind alleys abound. With twists and turns throughout, excitement and tension steadily mount, with a *denouement* true to Golden Age conventions. The finale is truly surprising and revelatory. One reviewer has described the solution as 'borderline genius yet utterly insane' (John F. Norris—Pretty Sinister blogspot, April 2013).

Stowe is a well-written and skilfully constructed story, which blends action, detection, human interest and romance to form a varied and effective first mystery novel. It also contains some witty dialogue and observations, with Loder's use of names and places which nod to other Golden Age writers and novels of the same period an amusing feature for genre enthusiasts.

Vernon Loder was one of several pseudonyms used by the hugely versatile and fecund Anglo-Irish author Jack Vahey (John George Hazlette Vahey), 1881–1938. In addition to the canon of Loder titles between 1928 and 1938, Vahey wrote initially as John Haslette from 1909 to 1916, resuming writing in the late 1920s as Anthony Lang, George Varney, John Mowbray, Walter Proudfoot and Henrietta Clandon. Born in Belfast, Jack Vahey was educated in Ulster and for a while in Hanover, Germany. He began his working life as an architect's pupil, but after four years switched careers and sat professional examinations with a view to becoming a chartered accountant. However, this too was abandoned, when Vahey took up writing fiction. He married Gertrude Crewe, and settled in the English south coast town of Bournemouth. His writing career was cut short by his death at the relatively young age of 57.

All of the Loder novels were published by Collins in the UK. From 1930 onwards, his works were published under their famous Crime Club imprint. Several of his early novels (between 1929 and 1931) were also published in the US by Morrow, sometimes under different titles. Loder had several series detectives—Inspector Brews, Chief Inspector Chase and later Donald Cairn—but Jim Carton makes his sole appearance in *Stowe*. The publisher's biographical note on Loder which appears in *Two Dead* (1934) mentions that his initial attempt at writing a novel (apparently never published) was during a period of convalescence in bed. Various colourful claims are made of Loder: he once wrote a novel on a boarding-house table in twenty days, which was serialised in both England and the US under different names, and published in book form in both countries; he worked very quickly, and thought two hours in the morning quite enough for anyone; also, he composed directly on a typewriter, and did not ever re-write.

Loder's entertaining and skilful novels are written in the simple, direct, smooth-flowing and occasionally jocular style favoured by Golden Age authors. His hallmark distinctives include complex and ingenious plots, full of creativity and invention, leading up to a major surprise and twist in the closing pages. A recurring theme often found in his works is that of the victim who falls prey to his own scheming. Despite his early popularity, Loder never quite achieved the first rank of detective novelists and the enduring status and fame which accompanies this, although original Collins jackets demonstrate that he was well-reviewed: 'The name of Mr Loder must be widely known as a reliable and promising indication on the cover of a detective story' (*Times Literary Supplement*); 'Successive books by Vernon Loder confirm the impression gathered by this reviewer that we have no better writer of thrill mystery in England' (*Sunday Mercury*); '. . . just the effortless telling of a good story and meticulous observation of the rules' (Torquemada in the *Observer*). Nevertheless, his works have remained out of print since the 1930s, and have been the purview of Golden Age collectors, among whom he has a dedicated following, with first editions scarce and commanding high prices.

Now Vernon Loder is emerging from obscurity—and rightly so. Despite the rather scant and cursory attention he has received in the major detective fiction commentaries, Loder has a number of proponents, including leading US writers on Golden Age fiction, John Norris and Curtis Evans, and deserves a better place in Golden Age posterity. I particularly recommend searching out some of his later titles—*Whose Hand* (1929), *The Vase Mystery* (1929), *The Shop Window Murders* (1930), *Death in the Thicket* (1932) and *Murder from Three Angles* (1934). Loder deserves to be rediscovered and enjoyed by a new readership, and this reissue of his important first novel *The Mystery at Stowe* augurs well for the revival of his popularity.

NIGEL MOSS
October 2015

CONTENTS

EDITOR'S PREFACE

MR Vernon Loder is one of the most promising recruits to the ranks of detective story writers, and this novel *The Mystery at Stowe* augurs well for his future popularity. He certainly knows how to provide a mystery baffling enough to satisfy the most exacting reader. He holds too a very definite opinion, with which we are wholeheartedly in agreement, that the task of the writer of mystery stories is not only to mystify, but to entertain. Consequently he has enlivened the more serious business of detection by the inclusion of several amusing characters.

But while appreciating to the full the entertainment value of the thriller, Mr Vernon Loder fully realises that nothing succeeds so well as really brilliant detective work, and that is the chief feature of his story. The reader may justly suspect every character of the murder of Mrs Tollard in that pleasant country house, and interest and suspense are cleverly maintained to the very last, when a well-engineered surprise awaits us. Jim Carton himself is a most interesting detective to follow. He is an unusual type and brings to the problem the fresh and alert mind of an Assistant Commissioner in West Africa. In that capacity he has investigated many criminal cases among natives. The fact that a tiny poisoned dart was found buried in the victim's back specially interests one who has special knowledge of African natives and their subtle use of little-known poisons in committing murder.

His experience had led him to support a theory that there were five primary motives for murder—anger, jealousy, greed, robbery and hate—and this test he applies in turn to the suspects in order to discover that most baffling thing in a murder case: a motive. Who? How? Why? These are questions which confront Jim Carton—and our readers.

THE EDITOR
FROM THE ORIGINAL DETECTIVE STORY CLUB EDITION
November 1929

CHAPTER I

WHEELS WITHIN WHEELS

'NED is full of vitality, and Margery hasn't a backbone even the X-rays could detect,' said Mrs Gailey, as she chalked her cue, and leaned over to take her shot. 'That's the trouble, I am sure, and if it wasn't for (Oh! rotten miss! I put on far too much side)—I mean to say only for her sweet temper, there would have been a dog-fight before this.'

Mrs Gailey, a vivacious brunette of about twenty-six, was known to be summary in her judgments, and better at jumping to conclusions than negotiating fences in the hunting-field. Miss Sayers, with whom she was playing in the billiard-room at Stowe, strolled round the table to where her ball lay, her face wearing an expression of mild scepticism.

'I don't see why there should be a quarrel, and I can't quite agree with you that she has a sweet temper,' she remarked. 'By the way, Netta, you've left me in a perfectly beastly lie under the cushion.'

She stabbed at the ball, and, by a marvellous fluke, effected a cannon. Mrs Gailey applauded ironically.

'I never heard her say a cross word in my life,' she observed.

Nelly Sayers played a losing hazard, and looked up when her ball rolled gently into the pocket. 'That doesn't prove anything either way. I don't say she has a bad temper. I only say we can't call it sweet till we know.'

'Wait till you're married,' said Mrs Gailey, with a wise look, 'you get different ideas of life.'

'I expect you do. You married people think we are a positive danger to your dear husbands. We have even to be careful where we smile.'

1

'You may smile at mine, when he comes down,' said her companion, laughing, 'but there is something in what you say. Margery is one of us, and we're bound to look on Elaine Gurdon as a poacher.'

Nelly Sayers foozled an easy pot, and came round. 'That strikes me as awfully silly. It isn't Elaine's fault that she is handsome, any more than it is yours.'

'A thousand thanks,' smiled Mrs Gailey, looking at her ball. 'Go on! I like to hear that sort of thing.'

'At any rate, she is jolly good-looking, and she has seen things and done things I should have funked.'

'But she has no nerves, and she enjoys it. She wouldn't be happy living all the year round in civilisation. If you enjoy anything there is no hardship in it.'

Miss Sayers sat down on the bank. 'I don't say there is. What I mean is this. She travels in all sorts of wild places, and has made one or two discoveries. But she hasn't the cash to go on.'

'I thought she wrote books?'

'So she does, but I suppose they don't make enough to keep her, and cover the expenses of travel as well.'

While she spoke, Mrs Gailey made twelve, and glanced up with a smile at the scoring-board, where apparently she only needed fifteen more for game.

'She might go to her bank for it.'

Nelly Sayers shrugged. 'Banks aren't too generous. In any case, Ned Tollard is only financing her expedition for the fun of the thing. He's interested in South America. Isn't he a director of the Paraguayan railway?'

'I don't know. I suppose so. But it sounds odd, and I know, if my husband spent half the day consulting a woman like Elaine Gurdon about maps and routes, and things of that kind, I should feel pretty hot about it. That's why I say she has a sweet temper. She never says a word, but sometimes I have caught her looking at Ned in a sad way.'

Nelly Sayers made six, and broke down. Mrs Gailey took her cue, deciding to risk the pot which would take her out.

'I expect she is like me. She doesn't think there is much in it.'

'Perhaps not. Oh! I've done it. That makes game, and I'm going into the garden. Coming?'

'No, thanks, I must write a letter.'

The house of Stowe, at which they were both staying for a week, had once belonged to a family more noted for warlike fame than wealth. Unlike the builders of the famous house of the same name, they never rose to be great lords or mighty men in the world. Stowe itself was really a very large manor-house, and the family had only parted with it in the nineties, when it had passed into the hands of Mr Magus, a miser and recluse, on whose death it had been sold to the present occupier, Mr Barley.

Mr Barley was fat, and fat-pursed. Rumour had it that he was extremely vulgar, but he was in reality a good-natured man who had not enjoyed a decent education, and was well aware of it. By sedulous cultivation he had picked up all his aitches, and learned to swallow those unnecessary ones that occasionally rose to his lips. He liked society, and though he never ranged in the higher branches, he was able to fill his house with decent people of the upper middle-classes, who could enjoy his hospitality without feeling or showing too open scorn for the humble upbringing of their host. Some of the younger guests did indeed call him 'Old Barley,' but most of them liked him, and some were not averse from accepting the tips he gave them with regard to finance.

At the moment when Mrs Gailey and Miss Sayers were playing a game of billiards, the house had only a few guests. Chief among them was Elaine Gurdon. Single, handsome, known as the heroine of an expedition into the wilds of Patagonia, and an enterprise which had penetrated the Chaco, she was sufficiently famous to secure a pretty regular place in the photographic galleries of the illustrated weeklies, and the chairmanship of gatherings at women's clubs, when travel was the topic.

Associated with her, occasionally in scandal of an ill-natured kind, which had originated in his offer to finance her next trip, was Edward Tollard. He was thirty years of age, a vital, good-looking fellow, fond of exercise and all open-air sports, and a junior partner in a banking firm. He came of a family that had enjoyed money for several generations, a kin that was neither bookish nor artistic, and his marriage, three years before, to Margery the daughter of Gellis, the impressionist artist, had surprised most of his friends.

Those who set store by Old Masters said that Margery was a Botticelli come to life; others said she had never really come to life at all. She was pretty, in a pale way, with very fair hair, blue eyes, a sensitive mouth, a long oval face. She looked excessively fragile, though she was rarely ill, and was in every way a strong contrast to her athletic husband.

There were also in the house, the two billiard players; a Mr and Mrs Head, who were inseparable, and had only one thought between them—bridge. Last came Ortho Haine, a young fellow who was much nicer than his unusual Christian name; and a little old lady reputed cousin to Mr Barley, called Minever. Mrs Gailey's husband was coming down for the week-end with several other people.

It is perhaps the fate of Botticellis come to life to look reproachful in a gentle way. That set of countenance in Margery Tollard, combined with the fact that her husband was proposing to finance Elaine Gurdon's next trip into the wilds, had given rise to gossip.

Margery did not hunt, or go out with the guns in the season; she did not care for walking, or yachting, or games. Her function in life was ornamental. She pleased the artists, and made sportsmen furious. This necessarily made a kind of breach between her and her husband, not an open breach it seemed. But, as he needed exercise and enjoyed it, there were a good many days when they were apart.

People said he was indulgent enough, would even accompany her to private views, where the pictures must have made him bite his tongue; to artistic functions, of a social kind, where he looked like a healthy tree among sickly saplings.

Then Elaine came back from her last pilgrimage, full of new plans. He had known her since she was a mere school-girl. He was interested in exploration, and in the country she had visited. He discussed the next trip with great interest, and, hearing that its success depended on finance, offered to help.

She had written a book, and was giving a series of lectures. If the proceeds of both left a deficit on the sum needed for the future, he was to make it up. Margery objected. She did not tell her friends, but she objected very much even to a Platonic partnership between her husband and the explorer.

Elaine Gurdon instinctively felt this trouble. She knew Margery, and never failed to call to see her when she was in town. They were at opposite poles in thought and action. Margery disliked her; Elaine had sometimes an impulse to shake the pale, shadowy, young woman she felt to be such a drag on Ned Tollard.

'If she even made an effort, I could forgive her,' she had told Nelly Sayers, 'but she won't move. She's the most selfish woman I know.'

That was indiscreet, but she was a woman who spoke out on occasion, and Nelly laughed.

'She certainly might buck up.'

The projected expedition was one to the hinterland of Matta Grosso, and as it was planned out, the expenses necessary to success seemed to mount daily. Elaine confessed that she would need five thousand more than her book and her lectures were likely to earn, and Tollard was willing to give that sum. But, first, they went into it together, to see where expenses could be cut down. Elaine insisted on that.

'I haven't much of a business brain, Ned,' she said to him. 'I know what I might spend, but I don't know what I need not. Then I want your advice about the route. I could cut out the last bit of the trip if necessary.'

At first it was decided that the consultations should take place at his house, but that was not a success. Margery was a sulky third, visibly impatient with their consultations, and ended by suggesting to her husband that they might be held elsewhere.

Mr Barley, having never been out of England in his life, had a fancy to be a patron of some foreign enterprise which should bring him into the public eye. He had heard some of the prevalent gossip, and asked Elaine down to stay with him, with two motives. She was lecturing at Elterham, and he had to be chairman. He had asked her as a favour to bring with her some of the many curios she had acquired in the trip through the Chaco, good-naturedly saying that he might be disposed to invest in some of the rarer objects for the adornment of his hall and library.

It was in part his second motive, an altruistic one, that had led him to invite Margery and Ned Tollard at the same time. A bachelor himself, he hated to see married people uncomfortable, or at loggerheads, and was preparing a plan to ease what he had heard was the tension in Tollard's menage.

Just about the moment when Mrs Gailey went out into the garden, and Miss Sayers went up to her room to write a letter, he intercepted Elaine Gurdon in the hall.

'Tollard gone out, Miss Gurdon?' he asked, beaming on her in his fat way, 'or have you another consultation on?'

She returned his smile. 'I think he and Margery drove over to Elterham. She wanted to order some book.'

'Good. Then I can annex you, Miss Gurdon, and have a little chat, if you don't mind.'

'Not a bit,' she said, her brown eyes twinkling, 'I am becoming quite a good saleswoman, you see. But, really, I find you are not such a shrewd buyer as I imagined.'

'I don't bring that home here,' he said, opening a door off the hall. 'Come along into the library, and have a cigarette with me. I have a little scheme I have been worrying out, and I'd like to hear what you think of it.'

She followed him, and he drew forward a comfortable chair for her, then closed the door, and came to stand with his hands behind his back in front of the empty fire-place.

'Now those curios I bought from, you are most interesting,' he began, when he had seen that her cigarette was alight. 'They mean a lot more to me than to you, for I never had the chance to go abroad when I was young, and I am too old for it now. It's a great thing that you can get about to all these strange places, and extend our knowledge, so to speak. Jography I have always been interested in, and now, it seems to me, I have a chance to get connected with it more directly.'

'I'll be glad to have you with me, Mr Barley,' she laughed, 'if that is what you mean.'

He smiled admiringly. What a fine woman she was, he thought. 'No, that isn't it exactly,' he said. 'I was thinking more of money. You want it, we have it, as the advertisements say!'

CHAPTER II

WHAT THE MORNING BROUGHT

FOR a few moments Elaine looked at him in silence. A little twitch showed itself at the corner of her mouth, and was gone. Her lips tightened a little, her gaze became speculative.

'What does that mean exactly?' she asked, when her silence had made him fidget, and uneasily stir his coat-tails behind his back.

He cleared his throat nervously. 'Nothing more than what I say, I assure you, Miss Gurdon. I hear that a good deal of money will be wanted for your new expedition. I'd like to have a hand, if not a name, in it.'

'You are suggesting financing me?' she said bluntly.

He nodded, relieved. 'That's it. I should like to. Name your figure, and I'm on. It would be a pity to spoil the ship for the sake of a hap'orth of tar.'

She considered that for a moment. She knew that the trip would be an expensive one. Barley had plenty of funds.

'Perhaps you haven't heard that Mr Tollard is backing me?'

He coloured a little, and she knew at once that someone had been talking. Her glance became slightly hostile. He fidgeted again, puffed gustily at his cigarette, threw it behind him into the fire-place, and smiled apologetically.

'Well, I understood so. Yes, decidedly I knew that. At least, I was aware that he was standing some of the expense.'

'What then?' said Elaine, and now she held his eyes, and her own had grown hard and challenging.

'My dear girl,' said Mr Barley, with symptoms of discomfort in voice and manner, 'now we come to a point that has been causing me some distress.'

'But does not directly concern you, perhaps?' she demanded.

'Not directly—no. But we are all friends here. I hope we are, and, er—'

'You think it unwise of me to accept financial help from Mr Tollard?' she interrupted fiercely.

'That is more or less what I meant to say,' remarked the kind old man. 'It may sound crude to you, the more so, Miss Gurdon, because I am not sure that you realise what people have been saying.'

'Or don't care?' she fired out.

'In this world we have to care,' he said gently. 'I'm old enough to be your father, my dear, and I tell you that we have to pay some attention to what others say, even if we have given them no cause to say it.'

'That simply isn't true!'

'Excuse me if I say it is. If not for oneself, there are others concerned. We never live quite alone and detached in this world. I was thinking of Mrs Tollard. She may be a weak woman, and a foolish, but I feel sure her husband's interest in this expedition gives her pain. Then she is aware of the gossip. There are always people about who are anxious to tell young wives what others say of their husbands.'

Elaine got up. 'I don't think I care to continue this.'

He reached out a fat hand, and put it on her arm. 'Do hear me out. I am sure you are everything that is discreet. Tollard too. I am quite sure of it. If I weren't, I should not insult you by saying what I have said. Look at it this way. You and Mr Tollard are old friends. You are interested in the same thing. No one of sense thinks otherwise, but his young wife has perhaps some of the natural jealousy we find in folk who haven't been brought up to keep a hold on themselves.'

Elaine's lip curled. 'You describe her neatly.'

'Very well then, is it worth while to sow discord between husband and wife, when you can avoid it by stepping the other way? Look at it that way. Let me give you a cheque for your work out there, and tell Tollard you need not trouble him. No one will know what I have just said to you.'

Elaine shrugged. 'It won't do at all. I know you mean well, but it won't do. Mr Tollard would see through it at once. It would be as blunt as telling him that I thought we were in danger of falling in love with one another. I refuse to take that attitude. Margery is a little fool. I hope she has not been complaining to you?'

'Not a word,' he said awkwardly, 'but I hear talk. I wish you would think it over. If on no other grounds, you might give me the pleasure of associating myself with your important exploration. It's a weak spot in me. I'm a bachelor and without anyone to carry on my name. I should like to be known as one who did a bit in the world.'

She shook her head. 'I am sorry. It is quite impossible. It would be an insult to Ned—to Mr Tollard. It would even seem to some a confession that there was something wrong. You must see that.'

'Mrs Tollard looks most unhappy,' he said.

'It's her own fault,' Elaine cried hotly. 'She has a pose. I detest her, if you must know! Like all the silly, backboneless creatures in the world, she thinks if she sits back in a chair, and smiles wanly about her, people will kneel at her knees all day and worship her. I refuse to pamper her wretched emotions. Mr Tollard and I have never been anything but good friends. I need not tell you I don't love him, or he me. I needn't say that a woman of my type who loved a man would not be as discreet as I have been.'

'I shouldn't have thought of asking,' he said simply.

'Then why should this miserable weakling parade a misery for which she has no justification, Mr Barley?' she cried hotly. 'She will end by making herself a laughing-stock, and ruining her husband's life.'

'Well, think it over, think it over,' said he, disconcerted by her vehemence. 'I am sure I meant no harm. It was just a thought of mine. I hoped it would do good. I hate to see folk unhappy.'

'I know,' she said, throwing away the stub of her cigarette, 'but I am afraid I have given you the only answer I can. Do you mind if I leave you, and go into the garden? I need a breath of fresh air.'

'Not at all. You have been very patient in listening to me,' he returned. 'I have a letter or two to write, so go by all means.'

Bitterness sat on Elaine's lips as she left him, and went out through the French window into the garden. Anyone watching her now would have understood, the spirit, the resolution, the fiery energy, which had carried her through a hundred perils. Poor old Barley was like the rest of them. Whatever he said, he was afraid Ned and she were on the edge of a precipice, dallying when they ought to have stepped back to safety.

As she crossed a strip of lawn, she heard a car come up the drive. As she turned the corner of the house she saw Tollard at the wheel. His face was white and set. Margery, beside him, had her eyes down, but she was white too, and drooping.

'The Madonna-lily pose!' Elaine said to herself angrily.

Neither of them appeared to see her. Tollard got down, and offered a hand to his wife, his face averted. She refused it, with a delicate shrug.

Elaine went away hurriedly. Tollard gathered up his wife's bag and books, which she had left on the seat, and followed her into the hall. She went upstairs without turning to look at him. In her fragile figure there was a lassitude that would have enchanted her Chelsea friends. Her pale face was that of a *Mater Dolorosa* of an Old Master.

Tollard put down books and bag on a chair, and looked about him uncertainly. Then he pushed open the door of the library, and greeted Mr Barley; who was not writing letters after all, but sitting in a chair, smoking and reflecting.

'Got what you wanted, Tollard?' he asked, turning to look at his guest. 'Good. I have been having a chat with Miss

Gurdon. I wanted her to let me have a share in the expedition, but she won't hear of it.'

Tollard shrugged. 'We have arranged that all right. By the way, Mr Barley, I shall have to go up to town this afternoon. Some urgent business I had not counted on. I am sorry to have to go in such a hurry.'

Mr Barley bit his lip. Surely Elaine had not had time to see Tollard and warn him? 'Just as you like, my dear fellow,' he replied. 'I suppose Mrs Tollard will stay on?'

Tollard nodded hastily. 'Oh yes. It's a personal matter. I felt sure you would understand.'

Mr Barley thought he did understand. Tollard was a man of fresh colour, and now he looked pale and tired. There was something up. Perhaps he and his wife had quarrelled. Surely it couldn't be a pre-arranged thing between him and Miss Gurdon? Elaine had told him bluntly that she did not love this man; but, if she did, she would hardly blurt it out.

'Perhaps you are going to make some arrangements for this expedition,' he said, hoping Tollard wouldn't resent his curiosity.

'No. Nothing. We have pretty well settled the thing now, and I have my own affairs to attend to. Miss Gurdon may set out at any time.'

Mr Barley nodded, reassured. 'All right. I had hoped to take you all to see Heber Castle this afternoon, but I can count you out. You must try to come down again soon.'

'I wonder what Barley is after,' Tollard said to himself as he left to go upstairs to his bedroom. 'And I wonder what he thinks. Some of those cats—'

He stopped there, and went upstairs quickly. As he passed the door of his wife's room, he heard her moving about with her slow, light tread. He shrugged, and did not go in.

He left at half-past two for town. By three, the other guests had filled two cars, and set off for Heber Castle, a show place in the neighbourhood that was open to visitors. Mrs Tollard did not go with them. She pleaded a headache, and did not come down after lunch. Mr Barley went in one car, with Elaine Gurdon, Nelly Sayers, young Haine, and Mrs Minever. Mrs Gailey, the two Heads, and a friend who had dropped in, took the other.

'I thought Margery looked awful at lunch,' said Mrs Gailey, as they drove along through the sun-soaked country. 'What a pathetic face she has.'

Mr Head grunted. 'I don't know really why she tries to play bridge. She has no idea of any conventions, and seems to think that the whole game consists in doubling.'

'Perhaps that is why she looks pathetic,' said the friend, with a smile.

Mrs Head frowned. Bridge was no subject for humour. 'She might think of her partners,' she remarked severely.

'And now Ned is going off suddenly,' said Mrs Gailey.

The friend grinned. 'There's the reason for the pathos. Young wife, departing husband! Why, some of them weep buckets!'

'Tollard looked a bit fed-up too, I thought,' observed Mr Head. 'Last night he muddled every hand.'

'Blow bridge!' thought Netta Gailey. She wished she were in the other car with Nelly Sayers, who could talk of interesting things without introducing some detestable hobby. In the other car, Miss Sayers was also seeking information.

'Mr Tollard left in rather a hurry,' she said to Mr Barley. 'Business, I suppose?'

'Men always have business for an excuse; we women are not so lucky,' grumbled Mrs Minever.

'Business,' agreed Mr Barley, avoiding Elaine's eye.

'If I had such a jolly pretty wife, I wouldn't let any business take me away,' said Ortho Haine enthusiastically.

'A single man doesn't know what a married man may do,' said Mrs Minever.

They picnicked in a lovely dell, duly made the tour of the castle, and returned in good time for dinner. Mr Barley's first duty on reaching home was to enquire after Mrs Tollard's headache. She herself was not yet visible, and her maid told Mr Barley that she was not sure if her mistress would leave her room that day.

'I hope she is not really ill,' said he solicitously.

'Oh no, sir. But she has a blinding headache, and will be glad if you will excuse her at dinner tonight, sir.'

'I shall have something sent up to her. You might perhaps ask her if she would care to see a doctor. I could telephone for Browne.'

'No, thank you, sir. She told me to tell you not to trouble, only please to excuse her.'

'Mrs Tollard will not be down tonight,' he told his guests, when they assembled at dinner. 'I should think it must be a touch of neuralgia myself.'

All expressed sympathy, though Elaine's face wore a look of slight scepticism, as if she doubted the cause of the *malaise*.

'She did look seedy this morning,' said young Haine.

'She is a pale type,' said Mrs Minever.

After dinner, Mrs Minever, the Heads, Mr Barley, and the Heads' friend, with Elaine and Ortho Haine, decided for bridge. Nelly Sayers wanted Mrs Gailey to go with her to the billiard-room, where they could discuss Margery and her neuralgia to their heart's content, but a fourth was wanted for the second table, so she sat down with a book.

At half-past eleven the last rubber had been played, and Mrs Minever closed her bag, and got up. She was followed by Mrs Gailey, Elaine, and the others, the Heads lingering almost to the last to discuss some incident in the evening's play. Then they too disappeared, and Mr Barley was left alone with Haine, who was yawning heavily.

'Fine woman, Miss Gurdon,' he said to his host, raising a desultory hand.

'Very,' said Mr Barley. 'Brilliant even. I have a great respect for her.'

'Doesn't seem to be much love lost between her and Mrs Tollard,' drawled Haine.

Mr Barley frowned. 'Oh, I shouldn't say that. But you're tired, Haine. What about bed?'

'Bed it is, sir,' said Ortho obediently. 'Good-night.'

Mr Barley retired last, looking thoughtful. Half an hour later, and the house was quiet. It was a still and warm night. Isolated in its park, there were no sounds from the main road that bounded the grounds on the south side.

Mr Barley fell asleep at twelve. He had tired himself speculating about Tollard and his wife. They would come round in time, he thought. These tiffs were a part of many married lives.

He was awakened about half-past five next morning by a sound. It seemed to him low but penetrating. He sat up in bed, and listened. A soft thud followed. He got out of bed, slipped on his trousers, slippers, and a dressing-gown, and was about to go out into the lobby when there was a knock at his door.

'Come in,' he said, in a disturbed voice.

He thought it might be his man. To his surprise it was Elaine Gurdon.

She wore moccasin slippers, and had on a silk dressing-gown over her night-dress. Her hair had been loosely coiled on top of her head, and held there by a long obsidian pin, with an amber head. He noticed that she was very tense, though she was in perfect control of herself.

'What's the matter?' he stammered.

She put a finger on her lips. 'Don't rouse anyone yet. Come with me, please. Mrs Tollard is very ill. She may be dead. I have just come from her room.' Mr Barley tried twice to speak. His face was ashen. He trembled as he stood staring at Elaine. Then he followed her out of the room, and down along the passage to the bedroom occupied by Margery Tollard.

CHAPTER III

THE DRESSING-GOWN

THE bedrooms on the right side of the lobby faced south. The one occupied by Margery Tollard had a door communicating with that formerly used by her husband, which was, of course, empty since his departure.

Still silent, but much shaken, Mr Barley followed Elaine Gurdon to the door, watched her turn the handle, and push the door open. Then he advanced ahead of her into the room.

Something in the posture of the figure that lay face upwards on the floor near the window told him that Mrs Tollard was dead. He stopped to stare for a few moments, passing his hand agitatedly over his forehead. Then, accompanied by Elaine, he went forward and looked down into the dead face.

It looked haggard and tormented, the lips drawn back from the teeth in an ugly way. He shuddered.

'I must send for the doctor at once. I don't understand what can have happened. Will you help me get her on to the bed?'

Elaine shook her head doubtfully. 'I don't think it wise. I have seen many dead people before now, and this doesn't look natural.'

'You can't mean murder?' he asked, his jaw dropping.

'I mean we had better leave her where she is,' said Elaine. 'Telephone at once to the doctor, and to the police. That is the only thing to do. I shall stay here until they come, or until you return.'

'Please do,' he said. 'I suppose we shall have to tell the others? Shocking affair, dreadful, awful! But I must telephone. That can't wait.'

He hurried out of the room, and slipped downstairs. He was anxious to alarm no one just yet, and at that hour most of the guests were wrapped in heavy sleep. It took him some time to get a reply from Dr Browne's house, but, when the sleepy man at the other end of the wire heard what had happened, he assured Mr Barley that he would drive over at once.

Mr Barley next rang up the police station. Another short wait here. Then he heard the sergeant's voice, hurriedly told him of the tragic event, and went upstairs again.

No one had been disturbed. Elaine was standing looking out of the window when he returned to the room. A great deal was required to shake her nerve. She had seen death too near, and too often, to lose control.

'You will notice that this window is wide open, Mr Barley,' she said in a low voice, as he went to her side, 'top and bottom.'

'So was mine,' he said, rubbing his hands nervously together. 'It was a very hot night.'

'At all events, remember it,' she said, so significantly that it rang in his head for long after. 'Is the doctor coming?'

'Yes, and the police sergeant. Dear me! Dear me! What ought I to do? The people here will be alarmed. Will it be wise to defer telling them?'

'For the present, yes,' she said.

'And later on I could make arrangements for them to go.'

She shook her head. 'The police may want to see them all.'

The thought of the police worried him. 'I think I must lock up this room then. We can't stand here. I don't like it. If we could have put her on the bed, it would have been different, but she looks terrible lying there.'

'Very well,' said Elaine. 'It's lucky most of the others are sleeping in the other wing of the house. Only Mr Haine is in this—beside my room, and her husband's.'

'Poor Tollard!' he said, 'I had forgotten him. What a blow it will be! How he will reproach himself for being away. But,

Miss Gurdon, surely it's possible she died naturally? She was not well yesterday, had a violent headache, and did not come down later—'

She touched him on the shoulder. 'We shall see all that later. We had better lock up this room. I must get dressed, and you too. The doctor might be here in a few minutes.'

He turned to the door. 'You are so practical. Yes, I must dress at once. I am sure Browne will be shocked when he sees her. But we mustn't talk here.'

He let her out, followed himself, withdrawing the key, and locking the door from the outside. He was far more disturbed than Elaine, unusually shaken for such a stolid and experienced man.

'Don't tell the others till after breakfast, if you can avoid it,' she whispered, as they parted outside her room.

He shook his head mournfully, and went off to complete his dressing. He did not shave. As he put on his collar he suddenly remembered that Miss Gurdon had not told him why she had gone into the dead woman's room. He supposed that, like himself, she had heard that extraordinary sound, and the thud. In the light of what he now knew, it occurred to him that the latter noise must have been the sound of Mrs Tollard's fall. In that case her death must have taken place at the most a few minutes before Miss Gurdon came to tell him that something was wrong.

That this should happen was troubling enough of itself to the good host and kindly friend, but in addition he had a liking for Mrs Tollard. It may have been that her rather pathetic face and air appealed to him; or her habit of speaking to him as if he stood in some protective relation to her. At all events he felt her death deeply.

He was sorry for Tollard too. The man had not seemed very happy of late. Probably there had been some slight marital differences, but these things fade away in the face of death. Ned would be horrified when he learned what had happened.

It was as well that most of the guests slept well that morning. One or two may have heard the doctor's car drive up, but at that early hour no one thought anything of it. Mr Barley, in a fret of impatience, let the doctor in, asking him to be as quiet as he could.

'A good many guests,' he added anxiously.

'I see,' said Browne, in a quiet voice. 'Will you lead the way, Mr Barley.'

Barley took him upstairs. In the passage near the door of Mrs Tollard's room, Elaine Gurdon stood waiting. Barley whispered an introduction, Browne bowed, looked curiously at Elaine, whom he had heard lecture, and waited till Mr Barley had unlocked the door.

He advanced into the room, and bent down to look at the dead woman. Mr Barley stopped near him, his heavy face quivering. Elaine slipped in, but remained near the door, her face intent.

Dr Browne pursed his lips, studying the face of Mrs Tollard carefully. Something he saw in it seemed to check him in an impulse to lift the body.

'Just a moment,' he whispered over his shoulder to Mr Barley.

Mr Barley stepped gingerly over to him, and listened to a few rapid words that Elaine could not catch. But, watching the doctor's moving lips, she thought she saw them shape the word 'Poison.'

'Yes, we had better wait for the sergeant,' replied Mr Barley.

Through the open window they heard a slight crunch of loose gravel. The doctor stepped over, glanced out, and nodded back at the others. Barley took this gesture to mean that the police sergeant had arrived on his bicycle. He left the room softly, but hurriedly.

Browne looked at Miss Gurdon. She approached him, and put a question in a low voice.

'What do you think? She was not very well yesterday.'

He shrugged. 'I prefer to say nothing for the moment.'

She nodded, and went back to where she had stood before. In a very short time Mr Barley ushered in the sergeant, who tried to cover his excitement by looking very grim and important. This sort of case had not come into his hands before.

He and the doctor spoke together in whispers for a few moments. Then, between them, they raised the dead woman into a sitting position, supported by their arms, being careful not to disturb the position of the lower portion of the body.

As they raised her, Dr Browne removed one arm suddenly, and glanced at the sergeant. 'Something here,' he said softly. 'Can you hold her yourself for a moment, sergeant? I felt something against my sleeve.'

The sergeant did as he was bid. Mr Barley stared eagerly at the two men. Elaine drew herself up, and seemed to be frozen by some sudden thought.

Browne put a hand to a spot beneath Mrs Tollard's left shoulder-blade, made a gentle plucking movement, and stared at something he held between his fingers. It looked to the others like a dark wooden sliver, or long thorn. The sergeant opened his mouth, restrained an exclamation, and fixed his eyes on this strange object.

'Lay her back again, please,' said Browne, his voice troubled.

The sergeant complied. Browne rose to his feet, and approached Mr Barley.

'If you will leave the room, and Miss Gurdon too, please, I will make an examination,' he said.

'But what is it?' stammered Barley.

'I am unable to say yet,' said the doctor.

Mr Barley, greatly shaken, advanced to Elaine, and told her that they must both retire. She nodded absently, and went out with him. The door was shut.

He turned to her when they were in the passage. 'Will you come down to the library, Miss Gurdon? We can't talk up here. There has been enough noise already.'

'All right,' she said. 'But, if I were you, I should telephone to the superintendent at Elterham as well. The sergeant does not impress me.'

'And to Tollard,' he assented. 'Dear me! Dear me! This is indeed a tragedy.'

He went downstairs to the telephone, and Elaine to the library. If it struck her as odd that the elderly and experienced business man's nervousness contrasted unfavourably with her own poise and practicality, she bestowed no further thought on it.

She was sitting smoking a cigarette when Mr Barley returned.

'I couldn't get Tollard at his house,' he said, 'but the superintendent is coming at once.'

'Good,' said Elaine, 'the sooner the better.'

He took his favourite attitude before the fireplace, and now his coat-tails positively swung like leaves in a gale.

'I believe that Browne has discovered something terrible,' he said. 'He found something. It may have been some species of weapon, though it was very small.'

'I had a glimpse of it,' agreed Elaine.

'It looked like a splinter, or a long thorn,' he said.

Elaine did not reply for a few moments. She appeared to be thinking quickly, trying to come to some decision. Then she looked him full in the face, and made an observation.

'I thought I recognised it. But we can make sure very easily. If I am not mistaken, you put up a trophy of some of my curios in the hall. We'll have a look at it now.'

He gave her a puzzled look, then nodded. 'I don't know what you mean, but we can go there if you think it will help us.'

She rose, threw her cigarette into the grate, and preceded him into the hall.

On one of the walls, at a considerable height from the ground, hung a small trophy of South American Indian arms. Chief among them was a blow-pipe and a little receptacle for darts.

'Get a step-ladder,' said Elaine, as he came behind her, and followed her glance upwards.

He stood still for a moment, his brows knotted, then went off. When he came back with a light step-ladder he had got in the kitchen, he began to adjust it.

'Lucky the servants have their own stairs,' he said in a low voice. 'I have asked them not to begin cleaning in this part of the house till I tell them. Grover was just coming down when I stopped him.'

She nodded assent, placed the step-ladder near the wall and mounted it before he could, stop her. With a quick hand she detached the miniature quiver for darts, and brought it down.

'There were six, weren't there?' she asked.

He gaped, beginning to see her point, then nodded vigorously. 'Yes. But surely—'

She took out the darts from the receptacle with the utmost care. 'I really ought not to have let you have these,' she murmured, 'but it can't be helped now.'

'There are only five,' he said, staring at the venomous things in her hand.

She nodded grimly. 'Just five. Now we know where we are.'

Mr Barley's eyes grew wide with horror. 'Then you think that thing upstairs—?' he began.

'I am sure of it,' said Elaine.

'But they were not poisoned surely?' he gasped. 'The other day, you know, you showed us how that pipe was used.'

Elaine nodded. 'The chief from whom I got those had a couple of dozen made for me. The poisoning is a later operation. Naturally, I used harmless darts.'

'Good heavens!' he cried, 'is that what you meant about the window being open?'

She nodded. 'I have seen people shot with those poisoned darts. Something in her face reminded me. But wasn't that a door opening upstairs?'

He left her, and went upstairs. He returned in a few minutes, followed by the doctor and the police sergeant. Elaine had removed the step-ladder by that time, and was standing near the door of the library. Mr Barley opened that door, let the two men in, and signalled to Elaine to accompany them.

'Sit down, gentlemen,' he said, when he had closed the door. 'Please sit down too, Miss Gurdon.'

They sat down. Dr Browne looked at Elaine, and then at Mr Barley. 'Well, Mr Barley, I am sorry to say that my conjecture was only too true. An alkaloid poison seems to have been the cause of death, and I have no doubt it had been placed on the point of the little sliver of wood I found implanted just under the left scapula, the shoulder-blade of your unfortunate guest.'

Mr Barley shot a glance at Elaine. 'I have telephoned for the superintendent at Elterham. He is coming. Perhaps we had better wait for him before we go any further.'

Dr Browne shrugged. The sergeant nodded. 'Very well, sir, that might be best. But perhaps I could make a few notes now.'

'Most of my guests are still abed.'

'I suppose so, sir; but you might tell me how you came to know something was amiss.'

'That, of course, I can do,' said Mr Barley, and coughed nervously. 'After that, if you will both be good enough to remain in this room for a while, I shall have breakfast sent into you. You see, I have the guests to consider. I should prefer not to alarm them now, but to inform them of the tragic event when they have breakfasted. They will then be at your disposal.'

Browne shrugged. The sergeant nodded again. Mr Barley went on: 'As for myself, I heard a curious noise a little while ago. It seemed like a sound made by someone in pain. It was followed by what seemed a dull thud. I got up hurriedly to dress, when I heard a knock on my door.'

The policeman noted that down. 'Yes, sir?'

'It was Miss Gurdon, who had come to tell me that Mrs Tollard was dying, or dead. It appears she had heard the sound, and gone in to see what was the matter.'

The doctor and the sergeant turned their eyes quickly on Elaine Gurdon. She nodded, her eyes anxious, but not afraid.

CHAPTER IV

A CURIOUS THING

Elaine Gurdon's aplomb had been the admiration of her friend. It had never been more apparent than now.

'Don't you think, on the whole, it would be wiser to—to allow the superintendent to hear my statement?' she asked, in a low but clear voice. 'It will save going over it twice. I did, of course, find Mrs Tollard dead, as Mr Barley says, but any light I may be able to throw on it may be better exhibited to your chief, sergeant.'

He plucked at his lip uncertainly. He was not very sure of his powers in a case like this, and it was unlikely in the end that the detective force in Elterham would allow him to take the thing up.

'As you please, Miss,' he said.

Mr Barley seemed about to say something; perhaps with reference to the darts, but a glance from Elaine stopped him. This glance was not noticed by the sergeant, who was putting away, his note-book, but it did not escape the doctor's eye.

In the end, it was agreed that breakfast should be sent into the library for the two men, Mr Barley was to inform his guests of the ocurrence after breakfast, and, on the arrival of the superintendent from Elterham, everyone in the house would be questioned as to their knowledge of the facts that might bear on the tragedy, or their (more probable) ignorance of anything throwing a light on it.

Only Dr Browne was slightly dissatisfied. He thought Elaine too calm and self-possessed for the occasion, and he could not forget how, at her lecture, he had seen her exhibit a blow-pipe, and tell her audience that, on occasion, she had shot birds for the pot with this primitive weapon. An idea in his mind that the alkaloid poison which had killed Mrs Tollard might be the well-known woorali, more scientifically known as curare, at once made the connection. There are few doctors who do not know how this poison was first used.

Added to that was her desire to postpone her statement, and the fact that it was she who had found Mrs Tollard dead. It was, it is true, not very obvious why she should prefer to tell her story to the superintendent, but it struck him as rather queer. The sergeant, of course, did not see that. He was a slow-thinking man, who could only get through routine duties.

He and the sergeant breakfasted together, the latter apologetic and ill at ease, until Browne assured him impatiently that he had messed in the trenches next a one-time convict!

Superintendent Fisher was slow in coming. The guests had assembled for breakfast when he came, accompanied by a detective-inspector of the Elterham force. They were shown into the room where the dead woman lay, and Mr Barley set to work with a heavy heart to play the host.

'Isn't Mrs Tollard coming down?' asked Ortho Haine, who had become rather a hero worshipper.

'No,' said Mr Barley awkwardly, 'not now. By the way, Haine, I'd like to hear what you think of my cook's new way of doing kidneys.'

Someone laughed, the transition was so rapid, but Haine, who was not imaginative, looked at his plate.

'I thought it was new to me—rather jolly effect, I should say, sir. What do you think, Head?'

'Quite piquant,' said Head. 'We must try this way at home, if your cook will give us the tip.'

So breakfast blundered on. When it was over, and the various guests were on the point of scattering, Mr Barley got up. He was very red in the face, and trembled a little.

'I have something to say to you all,' he began. 'Do you mind following me into the drawing-room? It's rather—er—important, and, well, I'll tell you there.'

The guests exchanged startled or amused glances, but followed him to the drawing-room, where they disposed themselves to listen.

Mr Barley opened his mouth, muttered one or two broken sentences, and turned appealingly to Elaine.

'Will you tell them, Miss Gurdon?'

They all stared with open eyes at Elaine, who rose, and glanced round. Her face was very pale, but her voice was measured and unemotional as she began.

'A tragic thing has happened,' she said. 'Poor Mrs Tollard died last night—or this morning, I should say. Please let me go on. We are afraid that something more is involved. I am sorry for Mr Barley, and sorry for you all, but the police are investigating. They are in the house at this moment. I think that is all Mr Barley wished me to say.'

For a moment there was a dead silence, then an uproar of voices broke out that Mr Barley had the greatest trouble to subdue. The two friends Miss Sayers and Mrs Gailey were in tears, Ortho Haine was demanding to know what had happened. Mr and Mrs Head (not very sure if they had a grievance against Fate or Mr Barley) were debating the question of leaving at once, while old Mrs Minever, without the slightest warrant, was saying that she had always known something would happen.

In all their minds was a general feeling that Elaine's composed demeanour and clear speech was a sign that she lacked heart. Or, perhaps, that is too sweeping, for Miss Sayers was a champion of Elaine's, and, when she had dried her eyes, grateful for the latter's calmness, which had prevented a general attack of hysteria.

Mr Barley looked about him pleadingly. 'Please, please!' he begged, 'I feel it as deeply as any of you. It is most unfortunate that this should have happened in my house, and at this time, when I have you with me. But we must face the fact. In ordinary circumstances I should not attempt to detain you here, but as it is, I must ask you to stay for a little.'

He seemed to have recovered himself again, but the Heads had not.

'My dear Barley,' said the husband, 'I am sure we can be of no use. We—'

Mr Barley raised his hand. 'It has nothing to do with me. The police will insist on examining all who were in the house at the time of Mrs Tollard's death. But I am sure it will be more or less formal.'

'I think Mr Barley is right,' said Haine. 'We all ought to help.'

'Of course,' said Mrs Gailey quickly.

The Heads at last assented with an ill grace, and Mr Barley told them all briefly what had happened. 'I shall ask the superintendent to put any questions he has to ask, as soon as possible,' he ended. 'It is a very serious matter.'

'Has anyone wired for Tollard?' asked Haine.

'I telephoned early, without result, and I have wired since. Now, if any of you would like to go to your rooms, or do anything in the matter of packing, please do. But you must be ready to come down when the superintendent asks for you.'

The Heads fled upstairs at once. It was a dreadful thought that they might have to go without their bridge for a day or two. They were not really callous people, but unimaginative, and obsessed by cards. Mrs Minever went behind them, full of her prophecies, and Ortho Haine went up to talk to Mr Barley. Elaine disappeared next, and Miss Sayers and Mrs Gailey, arm in arm, sedulously whispering, drifted out into the sunny garden.

'What does it mean?' asked Nelly Sayers, when they were out of earshot. 'It sounds beastly.'

Mrs Gailey nodded. She was very excited, and her eyes shone. 'Simple enough. Someone evidently hated her, and poisoned her. What a good thing it is Ned Tollard had gone.'

Her companion opened wide eyes. 'My dear Netta! What do you mean?'

'Nothing against Ned,' said the other hastily. 'Only you know how people talk. I thought Elaine was dreadfully calm. If I had been asked to tell the news, I should have simply blubbered,' she added.

'But you aren't used to speaking in public,' said her friend. 'Elaine is. I thought it was fine of her. You could see poor old Barley was simply dithering. In any case, Margery wasn't her relation. She never cared for her. If you and I were frank, we should say that we weren't really upset so much by Margery's death as by the way it was done. I am sorry for the poor soul, but I am sorry for a good many people.'

'Oh, I liked her. I agree with Ortho that she was very patient and really sweet, though she never said much to me.'

'Well, it doesn't matter much now,' observed Miss Sayers. 'The thing is, who killed her? I didn't quite follow what old Barley said about a dart. I don't think he was very clear, do you?'

'Oh, I got that part. Don't you remember a few days ago we were out on the lawn, and he asked Elaine would she show us how the savages fired off those blow-pipes?'

'Of course I remember.'

'And she did. Ortho said he never knew a woman could use one, and Ned said he didn't see why not. Even if it was a question of blowing hard—'

Miss Sayers nodded. 'He made a joke about women blowing their own trumpets nowadays. I remember—Go on!'

'Well, she brought out some little darts like thorns, with what looked like a bit of cotton-wool on the end, and hit the cedar with them several times.'

'But if she had missed, and hit one of us, we might have been poisoned too!'

'I don't think she would use that kind. I expect she has some without any poison.'

Miss Sayers nodded gravely. 'You mean it was one of the poisoned ones they found in poor Margery?'

'I am sure he meant that. When you said people talked, I thought of that at once.'

'But why should you, dear?'

'Well, we know it was Ned's business with Elaine's expedition that annoyed Margery.'

'But surely no one would be so wicked as to suggest—'

'Oh! wouldn't they? I don't know that it is wicked either. The police will fish about for evidence, and a motive, and they will know it was Elaine who had these darts, and knew how to use them, and it was she who found Margery.'

'But that has nothing to do with it. The finding, I mean. I can tell you, Netta, if the horrid police ask me if I know there was a split between Ned and Margery over Elaine, I shall say I have no idea. I haven't really. It isn't fair to decide that they were really divided just because Margery and he looked glum at times.'

'No, I suppose not,' said Netta thoughtfully. 'They want to know facts, not conjectures. I agree with you. I won't say a word about what I conjectured. Mr Barley said her window was wide open. Some burglar may have shot her from outside. If Elaine had done it, she wouldn't have been such a fool as to go in to find her dead.'

'Of course she didn't do it,' said Nelly. 'I am only afraid of Ortho Haine saying something. The Heads are too absorbed in bridge to know what is going on, but Ortho has been quite potty lately about Margery.'

'You mean he was in love with her?'

'No, I don't say that. He's a nice boy, and I like him, but he has Platonic passions. Last year he used to adore that bad-tempered tennis player; though I don't believe he ever met her! I am sure he thought Ned too material for Margery.'

'He is rather an ass,' said Netta. 'But perhaps we had better go in again now, and wait for the superintendent.'

The superintendent had already arrived, and was making an investigation of Mrs Tollard's room, in the company of the detective. As Mrs Gailey and her companion returned to the house, they saw two men momentarily at the window above. Fisher was tall and gaunt, a very grave man with a worried air; the detective-inspector was round and chubby.

'I suppose they have to measure, and do things like that,' said Nelly, as she entered the door.

Their evidence was not required at once, and quite half an hour had passed when the two officers from Elterham descended the stairs with Mr Barley, and went into the library. A minute later, Mr Barley emerged, and went for Elaine.

'They want to hear what you have to say,' he told her, in his worried voice.

She nodded, and accompanied him. When she entered the library she gave each man in turn a quick, observant look, then sat down, and folded her hands lightly on her lap.

'I understand that you wished to see me?' she said.

Superintendent Fisher bowed. 'Yes, madam. I understand that you were the first to discover the body of the poor lady upstairs. I should like to ask you a few questions.'

'Very well.'

The inspector had a note-book on his knee. He sucked his pencil-point meditatively, and bent an alert ear.

'What first attracted your attention to that room?'

Elaine replied clearly, 'My own room is next to it.'

'Not the room with the communicating door?'

'No, that was Mr Tollard's room. Mine is to the other side. I was rather restless last night, on account of the heat. It was just about dawn when I heard slight movements in the next room. A bed seemed to creak, as if someone were tossing on it.'

'Surely this is an old house, with thick walls?'

'I should think it is. But her window was open, and so was mine. At any rate, I heard these sounds. Later on, I heard what sounded like a moan. Mrs Tollard had not been well the day before, and I wondered if she was in pain. At last I got up, went into her room, when I heard a slight cry, and found her lying on the floor, dead.'

'Did you hear her fall?'

'No.'

Mr Barley interposed anxiously: 'Excuse me. I thought I heard a thud, though my room is on the other side of the passage.'

Elaine stared straight before her. 'When I entered the room, and saw her lying there, I put my arm under her, and tried to lift her up. Then something told me she was dead, and though I have had some experience in my travels of sudden deaths, I was so shocked that I let her fall back.'

'That will explain the bruise on the back of the head,' said the superintendent.

CHAPTER V

THE FINGERPRINTS

'HAS Dr Browne gone?' asked the superintendent, of Mr Barley.

'Yes. He had to go to an urgent case. He will be back later.'

'Then we must leave this question of the bruise till later. Now, Miss Gurdon, you are aware that Dr Browne believed Mrs Tollard died as the result of some alkaloid poison in which the point of a dart had been steeped. You know something of these primitive South American weapons.'

'Yes.'

'And you have heard of the use of curare?'

'I have seen it used in that way.'

'Then you will agree with Dr Browne that it was used in this case?'

She shook her head. 'I don't think so.'

Mr Barley started, looking puzzled. Even the detective gave her a glance of wonder.

'Why not?'

She frowned slightly. 'There are several ways of poisoning these darts. Some tribes use a poison that is unfamiliar to me. Some poison them with snake-venom injected by the snake into rotten meat. Some use woorali, which is also called urari, and curare here at home. But curare is not so deadly when it is stale.'

'I was not aware of that,' said Fisher thoughtfully. 'But your answer, Miss Gurdon, brings up another point. How could you, from merely seeing the body, assert that poison other than fresh poison was used on the top of the dart?'

'I have every ground for believing it,' she said steadily. 'Mr Barley has taken over some curios of mine. Among them

33

is a blow-pipe, and a little quiver for darts. There were six darts in the quiver when the trophy was hung up in the hall. This morning, in Mr Barley's presence, I took it down, and found only five.'

'Is this true, sir?' said Fisher quickly.

'Quite. I forgot to tell you.'

'Well, we shall go into that later. I want to hear more of these weapons, Miss Gurdon. For example, what is their range?'

Elaine looked down. 'It varies, just as the range of a bow and arrow varies, with the user. I should say sixty yards was a very long shot, and many people would not be able to aim accurately at that distance.'

'While the speed of the dart would not be great?'

'That is of no moment. The darts themselves, unless received in the eyes, say, would not do much harm. The savage relies on the deadly poison with which the dart is tipped.'

'So that a mere scratch would be fatal?'

'If fresh poison was used in the case of curare.'

'Then curare was not used on the darts in your possession?'

'No.'

'Have you any idea what it was?'

'No, it was one of the poisons I could not analyse.'

'So that it might be dangerous even when not quite fresh?'

'I thing so. I have heard that is so. I remember a boy, a native servant of mine, from that tribe, killed pacas with them, three months after we had left his tribe, though he had no means of getting a fresh supply of poison.'

'You think it possible from your experience that a man could shoot, say from the lawn outside, and kill a lady in the house?'

'Granting three things: a man who could use the blow-pipe, who saw Mrs Tollard at the window, and had a dart tipped with this particular venom.'

'Thank you, Miss Gurdon. That is a help to us. The window was open. You might go out, Warren, and investigate that point. And you might give out a general warning that no one in the house, servants or guests, should cross the lawn, or walk on the path under that window.'

The detective-inspector got up. 'Very well, sir.'

'Leave your notes with me.'

Warren handed over the note-book, and went out.

Fisher turned again to Elaine. 'I suppose it is rare to find an English person who can use a blow-pipe?'

'Yes. Some explorers can. Many don't trouble to learn, or find it too difficult.'

'Can you use one?'

'Yes. I was showing them here lately how it was used. Of course I used harmless darts.'

'Did anyone of your audience try a hand at it?'

Elaine bit her lip. 'One or two,' she said. 'Mr Haine tried, and Mr Tollard.'

'Is that the dead lady's husband?'

'He went to town before this occurred,' interrupted Mr Barley anxiously.

Fisher frowned. 'So he was not in the house last night?'

'No. He went to town.'

'Well, we shall see him later. But to return to this demonstration, Miss Gurdon, did Mr Haine or the other gentleman show any—er—proficiency?'

Elaine reddened slightly. 'Mr Haine couldn't get it out at all. Mr Tollard sent the dart a fair distance, but without any certainty of aim.'

'At least he could fire it?'

'Yes, to that extent.'

Fisher coughed.

Mr Barley looked annoyed. 'I have told you, superintendent, that Mr Tollard left for town.'

'I understood you to say so, sir,' replied the other blandly. 'Well, Miss Gurdon, I have no further questions to ask you now. You have helped us considerably. Thank you.'

'Who do you wish to see next?' asked Mr Barley, as Elaine bowed silently, and went out.

'I wish to ask you a few questions,' said Fisher. 'In the first place, have you any reason to believe that any of your guests had reason to dislike Mrs Tollard?'

'No,' said Mr Barley, setting his square jaw. 'None.'

'She was popular then?'

'Not perhaps exactly popular. She was a very quiet woman, retiring in a way, or dignified, one or the other. She had artistic tastes, and was perhaps too languid by temperament to mix much with my other guests.'

Fisher nodded. 'Her face is of that type, sir. I quite see what you mean. Now, how about her husband. Had they been married long?'

'Three years, I fancy.'

'They got on well together? I mean to say they were, in your opinion, an average married couple?'

'Granting a slight difference in temperament, they were. He is of a more sporting type.'

Fisher thought for a few moments. 'With a good many others in Elterham, sir, I attended Miss Gurdon's lecture. I had read about her in the paper before, and I think there was, the other day, some reference to a gentleman who was backing her financially in her next expedition.'

'Mr Tollard promised to make up any deficit, but that was pure good will on his part. I proposed to do the same thing myself, but had been forestalled.'

'They are old friends?'

'Yes.'

Mr Barley was disturbed. He saw where this line of examination would eventually lead. He felt with Netta Gailey that it was not for him to magnify marital differences of a trifling kind, in a case where they might take on an exaggerated importance. But he was saved any further trouble at that time, by the reappearance of Elaine Gurdon with the quiver she had taken down from the wall that morning.

'I think you ought to have these,' she said, without apology, and handing the quiver to Fisher. 'But be careful not to touch the points.'

Fisher thanked her, drew a dart gingerly from the thing, and studied the end. 'What is this? Cottonwool?'

'That is to make the dart fit the blow-pipe. It is a fluff of silk-cotton.'

'There was none of this on the dart which killed Mrs Tollard?'

'No, it would not remain on the dart, as a feather does on an arrow.'

'Thank you, Miss Gurdon,' said he, replacing the venomous thing, and laying the quiver on the table. 'Perhaps now you would ask Mrs Tollard's maid to come here.'

Mrs Tollard's maid came in a few minutes later, alone. She was very nervous, and had been crying, but her evidence did not amount to anything. She had been with Mrs Tollard three months, had found her a good, if exacting, mistress. She believed her to be a healthy woman, in spite of her looks, had rarely known her even to suffer from headaches. She was sure her mistress did not take drugs. On the previous night she had left her in bed, professing violent neuralgia. She had been told not to trouble any more. That was all she knew.

'So far as you are aware, she was happy with Mr Tollard?'

She stared. Mrs Tollard had always looked melancholy, to her mind, but she did not know it had anything to do with Mr Tollard, who was always most attentive. Ladies were different somehow. You couldn't always tell if they were happy.

'Quite true,' said Mr Barley when the girl had gone. 'That poetical, artistic type always looks to me in despair, but I believe that is only a pose.'

Fisher had been given a list of the guests, and now looked at it. He asked to see Mr Head first, and Mr Head came, with a countenance of protest, and an opening statement that he knew nothing about it. Fisher told him to sit down, and put a few questions quickly. Mr Head's only contribution to the evidence was the remark that Mrs Tollard might not have been well. The last time she had played bridge she had seemed very distrait. He went, and Mrs Head came in. She had much the same kind of inconsequence to deliver, and was soon dismissed.

'I think they will be of no further use to us,' said the superintendent, privately wishing he hadn't to waste his time on these bridge bores. 'You may tell them so, sir. Now what about Mrs Minever?'

Barley went for his elderly relation, hoping she would not put some silly interpretation on the event. Fortunately, he found her rather frightened by the prospect of examination, and determined to say as little as possible.

'I really don't know anything about any of them,' she said decidedly. 'They are Mr Barley's guests. I know Mrs Tollard said she had a bad headache, and didn't come down.'

She left, and Fisher consulted the roll again. 'Here's a gentleman, Mr Ortho—is that right?'

'Yes, Ortho Haine.'

'He seems to have been the only other man on that side. We had better have him in.'

Mr Barley went out, and Fisher scribbled rapidly. Haine came in, looking white and upset, but apparently determined to help the investigation in any way he could. It was quite true that he had developed a youthful but quite harmless passion for the dead woman, and was inclined to regard her as a sort of modern martyr to matrimony, but he was sensible enough not to enlarge too much on things that might be misconstrued.

'I heard nothing in the night, or early this morning,' he said, in reply to a question. 'But I am a very sound sleeper, and I was tired last night when I went to bed.'

'Did you not even hear Miss Gurdon or Mr Barley go into the room?'

'No. As a rule I do not wake until my tea is brought up. But there was none brought up this morning. I slept on until late. I did not hear Mrs Tollard was dead until this—until Mr Barley told us after breakfast.'

'Do you know Mrs Tollard well?'

'I have not met her very many times.'

'Did she impress you as a happy woman?'

Haine glanced at Mr Barley, and frowned. He hesitated for a moment, then spoke. 'I don't think she did. I may be mistaken. I should say on the whole that she—'

'Just a moment, sir,' said Fisher grimly. 'Could you say definitely that she was unhappy, or had any reason to be so?'

The word 'definitely' staggered Ortho. He was a conscientious fellow, and there was a world of difference between thinking that Mrs Tollard did not care for her husband's association with Miss Gurdon, and declaring in so many words that she was unhappy as the result of it.

'No, I couldn't say so definitely,' he remarked.

'Very well. Speculations are not much good to us, sir,' said the superintendent. 'Can you tell me if any of the ladies in the house were friends of the late Mrs Tollard?'

'They all knew her,' was the reply. 'Perhaps Mrs Gailey was most in sympathy with her.'

'And Miss Sayers?' asked Fisher, looking at his list.

'They aren't the same type,' said Ortho, who was young enough to divide humanity into types.

'Then I think I shall see Mrs Gailey next,' said Fisher. 'If you don't mind, Mr Barley, I shall question this witness privately.'

Barley started. 'I hope I have not been in your way?'

'Not at all,' said Fisher dryly. 'But please ask Mrs Gailey to come in. I have done with Mr Haine.'

Ortho bolted, much relieved, but Mr Barley was thoughtful and anxious as he went in search of Netta Gailey. Was it possible that the superintendent suspected something? It was odd his asking to see Mrs Gailey alone. If that young ass Haine had only held his tongue this ridiculous nonsense about Margery Tollard's unhappiness need never have come up.

'The police will be sure to make a mountain of this mole-hill!' he said to himself plaintively.

CHAPTER VI

FISHER LAYS A TRAP

It was certainly unfortunate that Ortho Haine had said even as much as he did. Superintendent Fisher had expected to hear that the dead lady had been a happy woman, but the earlier witnesses had not thought of saying so, and Haine had almost given him the impression that Mrs Tollard was unhappy in her married life.

'There's one thing certain,' said Fisher, as he sat waiting for Mrs Gailey. 'Mr Tollard left yesterday, so was not in the house last night. Mrs Tollard was most probably shot from outside. If that little fluff of silk-cotton had been detached in firing, as Miss Gurdon suggested, it ought to have been found. That is, if the criminal was indoors at the time. It might be possible, though, for someone to fire the dart through the keyhole of the communicating door. I must look into that. Come in!'

The last words he spoke aloud, and Netta Gailey entered shyly.

'You are Mrs Gailey?' asked Fisher. 'Good! Will you please sit down?'

She sat down, and began to fidget. He added in a reassuring tone: 'The questions I am going to put to you need not alarm you, Mrs Gailey.'

She nodded nervously. 'I don't know much, I'm afraid.'

'I gathered as much from Mr Barley. But I want to hear a little about the poor lady. I expect we shall find she was happy enough when alive, but some of the guests here have given me the impression that she was rather melancholy. Now, as another woman, and one more or less in sympathy with her, can you tell me your opinion?'

Mrs Gailey had come determined to say nothing. But the superintendent seemed so mild, and so casual about it, that she was not so careful as she had intended to be.

'Well, you see, she wasn't a sporty type. She liked books and pictures and things, while Mr Tollard was fond of sports.'

Fisher nodded indifferently. 'We mustn't let that influence us too much. Dozens of husbands and wives manage to rub along very nicely, even when they don't think alike.'

'Oh, of course,' she replied, more brightly. 'I don't say for a minute that Ned Tollard made her unhappy.'

'I don't suppose he did,' said Fisher, giving her a keen look. 'No one has dared to suggest that, I hope.'

'Not suggest it. Oh, no,' she cried. 'She was rather languid, you know, and had a rather melancholy face. You see, Mr Tollard was only giving money to this expedition. I never saw anything in it myself.'

Fisher smiled inwardly. It was not for nothing that he had wished to see this lady in Mr Barley's absence.

'Too absurd to suggest it,' he said. 'With a big thing like that in view, there would be a lot to discuss and talk over?'

'Miss Gurdon used to visit their house, with her maps and plans,' she agreed. 'I can assure you it was quite above-board. You do see that, don't you?'

'It seems hardly worth discussing,' he said casually. 'But let us leave that, and come back to Mr Tollard. He only left here yesterday. I presume you knew he was leaving?'

She reflected. 'No. That was rather a surprise. We were all going to picnic at Heber Castle, in the afternoon, and he had driven his wife over to Elterham to get some books in the morning. I saw them come back in the car, but did not speak to them. It was later we heard he had to go back to town on business.'

'I hope the drive did her good—I mean to say, how did she seem when you saw her?'

Netta Gailey gave a sudden start. Was it possible that this horrid man was pumping her? Had she said too much already?

'Oh, all right,' she said hastily.

Fisher had been watching her face. 'Do you mean happy?'

She squirmed a little, and he saw that too. He came at her suddenly with a verbal thrust.

'You thought not? You felt that she was not quite at her ease?'

Netta gasped. 'Oh, I don't know. She seemed a bit upset, perhaps, but she had a bad head later, and perhaps she felt it coming on.'

It had dawned on her that her conjecture was right. He had been drawing her on. She rose, much perturbed.

He got up, and rang a bell. 'Please sit down for a few moments,' he said, and began to scribble in his note-book as she resumed her seat.

Grover, the butler, came in. Fisher asked him to send in Miss Sayers, and went on writing. Miss Sayers appeared in a minute, and glanced woefully at Netta. The superintendent suddenly seemed to jump up, and be standing between them.

'Thank you, Mrs Gailey, that will do,' he said.

Netta went out, without a chance to warn her friend. Fisher courteously asked Nelly Sayers to sit, and stood near her, his hands behind his back.

'I am sorry to trouble you, Miss Sayers,' he began, 'but duty is duty even when it is not very pleasant. Mrs Gailey tells me that Mrs Tollard returned yesterday from a drive with her husband, looking rather upset. Between you and me, I am not disposed to lay much stress on Mr Tollard's connection with this expedition, but I get the impression that Mrs Tollard, perhaps, did not quite like her husband's interest in it.'

Nelly Sayers was not vivacious, and quick, but she had at the back of her more common-sense than her friend Netta.

The trouble was that she did not know what the latter had told the officer.

'I think it's rubbish,' she cried. 'She had nothing to complain of.'

'Unfortunately, people do not require to have grounds for complaint,' he said shrewdly. 'Did you see her return from this drive?'

'Yes, I did.'

'And you formed the same impression?'

She bit her lip. 'Women have their off-days. I have myself.'

'That will do, thank you,' said Fisher gently. 'I shan't need you more at present, Miss Sayers.'

She went out, inwardly fulminating at Netta for being such a fool. When she had gone, the superintendent took up the quiver again, and was examining it, when the detective-inspector came in.

'Not a sign, sir,' he said. 'I have made a careful search of the grounds within a radius of a hundred yards of that window, and I can see nothing. The ground is hard after the drought.'

'Are there no beds, or shrubberies?'

'Yes. I paid special attention to one that lies about thirty yards from the window. The shrubs are pretty thick, and could hide a man well, but no one seems to have walked on the soil under, or near, the bushes.'

'It's pretty still,' said Fisher, giving a glance out of the window. 'I don't think there was any breeze during the night either. Have a careful look around again, see if you can trace a bit of fluffy stuff, like the silk-cotton on these darts. When you have done, come up to me. I shall be in the room next that occupied last night by the dead lady. The one with the door communicating.'

'Where her husband slept the previous night?'

'That's it.'

The Heads were driving away when the superintendent went upstairs. He met Mr Barley on the way, asked him if Mr Tollard had yet arrived, and continued his way.

Mr Barley had been talking to Nelly Sayers and Mrs Gailey. He looked at them earnestly as Fisher disappeared.

'I wish Tollard would come,' he said, in an exasperated voice. 'Are you sure the man believed he had something to do with it?'

'Quite sure,' said Nelly Sayers. 'Netta made such an ass of herself. She let it out that there had been gossip about Elaine and Ned. When I went in, I didn't know how much or how little she had told him. He suspects Ned, I am sure.'

Netta was too troubled to defend herself. 'Perhaps Ned will be able to prove where he was?' she said.

'I hope he will,' said Mr Barley.

Grover answered the front door bell as he was speaking, and came to him in a few moments with a telegram. He tore it open, and passed it to Mrs Gailey after glancing at it. It read:

'Mr Tollard left last night for Ventnor. Have wired.'

'That will be from his secretary,' said Mr Barley, much relieved. 'Of course I never believed he had anything to do with it, but I had better show it to the inspector now.'

Nelly and Netta separated and went to their rooms. Mr Barley went in search of Fisher. The sergeant from the village had already gone away, to be pestered by the inhabitants of the hamlet with regard to the tragedy, news of which had already filtered down there.

Ortho Haine was in the drawing-room talking to Elaine Gurdon. He was still excited and indignant, and though she did not seem to be aware of it, a faint hostility to Elaine pervaded his mind. Whatever had happened, he told himself, she was the indirect cause of it. She had been very indiscreet in associating with Tollard, who had apparently a jealous wife. Why hadn't she touched old Barley for the money? Apart from that, it was one of the beastly darts she had brought to the house that had done the mischief.

'She must have been shot by someone outside,' he said. 'It wasn't done from indoors, I'll swear; but her window was open, and you know there is a little shrubbery opposite.'

'I know there is,' she returned. 'But who would do it? And the blow-pipe I sold Mr Barley is still in the hall.'

'They ought to examine it for fingerprints,' he said.

'No doubt they will,' said Elaine. 'But I don't see that it will be much use. I had it the other day, and so had you; and so had Ned Tollard. All our fingerprints may be on it.'

'But no one could charge me with it,' he cried.

'And I am in the same position,' she remarked. 'As for Ned, he was not here.'

'There may be other prints.'

'But how could an outsider know where it was? And how could he return it, even if he stole it first?'

'I don't know. It's very odd. But I hope they catch the beast who did it! I would like to skin him!'

Elaine did not reply. She got up from her chair, took a turn up and down the room, and went out.

The superintendent had made a careful examination of the room formerly occupied by Mr Tollard, and was joined there by the detective, who reported that he had found nothing incriminating in the garden.

'Then we had better get that blow-pipe, and have it packed, and sent back to be examined for fingerprints,' said Fisher. 'Come along.'

As they descended the stairs, they heard a ring, and saw Grover cross the hall to the front door. Mr Barley had already handed over the telegram, which apparently gave Tollard an alibi. They paused for a moment, then saw Grover backing into the hall, to admit the police sergeant, who was accompanied by a fellow of twenty-four, or five, dressed in moleskins, and wearing gaiters of an under-keeper.

'What's up now?' asked Fisher, going across.

'A new witness, sir,' said the sergeant, full of importance at his find. 'This is Jorkins, sir.'

'Bring him into the library,' said Fisher, leading the way.

When, they were settled there, Fisher asked the man to tell what he knew. It was simple and clear enough, though it was difficult to decide exactly what bearing it had upon the murder.

Jorkins had passed across the park just after dawn, he said. He had happened to look towards the house, and in one of the windows on the first floor he had seen a lady standing.

'Are you sure of the window?' asked Fisher.

'Yes, sir,' said Jorkins. 'Sergeant showed it me.'

'Very well. Go on.'

Jorkins cleared his throat nervously and continued. He had only seen the lady for a moment. Then she had disappeared. He did not know if she had walked back, or to one side. She had just disappeared.

'Might she have fallen?'

Jorkins agreed that she might, though he could not say.

'You are sure it was a lady?'

The witness was quite sure. He had seen that she was wearing something flowing, even at that distance.

'A white night-gown, perhaps,' said Fisher.

The man shook his head. He was quite certain that it was not white.

'Mrs Tollard was wearing a dressing-gown, sir,' the inspector reminded his superior.

'So she was. We are not sure that this fellow did actually see Mrs Tollard, though. Pale green was the colour of that silk thing, I should say.'

'Yes sir,' the inspector agreed, 'a pale tint.'

'What colour was this flowing garment?' the superintendent asked Jorkins.

'Red, sir,' said the man.

Fisher started, and looked at his colleague. 'That's odd! As clear a suggestion that an intruder was in the room as one could wish for.'

'Looks like it, sir.'

'While the fact that this intruder was dressed in what seems like a dressing-gown suggests that someone in—' he stopped short, remembering that Jorkins was listening.

'Shall I make inquiries about that now, sir?' asked the detective.

'At once, please,' said Fisher.

CHAPTER VII

A STRANGER IN RED

THE detective-inspector found Mr Barley wandering about the house restlessly, and asked him if he could get the lady guests, and also the female domestics together, so that he might question them as speedily as possible.

'Why all the women only?' asked Barley curiously.

'Because we have a new witness, sir, who declares he saw a woman's figure at that window early this morning.'

'Mrs Tollard herself?'

'We are not sure, sir.'

'Very well. I'll have them all called.'

He ushered the detective into a large dining-room, and went off on his errand. Within ten minutes he had a small congregation of women in the room, some in tears, some hostile, most nervous and suspicious.

'A lady was seen at the window of Mrs Tollard's room early this morning,' said the detective clearly. 'A witness who saw her declares that she was wearing a red garment, probably a dressing-gown. If any of you have a garment of this kind in use, or know of any in use in this house, will you please let me hear of it?'

They looked at one another wonderingly, and the cook held up her hand, as if she were a child at school trying to attract the teacher's attention. She wore a red flannel gown, it seemed, and was ready to show it to anyone, but not a hand had she had in anything to do with the poor dead lady.

'We don't think of such a thing,' said the detective, 'but someone might wear another's garment, you see.'

Elaine spoke up suddenly. 'Perhaps, inspector, it might be better if those who have dressing-gowns told you in turn what colour they are. Personally I prefer blue. I was wearing a pale pastel shade of blue this morning when I found Mrs Tollard. Mr Barley will corroborate me in that.'

'Thank you, miss, a very good idea,' said the detective. 'Now, we'll begin with this lady on the right.'

'Mauve!' snapped Mrs Minever.

'Maize,' said Mrs Gailey.

But most of those who possessed dressing-gowns preferred some shade of blue. One or two wore pink, but they were under-servants who slept in the same bedroom, and were not likely to be connected in any way with the tragedy.

The inspector dismissed them, and conferred for a few moments with Mr Barley. Then there was a knock at the door, and Dr Browne came in.

'Ha, Warren,' he said to the inspector, 'is the superintendent here?'

'Yes, sir, in the library, I know he wants to see you.'

'Come along, Mr Barley,' said Browne. 'We may as well go into this at once. I have another urgent case I must get to as soon as possible.'

Jorkins had been dismissed, and Fisher was making notes of his evidence when the doctor and Mr Barley entered behind the detective.

'I am glad you are here, doctor,' said the superintendent. 'There is a point I want to go into with you. I wonder, Mr Barley, if you would be good enough to fetch Miss Gurdon here. In this case she is an expert witness, from her knowledge of those darts.'

When Barley had gone, he looked at Warren. 'Any luck about those dressing-gowns?'

'I am afraid not, sir. Only the cook had one really called red.'

'Right! We must examine all the garments of that kind later.'

Browne shrugged. 'What's your point?'

'About the dressing-gowns?'

'Good gracious, no, man! I'm not a draper! I mean about the dart.'

'If you will wait, please, till Miss Gurdon comes. Ah, here she is. Miss Gurdon, you can help us now. We are assuming that the dart was fired by someone standing outside with a blow-pipe. We assume that he would hide in the little shrubbery about thirty yards from the window. That would be about the range.'

'I understand,' said Elaine.

Fisher turned to the doctor. 'Now, sir, was this dart deeply seated in the wound or not?'

'Pretty deep,' said Browne.

'It had done more than merely penetrate the flesh, though it had first to penetrate two thicknesses of cloth, the night-dress and the dressing-gown?'

'Yes. Both cloths were pretty flimsy, but the dart had gone well in.'

'Thank you. Now, Miss Gurdon, do you think a dart fired at the range I have mentioned would penetrate human flesh deeply, after going through two thin cloths?'

She considered for a few moments, then shook her head. 'I don't think so. The dart flies with considerable velocity, but, unless it was directed by an expert, I am sure it would not go deep at that range. It is unlikely, in any case.'

'Then that does seem to spoil our theory of its having been fired from outside,' murmured Fisher.

Browne shrugged impatiently. He was not a very mild man at any time.

'Nothing whatever to do with it,' he declared. 'You are forgetting that she was lying on her back when found. Even if the dart had only just entered the skin, it would be driven deeper when the free end of it came in contact with the floor in her fall.'

'And when I raised her up, on going into her room, I was so shocked that I let her fall back a second time,' said Elaine.

'There you are,' said Browne abruptly. 'I've seen that blow-pipe. It's a long clumsy thing to hold. I don't think anyone could use it well in the confined space of a room.'

'It might have been shot through the keyhole of the door of the room communicating with Mrs Tollard's, doctor. There was no key in that.'

'Stuff and nonsense! The blower would be more than seven feet away from the keyhole. The mouth of the pipe would cover that up. How could he see to aim at someone in the other room? No, she was shot from outside, if she was shot at all.'

The superintendent agreed rather ruefully. 'Well, we must wait till Mr Tollard turns up. I don't think we can do anything more than make arrangements for the post-mortem, and the inquest. Mr Tollard was the only relation who stayed here lately, but was not present last night.'

'In the Isle of Wight,' said Mr Barley.

'Presumably in the Isle of Wight,' agreed Fisher, but stressing the adverb.

'I should prefer not to have the body sent to Elterham,' said Barley quickly. 'I have no objection to the inquest being held here.'

'We shall decide that later,' said Fisher. 'Now, I shall examine the servants in detail, then return to Elterham. We'll take the blow-pipe and the darts back with us.'

A quarter of an hour later, the police left for Elterham. Dr Browne had a few minutes' chat with Mr Barley, and went off to his case. Mr Barley himself had had a little conversation with each of his guests, and was relieved to find that none of them objected to remaining until after the inquest.

Ten minutes after that, a wire came from Tollard. It had been handed in at Ventnor, Isle of Wight, and said that he was crossing at once to the mainland, and driving over at once.

'I expect a fast car will bring him here sooner than cross-country trains,' Barley said to Elaine, to whom he showed the wire. 'I'll hate telling him all about it, but I can't put any more trouble on you.'

That afternoon he began to suspect that there was a division in his house party, and it was obvious that the members of it were taking sides in the matter of Margery Tollard's death.

Mrs Minever, Ortho Haine, and Netta Gailey talked a great deal together; while Miss Sayers and Elaine (the initiative coming from Nelly) appeared to be seen more together than ever before.

Mrs Gailey had wired to her husband, putting off his visit, and was very eager to support her friend even to the point of indiscretion. This division, which gradually grew, came with Elaine's decision not to leave the case altogether to the police, but to make some enquiries herself.

'I don't see why she should,' said Haine to Mrs Minever. 'It seems odd that she is so much to the front in this.'

'Well, they may say she is too much interested in Mr Tollard,' snapped the elderly lady. 'I knew what would come of it.'

'But can we say that anything has come of it?' asked Netta Gailey timidly. 'After all, Mr Tollard was away last night.'

'That's true,' said Ortho. 'This wire proves he was in the Isle of Wight right enough.'

'I never said he wasn't,' grumbled Mrs Minever. 'All I say is that, with his wife dead, he is free to do what he likes.'

'I see what you mean.'

Haine shook his head. 'Oh, we can't go as far as that yet. Being interested in a married man is one thing, and disposing of his wife is another.'

'I never said anyone disposed of his wife, Mr Haine. I only say he is free now.'

'You don't think he wants to marry Elaine, do you?' asked Netta.

Mrs Minever became alarmed, and drew in her horns. 'I don't say anything. I know nothing about it,' she observed.

But the thought she had expressed did linger in their minds. Margery had been no companion to her husband. She had been in the way. If Elaine really was in love with Ned Tollard, the way was open.

'What troubles me is this,' said Ortho, in the ardour of his championship. 'So far as we can see, that dart must have been shot out of the blowpipe. Very well! The police will look for fingerprints on it.'

'How do they do that?' asked Netta.

'I don't know the exact process, but that is what they will do. Now, that day on the lawn, Miss Gurdon brought out the blow-pipe, and let us try our hand with it.'

Mrs Minever nodded. Netta looked interested. 'You aren't worrying about the possibility of their suspecting you, Ortho?'

'Of course not. But they will find three sets of fingerprints on it—mine and Mr Tollard's and hers.'

'What's the point of that?' asked Mrs Minever bluntly.

Haine bit his lip. 'I thought you would see it at once. It's only hypothesis, of course, but that is the kind of thing the police will put to themselves.'

'What hypothesis?'

'If they begin to suspect Miss Gurdon, they will ask if she didn't arrange, that demonstration on purpose.'

'I'm very dense, I suppose,' observed Mrs Minever, shaking her head impatiently. 'For what purpose?'

'Oh, so that she could say any fingerprints on the blow-pipe were those she made when she showed us how to use it on the lawn.'

'You are clever!' cried Netta. 'I never thought of that. Why, it does look suspicious, doesn't it?'

Mrs Minever expressed disbelief. 'I don't think so at all. If she is in love with Mr Tollard—I don't say she is!—she would hardly have let him handle the nasty thing, for fear he might be suspected.'

'It's horribly puzzling,' said Netta.

While they were talking, Mr Barley had found Elaine and Miss Sayers in the billiard-room.

'I am relieved to find that Mr Tollard was right away from here after all,' he said, as he sat down, and began to fan his hot face with a handkerchief.

'Who could have suspected him?' said Elaine, rather coldly.

'The police did,' said Nelly drily. 'I know they did. They fished for information from Netta, and they tried to pump me. It will be a nasty smack for them when they hear he was in the Isle of Wight really and truly.'

Elaine reddened. 'No one who knows Ned could think such a thing.'

'We don't,' said Mr Barley. 'But it's a puzzle to know who had a motive. She wasn't an aggressive woman, or mixed up in politics or anything that might make her enemies, and I doubt if in this country any controversy would lead to murder.'

'I quite agree,' said Elaine. 'My travels perhaps have done something to harden me, but I was really terribly shocked when I went in this morning, and found her dead.'

'I am sure you were. I suppose we can only leave it to the police?'

'I intend to do more,' said Elaine, her mouth growing firm. 'We can't get away from the evidence of that man Jorkins, who saw a woman in a red dressing-gown at the window.'

'But it couldn't have been cook,' cried Nelly.

'Of course not; but someone may have *borrowed* that garment of hers. At any rate, there was another person present in the room this morning.'

'But she must have been dead then, or surely she would have cried out?'

'Margery? I should imagine so. At all events I am going to look into it on my own. I suppose you don't mind my fossicking about the house, Mr Barley.'

'Not at all,' he said; for, now that Tollard seemed to have an alibi, he could not help feeling that suspicion might fall on Elaine. He did not believe for a moment that she had anything to do with it, but the police knew nothing about her, and might regard her as a possible criminal, inspired by a passionate motive.

The butler entered suddenly. 'A gentleman to see Miss Gurdon,' he said. 'He is waiting in the hall, sir.'

'Did he give his name?' asked Elaine, with a look of surprise.

'Yes, miss. Mr Carton.' He advanced with his tray, on which lay a card, and held it towards her.

Elaine looked at the card, and a faint colour flowed into her cheeks. Then she looked at Mr Barley.

'It's—it's an old friend of mine,' she said. 'Will you excuse me?'

CHAPTER VIII

MR CARTON INTRUDES

THE man who awaited Elaine in the hall was a tall fellow of about twenty-seven. While not handsome, he had an attractive and humorous face, much tanned by sun and wind, and an air of distinction that even clothes of a colonial cut could not altogether hide.

'Hello! Hello!' he cried, as he saw her. 'Didn't expect to see me, did you?'

He grasped her hands warmly, admiration in his eyes, and Elaine returned his grip, gasping a little with surprise, a thing unusual with her, and a sign of unfamiliar emotion.

'My dear Jim!' she cried, 'it is really you after all? I wondered—I thought there must be some mistake, when I saw the name on the card. But you have changed.'

'Grown up,' he assented, laughing. 'You found me a cub once. Talking about changes, why, you—are looking wonderful. If I was a cub, you were a lanky awkward thing, to be frank!'

Elaine suddenly remembered that they were talking in the open hall. 'Will you come into the library?—I thought you were in Africa.'

'Correct,' he said with a twinkle, as he followed her. 'I was in Africa—Nyassaland, to be precise. I got home three days ago, looked round your old haunts, then came on your name in a paper. You looked almost too high and mighty for me. A lecturer and explorer, by Jove! But I chanced it. I saw you were at Elterham, gutted all the social announcements, and read that you were the guest of a Mr Barley—here. I wonder if he will think it cheek, my coming?'

Elaine bit her lip. 'I don't think so. He is very kind.'

'Tell him I once proposed to you,' he laughed, 'and have been very humble since. Nothing like the wilds for taking the starch out of you, and showing you that you are only a speck in the universe, what?'

She did not smile. She had to tell him what had happened. He could hardly have come at a more awkward moment.

'Look here, Jim,' she said, 'a rather terrible thing has happened here—in this house. One of the guests, the wife of a friend of mine—but you know Ned Tollard?—'

'Of course,' he said, staring, and anxious.

'Is dead, they fear was murdered in her bedroom early this morning.'

He exclaimed sharply, bent his brows, and spoke. 'I had better clear out then. I am sorry. Ned's wife? He was unmarried when I was last home. Do they know who killed her?'

She shook her head. 'I had better tell you all about it, then I should like you to see Barley. Will you listen quietly, please, to what I have to say, and not interrupt until I have done.'

'Oh, I'll listen,' he said, seeing now the marks of trouble on her face. 'Fire away.'

His face expressed surprise, horror and indignation, as she went on. When she had finished, he looked straight at her, and put a blunt question.

'Look here, Elaine, I apologise in advance if I hurt you, but there isn't anything in this business with Ned Tollard?'

'Of course not,' she said proudly.

'And Ned isn't likely to have done it? He wasn't that type of fellow, but I just ask.'

'Could you think him guilty of such a thing?'

'No, though one sees some dashed queer things where I have been. One fellow I knew killed his brother and bolted. He was the mildest man out, and we never knew why.'

'He was in the Isle of Wight. He is coming here today.'

'Good! The nasty fly in this ointment is the fact that someone used one of your darts. That's rotten!'

'It's unfortunate.'

He pursed his lips. 'More than that. You see, Elaine, since I saw you, I've been a bit of a policeman myself.'

'A policeman?'

'Well, a sort of Assistant Commissioner among the natives. I had to nose out a good many crimes, and I think I am pretty good at it.'

'This is different,' she said.

'Only in details,' he said. 'All crimes are much the same. When the negro kills a man or woman, he hasn't any esoteric motives. It's anger, jealousy, robbery, or hate, just as at home. There are about five primary motives, as there are five primary colours. But to come back to this inopportune visit of mine, don't you think I ought to buzz off, and see you another time?'

'Please don't,' she said. 'I want you to come with me to see Mr Barley.'

'I'd rather not,' he replied, lighting a cigarette thoughtfully. 'Perhaps you would see him, and just mention that I didn't know of this tamasha.'

'Very well,' said Elaine, 'I'll go at once.'

She was back in a few minutes with her host, and introduced the two men briefly.

'Mr Carton and I are old friends, but I haven't seen him for six years,' she said.

'Glad to meet you, Mr Carton,' said Mr Barley. 'I suppose Miss Gurdon has told you of the terrible trouble we have had down here.'

'She has, sir, and I'm confoundedly sorry. I don't think I ought to hang about any longer. I shall only be in the way.'

Mr Barley shook his head. 'I can't let you go off like that, after coming so far. Stay to dinner, if you can, and we can put you up for the night. I wish you would. I'm a poor host with all this trouble to worry me.'

'Couldn't think of it, sir,' said Carton gratefully. 'I'd better get back to town at once.'

'There is no train after the four-fifty,' said Barley. 'It isn't a very cheery house to invite you to just now, but I can't see you stuck. The inn at the village is not fit for a pig.'

Carton considered. 'Very well, sir, I'll accept your kind suggestion, and I may be able to help a bit, perhaps. I have some experience of police work.'

Mr Barley raised his eyebrows. 'I am afraid it is in the hands of the regular police, Mr Carton.'

'Jolly good fellows, too,' said Carton. 'But two heads were always better than one, and witnesses have a way of shutting up when an official gets on their track.'

'At all events, I am pleased to have you. You will be company for Miss Gurdon. She tells me you know Tollard.'

'I was at school with Ned. A very good sort, too. Ned's people, and mine, and Elaine's, lived within a mile of each other in Bucks.'

'Really? Mr Tollard is rushing here by car. It will be a sad business meeting him.'

'Let me see him for you,' said Jim Carton readily. 'He may take it better from me.'

Elaine broke in. 'There is something in that. Mr Barley has too much on his hands already.'

'Let me know when he arrives, and I'll have a talk with him,' said Carton. 'It's awfully good of you to put me up, sir.'

'Oh, that's all right,' said Barley. 'You'll excuse me now, won't you? I have several things to see to, and the superintendent may ring me up at any time.'

When he had gone, Elaine turned to Carton. 'I think it was a good idea to suggest telling Ned. Poor Mr Barley is dreadfully upset and fussed. Sometimes he looks as if he was going to break down.'

'Doesn't Ned know anything about it?'

'Of course he knows that she is dead, but unless—No, it could not be in any of the papers yet.'

'You mean, he does not know she was murdered?'

'That's it.'

'I thought the old chap might think it funny, my suggesting seeing Ned first. I'm a stranger here, after all.'

'Mr Barley has got to the point where he is only too glad to get anyone to take the responsibility off his shoulders. It is wretched for him, really. It will get into all the papers, and he may be haunted by journalists.'

'I know.' Jim Carton looked at her thoughtfully, and added, 'I think I should like to take a look at that window from outside—the window you told me about. I might see something.'

'The detective searched the lawn and the shrubbery thoroughly. And the superintendent gave orders no one was to go out there.'

Carton shrugged. 'Well, I am a stranger, and did not hear the instructions! You see, Elaine, out where I was we get a bit more practice in open-air tracking than they do here. We were up against hard ground, too, that doesn't show spoor much, and the men we went after were used all their lives to treading warily, covering up their tracks, and all the other little games savages are so expert at.'

'Do you think you could get any information?'

'I might. There's the shrubbery. If a fellow hid there, he must have moved the branches and leaves. Signs that a town detective wouldn't see, might convey a good deal to me.'

Elaine went to the window, and pointed out a shrubbery about twenty yards to the right. 'If you think you can, you had better slip out now, Jim. I can't take any responsibility, but this may be your only chance if the police come back.'

He smiled, and advanced to the French window, which was latched. 'Right! I'll risk it! You don't know what I'm doing. You can say I had a touch of the sun in Africa, if you like!'

He slipped out, and went across to the shrubbery at once. Elaine sat down, and bent her gaze on the floor. She was thinking quickly. Her eyes were absent. Once or twice she frowned. Once a little smile flickered on her lips, and was gone.

Carton's quick eyes were roving about the shrubs outside. He bent down and examined a twig here, a leaf there. He studied the dry soil under the bushes, and frowned when he saw the distinct mark of a large boot.

'The policeman's mark,' he said. 'That broken twig is his job too. The sap is too fresh; especially with this sun so hot.'

He had concluded his examination, and was stepping out of the shrubbery, when a window was thrown open on the first floor of the house, and a youthful but angry voice addressed him.

'What the devil are you doing there, eh? Don't you know no one is allowed to walk there?'

Carton looked casually up, to see Ortho Haine's flushed face staring down at him. 'Oh, sorry,' he apologised. 'Are you the inspector?'

Haine glared at him. 'I'm a guest here,' he said sharply. 'But get off the lawn at once.'

Carton raised his hat ironically, and returned to the library through the French window.

'Who's the angry boy-scout above?' he asked.

Elaine repressed a smile. 'Ortho Haine,' she said. 'He's a very decent boy, but is rather excited just now. You see, he doesn't know who you are, and he was rather a worshipper of Margery Tollard.'

'Oh, is that it? Well, to avoid further trouble, perhaps you would introduce me to some of the other guests.'

'Of course,' said Elaine, then glanced at him. 'You brought nothing with you, of course?'

'Not a clout. I never thought the old sportsman would invite me to stay. I expect he won't mind my turning up to dinner in these, though; considering the occasion.'

'I'm sure he won't, and Haine might lend you pyjamas.'

'From his voice, he didn't appear joyfully impressed by me, but you never know,' said Jim.

Ortho Haine was rather unpleasantly surprised when, after running downstairs to tell Mr Barley that a strange man was on the lawn, he met Elaine with that very fellow, and was promptly introduced to him. After shaking hands, and staring almost rudely at the newcomer, before he recollected himself, he muttered an apology.

'I didn't know you were a friend of Miss Gurdon's,' he said sheepishly. 'I thought you were a reporter.'

'And I mistook you for a policeman, so we're square, Mr Haine. As a matter of fact, Mr Barley knew I could not get back to town, and took pity on me.'

Elaine led the way then into the drawing-room, and made him known to Mrs Minever, Nelly Sayers, and Mrs Gailey. The latter, who was always a romantic, at once took particular interest in Carton, wondering if he were in love with Elaine. Surely he must be, or he would not have rushed down to see her so soon after his return to England.

Elaine left them, saying she must ascertain in which room Mr Carton was to sleep.

'How exciting to have been in Africa,' Netta cried. 'But then, things are horribly exciting here. It is most terrible, isn't it?'

'Very tragic indeed,' he said soberly. 'I knew Ned Tollard before I went away.'

'But not Margery, perhaps?'

'His wife, no. I have been away some years.'

'Have you known Elaine long?' she asked ingenuously.

'A good many years,' he said, with a look in his eye that stirred Netta's romantic instincts again.

Meanwhile, seeing the new visitor engaged with Netta Gailey, Haine had gone to the further end of the long room with Mrs Minever and Nelly Sayers. The impudence of Carton, in ironically raising his hat and mistaking him for a policeman, when he challenged him from the window, still rankled.

'Seems an odd fish,' he remarked in a low voice to Nelly. 'I suppose he's all right though.'

'He is evidently one of Miss Gurdon's worshippers,' said Mrs Minever waspishly.

Nelly was torn between two impulses: to agree with Haine and the old lady; and to champion the attractive stranger.

'He doesn't know anything yet, you see,' she said, compromising between the two camps.

As she spoke, Elaine came hurriedly back. She did not look at any of the others, but went straight up to Carton.

'Ned has come,' she said, in a low but clear voice, 'but you need not go. Mr Barley happened to be going down the hall, when Ned arrived.'

Haine turned to Nelly to whisper, 'Why should he go anyway?'

'Hush!' said Nelly fearfully, 'he'll hear you!'

CHAPTER IX

THE HUSBAND

IF anyone doubted that Ned Tollard had loved his wife, his appearance when he arrived at the house was sufficient to dissipate the doubt. He looked as white as paper, his eyes were red-rimmed, and he walked with the tremulous gait of a man crushed under some great burden.

Mr Barley, much moved himself, ushered him into the library, locked the door, and at once told him what had happened. Fortunately, there was no one in the hall when they left the room together, and ascended the stairs. They parted on the landing, Mr Barley remaining standing near the head of the stairs, while the bereaved husband went on to the room where his wife lay.

When he came out again in ten minutes, he walked with a decisive step, his eyes were full of determination, and he had recovered command of his voice.

'I must pull myself together, Mr Barley,' he said. 'What is done is done, but we can make sure that the ruffian does not escape punishment. Are the police in the house?'

'They were here, but they are gone. No doubt Superintendent Fisher will be back. He was anxious to see you.'

They returned to the library, and hardly sat down before a heavy vehicle came up the drive. Mr Barley excused himself and went out to see what it was. When he came back, he told Tollard in an awed voice that the body must be removed to Elterham for the post-mortem. The town was nearly twenty-five miles away, and the ambulance had arrived.

Tollard held his hand over his eyes for a moment, then looked up. 'I suppose it must. I can't go up again now. Tell them I identify the body, and will do so in public when required. Is the superintendent here yet?'

'He came with them, and wants to ask you some questions. Are you fit to see him?'

Tollard's mouth grew grim. 'Yes. Show him in here. If any man can help me to punish the damned ruffian that did it, he's welcome.'

'What a fool I was to think there was anything in this business between him and Miss Gurdon,' said Barley to himself, as he went in search of Fisher.

The latter entered the smoke-room a few minutes later, introduced himself, and exchanged a few words with Tollard. Then at the latter's bidding, he sat down, and put a question.

'You were in the Isle of Wight last night, sir, I understand?'

'Yes. I left London pretty late, but a friend of mine who has a small steam yacht at Lymington took me over.'

'I understood Mr Barley to say you went away on business.'

'I may have said so,' replied Tollard, giving him a steady look, 'but, from your point of view, it is most important to know where, and not why I was in any given place last night.'

'That is true, sir,' said Fisher, conscious of an evasion, but not quite sure if he ought to pin it down.

'Very well. I called at my house in London before I left town. My secretary saw me. If you will communicate with Mr Charles Dodd, S.Y. *Triton*, Lymington, Hants, he will tell you that I was on the yacht with him.'

'Thank you, sir.'

'And now,' said Tollard, with some bitterness, 'having disposed of the possibility of my having killed my wife, to whom I was deeply attached, let us get back to common-sense! Some woman in a red dressing-gown was seen for a moment at my wife's window, this morning early. Have you traced her?'

'No, sir. We can't understand that. Unless a woman climbed in through the open window, we don't know how she got admittance. There were no fingerprints on the sill, and no outer door of the house appears to have been tampered with. The windows on the lower floor were, of course, closed and fastened last thing by Grover, the butler.'

'Is anyone in this house in the habit of wearing a red dressing-gown?'

'Only the cook, sir,' said Fisher, and suddenly remembered that he was being examined—a reversal of his proper rôle.

'If you don't mind, sir, I prefer not to answer any more questions,' he said, rather sharply. 'As far as I can see, sir, we can be pretty certain that you were out of the district last night, and that being so, we have nothing further to ask.'

Tollard nodded. 'Very well. But you can, perhaps, tell me if you have any clues yet. Surely the number of people capable of using a South American blow-pipe is limited?'

'No doubt it is, sir. When I tell you that your fingerprints are likely to be found on the blow-pipe in the hall here, you will understand why we had to question your whereabouts.'

'I tried to use it once here,' said Tollard, with a keen look.

'Quite so, sir. But having used it some time ago you will see for yourself what might be reasoned.'

'That is all you want of me, then?'

'That is all, sir. I presume you are ready to attend the inquest. It will be fixed for Monday, I think.'

'I said I should be ready to identify in public.'

Fisher nodded. 'I should say that the enquiry will be adjourned, sir. The evidence of toxicological experts will be required, and their reports on the nature of the poison tipping the arrow may take some time to prepare. In any case, we shall not be ready by Monday with sufficient evidence to get a proper verdict.'

Tollard rose. 'What I want to satisfy myself about is the way the investigation is being carried on.'

'That you will have to leave to us, sir,' said the superintendent stiffly.

'Are you going to ask for the assistance of Scotland Yard?'

'We don't contemplate it yet. We have adequate forces at our disposal, sir.'

'I hope you have,' said Tollard sombrely.

He left the room, and went in search of his host. Mr Barley was hovering about the hall, like a distracted foster-mother of chicks, and took him at once to the drawing-room, where Elaine and Jim Carton were talking softly by the window.

Elaine went up to Tollard with outstretched hands when he came in, her face showing some emotion when she saw how much the tragic news had changed and aged him. She murmured a few words, and then turned to Carton, who had watched their greeting with a thoughtful and not very approving eye.

'You know Jim Carton,' she said. 'He heard I was here, and came down to see me.'

'Of course,' said Tollard, staring for a moment at his old acquaintance. 'I haven't heard of you for years, Carton.'

They shook hands, and Carton spoke his sympathy. Grover came in at that moment, and said the superintendent would like to see Mr Barley and Miss Gurdon before he left. They excused themselves, and went out. Carton sat down, and fixed his eyes on Tollard.

'This is a damned ugly business,' he said. 'I'm more sorry for you than I can tell, old man.'

Tollard sat down. 'Terrible. I only hope these police here are competent to unravel it. I can't say that the specimen in the other room impressed me much. He seemed almost inclined to believe that I might have had something to do with it.'

Carton stretched out his long legs. 'I know how you feel. I should feel the same, though it is not a very logical attitude.'

Tollard glanced at him quickly. 'Why not?'

'Because you can't be logical without looking at both sides. You haven't done anything; therefore you wonder why you are questioned about your movements. But the police don't know you, they don't know what you have, or have not, done. They are bound to thrash out—especially in this case.'

They were men of very diverse temperament and outlook. At this moment Tollard began to feel a sensitiveness about Carton's attitude that resulted in the faintest shade of hostility.

'Why especially in this case?'

Carton shrugged. 'Excuse me, old man, if I sound sententious. But, as I was telling Elaine a little while ago, I had some police work of a kind to do in Africa. It was part of my job. It gave me an insight into the feelings of those whose duty it is to investigate unpleasant things.'

'You haven't answered my question, Carton.'

'I'm coming to that,' replied Carton bluntly. 'Being away, I have got out of touch with our set, but, to be quite frank, I can see some people wondered at your backing Elaine financially.'

'I wish they would mind their own business.'

'Quite. It would, be easier for everybody. But I am trying to look at it as the police will. They hear gossip about this, they wonder if—well, perhaps I had better say no more about it.'

Tollard flushed. 'You have said enough to tell me what you mean.'

'What the police may mean.'

'The police then, if you prefer it. If they are such lunatics as that, they will suspect Miss Gurdon next.'

'Probably they do,' said Carton, frowning.

Tollard started. 'You don't mean that. How could they?'

'Very easily. She can use a blow-pipe. She found Mrs Tollard. She has no witnesses—could not have in the circumstances—to prove that she was in her bedroom from the moment she retired to bed, till she went into that room early in the morning.'

'You are taking a rather brutal line of supposition, Carton.'

'Possibly; murders have a way of being brutal, and the police know it. There's a good old saying that the man who keeps furthest away from the precipice has the least danger of falling over.'

'You are suggesting that it was injudicious of me to offer to finance Miss Gurdon?'

'To put it plainly, yes. I don't mean that there was any harm in it, but the most harmless things lead to the greatest trouble sometimes.'

'They would actually go to the length of thinking that I had a guilty passion for Miss Gurdon, and that she, or I, tried to remove my wife!' Tollard cried hotly.

Carton shrugged again. 'They are bound to take every possibility into consideration. You must see that. Don't think me a cold-blooded fish for talking like this. If a man is going to defend himself, or someone else, the more he knows about the likely line of attack, the better able he will be to meet it. I can assure you that my interest in Elaine more than equals your own.'

'That sounds cryptic.'

'I am sorry if it does. I hope you don't think I have no sympathy for you, Tollard. The fact is, I once proposed to Elaine. She turned me down. But I came home to try my luck again.'

'Now I see.'

'Good! I have the greatest sympathy for you in your trouble, but, naturally, Elaine stands first in my mind. I can foresee that the police may suspect her, and I can't forget that they can only suspect her because she and you were arranging this expedition together, and seeing enough of each other to cause gossip—probably malicious.'

'Certainly malicious.'

'But just as damaging when one does not know the rights or wrongs of the case.'

Tollard bit his lip. 'Anyone might have heard the whole details. Elaine wanted money for her next trip, I came to her help with a promise. Naturally, since I had offered financial assistance, she consulted me about details. There was nothing more than that in it.'

'I am sure there wasn't,' said Carton. 'But it is like a super-stition that there are human beings in Mars; a scientist may deny it, but others will still believe, because there is no means of proving it one way or the other.'

Tollard nodded. 'What about this woman in red?'

Carton was glad they had left the more controversial topic. He looked down thoughtfully. 'That is really interesting, I mean to see the man Jorkins about that.'

'Are you taking up the case too?' asked Tollard, rather impatiently.

'In a way I am,' said Carton, discerning the fact that the other had begun to dislike him on account of the necessary home-truths he had delivered. 'If I can prove that there was a woman in the room this morning early, I shall have a defence.'

'Unless this superintendent fellow says it was Elaine.'

'It is possible he may.'

'Though, of course,' said Tollard thoughtfully, 'Mr Barley says Elaine was wearing a pale blue dressing-gown when she entered his room.'

'That proves nothing, I am afraid.'

Tollard looked at him sharply. 'On the contrary, it seems to my infantile mind to prove everything!'

He felt rather bitter, but his companion made allowance for that and did not resent the implied sarcasm.

'Strictly speaking, no. If we can imagine Elaine to have done such a thing, she would realise the importance of the colour, and purposely show herself to Barley in a blue one.'

'Very elaborate precautions, Carton.'

His tone stung Carton this time. What the devil was the fellow driving at? Why was he so snappy? Surely there could be nothing in the common gossip after all?

'Considering the provocation I have sometimes received,' he drawled, 'I have committed very few murders; but, if I were going to commit one, I think I should take rather elaborate precautions to cover up. But we'll drop that theory for the moment, if you don't mind. When I see Jorkins I may get further light on this supposed intruder.'

Tollard calmed down. 'I hope you can. I suppose you know more about this sort of thing than I do. But what can you ask the man the police did not ask him?'

Jim Carton raised his eyebrows. 'I didn't ask him, I mean the superintendent, but I haven't heard from anyone if Jorkins was questioned about the position of the woman, if she was facing inwards or outwards.'

'How does that affect the issue?'

'In several ways. For example, if he saw a woman's hair, he might be sure it was a woman. Men nowadays do wear silk dressing-gowns, and light ones too.'

'By Jove!' cried Tollard, studying his companion with more interest. 'That never occurred to me.'

CHAPTER X

DID TOLLARD LOVE HIS WIFE?

THE superintendent had gone, and dinner was served. It was a gloomy meal, for no one cared to trench on the subject of the tragedy, and the circumstances precluded conversation from proceeding in a lighter vein. Only Carton saved the dinner from disaster, by telling some of his experiences in Africa, which were neither criminal nor amusing, but sufficiently interesting to fill a gap.

Mr Barley had rather unwisely put Tollard at some distance from Elaine Gurdon, a blundering exercise in what he thought tact, that provoked comment in the minds of Ortho Haine and Mrs Gailey. The former had his own opinions about Tollard, and they were not very flattering ones.

The next morning Tollard sat writing letters until lunch time. Mr Barley went over to Elterham with Haine and Miss Sayers. Netta Gailey sat up in Mrs Minever's sitting-room, and Carton, finding himself alone after breakfast with Elaine, suggested a walk.

'I don't feel much inclined for it,' she said.

'I wish you would come,' he replied. 'As a matter of fact, I am going on a little errand that may interest you.'

'What do you mean?'

'I want to see Jorkins. So far as we know, the police have not turned up today. I should like to get in before them if I can.'

'He's an under-keeper,' said Elaine. 'I think he has an outlying cottage near that big fox-cover.'

'By the way,' said Carton, rising leisurely, and pushing his coffee-cup aside, 'you haven't a red dressing-gown, have you?'

She started. 'No.'

'Never had one?'

'Of course not. Do you think I should have been silly enough not to say so, if I had? Why, I insisted on the superintendent going through all my trunks when you were talking to Ned yesterday evening.'

'Good! Well, we'll get on the track of Jorkins now. Run up and get on your things. I don't want to let it out where I am going. And Elaine.'

'Yes?'

'Don't be shirty if I face facts. Tollard got his wattles up when I suggested that the police might suspect him or you. The ostrich doesn't stick its head in the sand, but, if it did, it would show what an ass it was.'

'Ned is upset,' she remarked.

'All the more reason for us to keep our heads. This is going to be a jolly awkward enquiry, and sneering at the police methods doesn't do anyone a ha'p'orth of good. They're only human, you see. Tollard's naturally shocked and upset, but what I can't understand is this—'

He paused awkwardly, and studied her face. She did not look at him, and he went on with more determination.

'His friends here talk as if he hadn't been frightfully enamoured with his wife.'

'I'll run up now and get ready,' said Elaine, as if she had not heard him. 'I shan't be long.'

When she had gone he went, out into the hall, got his hat and stick, and waited for her under the porch.

'Rum,' he said to himself doubtfully. 'What's the game, I wonder? Perhaps they were all mistaken. You never can tell with a man and his wife.'

A minute later Elaine came down, and they set off across the park to a little gate that broke the wall on the east side.

'You can see the big cover on that little hill over there,' Elaine said, pointing. 'I believe Jorkins is a single man, and does for himself.'

Carton nodded. 'If someone was hiding in the shrubbery near the window, the fellow ought to have seen him. Keepers have good eyes.'

'But there would hardly be a woman in the room, and a man outside,' she objected.

'No. One does away with the other. But we have to prove who was there.'

She reflected. 'Surely the coroner's jury will think it—must think it was a woman?'

'Coroners' juries don't settle things. They are there to find the cause of death. If the police are not satisfied, they will go on enquiring. Besides, as I told Tollard, it may have been a man. Apparently this Jorkins based his supposition on a long flowing garment. That may mean a dressing-gown. A man may wear one.'

'But what men were there in the house? Only Mr Barley, Mr Haine, and Mr Head.'

'And Grover. What of that? If we are going to except anyone, we may as well give up. Of course I had to know it, but it seems strange to me that neither you nor Tollard seem to have any idea of the necessity of keeping an open mind. You're like some people during the War. They had met a decent German, or Hungarian, or Turk, and couldn't believe that people they thought nice might be very nasty indeed.'

'No, I suppose you're right. I would never suspect Mr Barley or Mr Haine.'

Carton cut the head off a thistle with his stick. 'Look here, Elaine, let me hear about these collogues you had with Tollard. I'm on your side every time, but I ought to get a line on that.'

Without turning to look at her, he felt that she had stiffened.

'In what way?'

'Well, when you started to talk it over. Where did you meet?'

She considered for a moment, her colour rising. For a moment her lips took a mutinous turn, then she replied rather coldly.

'At his house, of course.'

'Thanks. What about his wife?'

'Margery? Oh, she was there.'

'Did she take any interest—join in, eh?'

'No, not often.'

'But she wasn't very keen on it?'

Elaine frowned. 'Don't you think I may have enough of this sort of thing at the enquiry?'

He looked at her earnestly. 'There! That's what I feared. That is what I meant when I told you not to fly off the handle when I wanted to hear things. I tell you this is serious. You may be as innocent as a babe unborn. I have no doubt you are, but I wouldn't like to bet that the police don't try to mix you up in it.'

'I am afraid of that,' said Elaine.

'Naturally. There are such things as miscarriages of justice, even in this country. I'm jolly well going to see that you get clear of it. But I can't do that unless I know exactly how things stand.'

'Go on then,' said Elaine composedly.

He looked relieved. 'I may take it that Mrs Tollard wasn't very keen on the thing?'

'No, she wasn't.'

'She never told you so?'

'Not directly. I believe she hinted to Ned that the talk bored her. She wasn't interested in travel.'

'Right. You met elsewhere to talk the thing over? It was only if there was a deficit in the proceeds from your book and your lectures that he was to weigh in with extra funds?'

'Yes. But it was very likely he would be called upon. He is a director of a company in Paraguay. He was on the board of a new company that thinks of running a railway in lower Brazil.'

They had come to the little gate in the park wall. Carton let her out, and followed her across a narrow road to a stile giving on a field-path.

'I suppose,' he said tentatively, when they were on the path, 'Tollard was in love with his wife?'

She stood still, and looked at him. 'Why ask me that? He married her. I suppose he was in love with her.'

'When he married. No doubt. But I gather that they were not much together.'

'They had different tastes.'

'You don't know if they quarrelled?'

Elaine walked on. 'I really must refuse to say any more, Jim. I don't know anything about it. Ned is not the sort of man to talk about his wife.'

'Then I take it he didn't,' said Carton. 'Sorry if I worry you, old thing, but I don't want to move in a fog.'

'You had better leave it to the police,' she said.

'Hanged if I do!' he said obstinately.

They walked on in silence. With all his zeal for her cause, perhaps because of it, Carton felt that his position was an awkward one. If either Ned Tollard or Elaine had been able to appreciate the situation properly, things might have been easier. As it was, he must appear to them inquisitive and officious above the normal.

He had an impulse to abandon any part in the investigation, and apply himself to his wooing. That would be easy. He would not be disliked, or parried when he asked questions. But he was not the kind of man to take the easy road in preference to any other.

He fell to studying Ned Tollard's character as he tramped on by Elaine's side. At school Ned had been a sporting boy, as he was now a sporting man. With it, he had been frank, generous, easy to get on with. He seemed different now. Was that change a recent one; the result of the tragedy which had just taken place? Or was it of old standing, a deterioration since his marriage?

On the one hand, bearing and voice and everything spoke to a man distracted and on edge, on account of his bereavement. To set against that was Elaine's admission that he and his wife had had differing taste, which had set them rather apart, and her omission when he asked her for closer details. There was also the gossip, which might be fundamentally incorrect, but had not arisen out of nothing.

And yet, as Carton told himself uneasily, it did not seem to matter much either way, so far as Tollard was concerned. He was away at the time, and he had what looked like a fool-proof alibi.

'What do you know of Mr Barley?' he asked, suddenly coming out of a reverie.

Elaine started. She too had been thinking. 'Mr Barley? Oh, I like him. He is very generous and kind.'

'Yes, but what do you know of him?'

'Not much more than anyone else does, Jim. I believe he is a retired financier.'

'That isn't altogether a testimonial—may not be anyway. Finance covers a multitude of fishinesses.'

She smiled faintly. 'He knows one or two people I know, and when he heard I was lecturing at Elterham, he wrote and mentioned the names of two, and asked me would I come on a visit.'

'Was Tollard one of them?'

'Yes. Ned says he had a good reputation.'

'Why did he ask you? Is he a traveller?'

'Not at all, I believe. But, as he put it to me, he had no chance of marrying, and wanted to get associated with a geographical discovery.'

'What the dickens for?'

'Well, it was an ingenuous thing to say, but I know what he meant. He has no children to carry on his name.'

'Funny old chap! He wanted to be known to posterity by a side wind.'

She nodded. 'Something like that.'

Carton wrinkled up his eyes, a way he had when he thought himself on the track of something. 'But the fact that you were a guest here would not help him much.'

'It wasn't that, quite. He volunteered to come to my help with funds for the next expedition.'

'Since you came here?'

'Of course.'

If she expected him to pursue the subject further she was mistaken. They had neared the edge of the cover, and saw a small cottage on the rim of it.

'That's Jorkins' place, I take it?'

'I think it must be.'

'Looks to be shut up,' said Carton, as they advanced. 'The oak is sported, and there doesn't seem any smoke from the chimney.'

'I hope we haven't come all the way for nothing.'

'Hope not. We'll soon see.'

They advanced to the cottage, only to find the door locked, and the place empty. They looked in at a window, but could see no one.

'He may be back for his lunch,' said Jim.

As he spoke a keeper came out of the cover, a gun on his arm, and advanced, touching his hat to Elaine.

'Did you want to see Jorkins, miss?'

'Yes, we did. Is he away?'

'Afraid he is, miss. He had a job I give him this morning to get some rabbit netting from Elterham, or leastways order it.'

'Then he will be back later?'

'No, miss, not along of this murder up at the big house, he won't. This be Saturday, and he has to give evidence at the inquest Monday. Police said he had to come, and gave him a paper about it.'

'A subpoena,' said Carton.

'That's it, sir—a suppeeny. He has a married sister living over to Elterham, and he said to me might he go to stay on there, after he'd ordered the netting, and save a journey back and forward. So I said he could, knowing Mr Barley wouldn't mind.'

Carton nodded. 'Thank you. I'll see him again another time. Well, Elaine, we'd better hurry back to lunch, I think.'

CHAPTER XI

SUPPRESSIONS

A FEW of Mr Barley's guests wandered into the billiard-room after lunch, and after a faint-hearted attempt to play pool, sat down on the bank to smoke and chat.

Carton and Elaine were there, with Ortho Haine and Nelly Sayers. All of them kept studiously away from the topic that most intrigued their minds, and the conversation, growing more and more desultory, threatened to die of sheer inanition, when Tollard came in, hat in hand.

'I must get a breath of fresh air,' he said, looking at Elaine, after a short look at the others. 'What about a walk?'

Carton expected Elaine to say she was tired after her trudge over the fields that morning, but she only nodded.

'I don't mind.'

'Come along, then,' said Tollard. 'Three or four miles' tramp will do me good.'

'Elaine has done her bit already,' said Jim.

'Oh, if you're tired!' said Tollard.

'I shan't be a minute,' said Elaine, smiled faintly about her, and went out. Tollard nodded casually to the others, and followed her. Ortho Haine looked discontentedly about him.

'Come for a spin in my jigger, Nelly?'

Miss Sayers shook her head. 'Not now, thanks, but don't let me keep you.'

'If you won't, you won't,' he said sulkily, and lounged out.

'He never smiles on me,' said Jim Carton, as the door closed. 'I am not in his good books.'

She laughed. 'He's young.'

'That must be the disease. I say, Miss Sayers, that poor thing who is dead quite perplexes me. She seems to have been so fascinating to some, and so unattractive to others.'

'She was like that,' said Nelly. 'I suppose some people would think her perfectly lovely. She had an oval face and the fairest of hair, and melting soft eyes—the kind you see in a Greuze. Then she was very slim and graceful, and had an odd way of moving. It wasn't quite walking. Sinuous, you know, that sort of thing.'

'Was her conversation as attractive as the rest of her?'

'No. She hadn't much—at least to me. I always thought her very silent. I don't know that I should call her sulky, but you know what I mean.'

'The blow seems to have stunned Tollard anyway.'

'That's the funniest part of it,' she said. 'Of course I expected him to feel it, for he is a good sort, but I imagined he wouldn't be exactly crushed.'

'It surprises you?' said Carton.

'Well, in a way. You see, though there was nothing in it, he seemed so keen on Elaine's trip. I don't mean to say a married man ought to have no interests outside his home, but most of them felt that if he were very happy with his wife, he wouldn't stay far away from her.'

Carton nodded. 'It's puzzling, isn't it? But you can see he is sincere about it now. He really is terribly cut up?'

He meant this as a question, though he did not accentuate that. She agreed without hesitation.

'Of course. He looks almost a wreck.'

Carton looked her straight in the face. 'We need not doubt it. Lots of fellows who are married happily enough think they have a whole lifetime before them. They wake up when their wives die, and are horribly shocked to discover that even wives are mortal. In confidence, Miss Sayers, I may tell you that I know too much about Elaine ever to suspect that she would encourage Tollard. We mustn't make too much of this, or get things out of proportion.'

'Oh, I never thought she would,' cried Nelly. 'And I do see what you mean. If anyone talks about them that way again, I'll manage to work that in.'

'I wish you would,' he said, having got from her all the information he could.

Later on, Mrs Minever happened to sit near him, and, without asking for them, he was favoured with her views. When he managed at last to get away from her, he was frowning a little.

Justifiably or unjustifiably, most of Tollard's acquaintances had formed the opinion that he did not get on well with his wife. Most of them, until his last appearance after the tragedy, had suspected him of a latent *tendresse* for Elaine. About Elaine herself opinion was divided. Mrs Minever and Mrs Gailey half believed Elaine had encouraged him.

This made him angry with Ned Tollard. The fellow, if the reports about tension in his home were true, ought to have had more discretion.

Most of the guests went early to bed that night. Carton sat them all out, and found himself at last with Mr Barley, smoking a final pipe.

Elaine had told him of Mr Barley's offer, and he wanted to probe a little deeper into that. Barley had probably been an experienced and successful financier, but aptitude in business does not always make a man an expert in other affairs. The elderly man was only sophisticated to a point. In his own home he showed himself kindly, unreserved, simple-minded.

'I suppose this kills Miss Gurdon's expedition,' said Jim, feigning to be busy with a pipe that drew badly.

'I'm afraid it does, for the time at least,' said Mr Barley. 'I am really very sorry, for she is so keen on it, and her mind was quite taken up with the idea.'

'I think it was unwise of Tollard to offer to back her,' said Jim. 'But he won't repeat that error. I wish I could do something myself.'

'In what way, Mr Carton?'

'Well, you suggested that she might take it up later. Funds will be just as necessary then.'

Mr Barley waved his pipe. 'I can come to her rescue, as I tried to before.'

'That's good of you, sir. I think Elaine told me she had had an offer from you. What a pity you didn't get in first.'

'I think it is, but that can't be helped now. But perhaps—who knows?—she may settle down, and get married, and then she won't want to go gallivanting about the world.'

Carton looked at him so sharply that he added awkwardly, 'I don't mean Tollard, of course. I wondered if you now—' he smiled kindly, and glanced at his guest.

Carton smiled. 'I admit, sir, you made a good shot. Between you and me, I am inclined to resolve the prospected next expedition into pleasant nothingness.'

'I wish you luck,' said Barley, that confirmed sentimentalist. 'You've known her a long time?'

'Long enough to decide that she was worth waiting for, sir.'

'That's the right spirit, my boy,' cried Barley. 'I don't know what your chances are, but you have my best wishes.'

'I wish I knew myself,' said Jim thoughtfully.

Ever since the tragedy Mr Barley had been bursting to confide in somebody. Here was a young man who had known Miss Gurdon for years, who was in love with her; a nice fellow, and a very intelligent one. He fell to the temptation to be expansive.

'Since you are so interested in Miss Gurdon,' he began, after a look about him, 'I think I may as well tell you what has been worrying me.'

'Unless you feel sure that you want to, sir—' began Jim.

'I am quite sure you will keep it to yourself. I should like your opinion. The other people here seem to have taken sides so strongly that I don't care to ask any of them. I think you have heard some of the gossip that was flying about. Very well. I heard it too. I have known Tollard for a year or two. I like him. I liked his wife too, though she was not exactly the sort of woman who would take to a fossil like me. But when I heard this talk, I thought I would like to put things straight if I could. Officious, perhaps, but I meant well. I hate to see people unhappy. I was very unhappy once in my young days, and I thought I would have a shot at putting things right.'

'It was a kindly impulse at all events, sir.'

'From what I saw of Tollard and his wife I did not think that any real damage had been done, Carton. I felt that they were beginning to drift apart. Then I got a notion I should like to see the lady who was said to be causing the trouble. I knew she was famous in her way, but I thought her face would tell me more about her than the newspaper paragraphs.'

'No doubt.'

'So I asked Tollard and his wife here, and I asked Miss Gurdon at the same time. I happened to be the chairman at her lecture in Elterham. If I had thought to find her what is vulgarly called a "vamp," Carton, I was much mistaken. I took to her from the first. I decided, rightly or wrongly, that she was not the kind of woman to make hay of her friend's happiness.'

'You were right there.'

'I thought so. I think so still. But I am enough of a man of the world to realise that circumstances are sometimes stronger than the people they surround, and in any case, I felt that this association of her husband with Miss Gurdon was making the wife unhappy. It occurred to me that I might remove the cause of quarrel.'

'I don't think you went astray in that.'

'Perhaps not. Though, since this terrible business, I am beginning to doubt if it is wise for any outsider to try to compose quarrels. However, Tollard was backing Miss Gurdon, and I had a talk with her and offered to supply her with the necessary funds. If she had accepted she would not have been dependent on Tollard, these long consultations with him would have been rendered unnecessary, and Mrs Tollard would be easier in her mind.'

Carton smiled. 'You were generous enough, sir.'

'Oh, I have plenty of money. A few thousands is not so much to me as to some people. But it was in the interview with Miss Gurdon that I must have made some error in tact.'

Carton nodded. 'May I hear what it was?'

'I am not a diplomatist, and I suppose I was nervous and showed my hand. She was clever enough to see what I was getting at, and refused my offer.'

'On what grounds?'

'She said, naturally enough, that if she went to Tollard and turned his offer down after accepting it, he would think she was afraid of the situation. She was also afraid that people who heard of it would draw the obvious inference, I think some of them would have done so. After that, I was foolish enough to hint that Mrs Tollard was unhappy about it, and she fired up a little, so that I was glad to drop the subject.'

'But why should she fire up?' asked Carton, with a puzzled air. 'You had made a generous offer, with the best of intentions.'

'Well, you see, she did not like Mrs Tollard. She seemed to have a grievance against her. I know what she meant. She is herself a woman of action and resolution, and Mrs Tollard was a languid, rather aesthetic kind of woman. They didn't hit it off, and Miss Gurdon told me plainly she thought Mrs Tollard was spoiling her husband's life.'

Carton frowned. He had found Tollard changed. Had Elaine changed too?

'It would not be wise to repeat that at the inquest.'

'I don't intend to, Carton. I know a bit about the law, and when I give evidence in a court of law I confine myself strictly to what I know. I should never dream of quoting hearsay, or other people's gossip. That is fatal.'

'Absolutely. However, you got the idea that Mrs Tollard was unhappy, probably jealous. It is a curious thing that that opinion gained ground, while I have met no one yet who ever heard Mrs Tollard complain.'

'That's true. She never complained to me. I hope I was mistaken. I may have been. Tollard evidently loved his wife. Life is an odd thing, Carton; it isn't lived on the surface.'

Carton knocked out his pipe. 'You will have someone to represent you at the inquest?'

'My solicitor will watch matters for me. He is coming down tomorrow. If she consents, I shall ask him to represent Miss Gurdon as well. The police may have some evidence we are not aware of.'

'The inquest will be adjourned very likely. In that case you might ask your solicitor to watch for police omissions rather than evidence.'

'You think they may suppress something?'

'It's possible. If, for example, they suspect someone, and have not sufficient evidence to go on, they will pass over that person as lightly as possible.'

'Not to alarm them prematurely?'

'Exactly.'

'What do you think of this woman in red?'

Jim Carton shook his head. 'I can't form an opinion yet. The man saw someone, but we have no idea who it was. It seems unlikely that anyone intruding for the purpose of murder would show himself at the window, even if it was still early morning.'

'No. I suppose not. But he must have seen someone.'

'It does not seem to have occurred to anyone yet that Elaine—Miss Gurdon, went in there. Perhaps at the very moment when the man was passing across the park.'

'Oh, it did occur to me, but she was not wearing red.'

'Did you look at the clock when you got out of bed, and went across with Miss Gurdon to see to Mrs Tollard?'

'I have no clock in my room. I can't bear a tick at night. I keep my watch under my pillow, but in a thick chamois case.

In any case, I did not expect to find Mrs Tollard dead. When I returned to dress I was too upset to look.'

'That is unfortunate. Did Elaine say what time it was she got up and went into the other room?'

'I don't think she did. She said she was awakened by a sound of a restless sleeper next door soon after dawn, but I don't think she knew the exact time. She did not mention it to the superintendent.'

'Then we have no means of relating events to time,' said Carton. 'But you are quite right. No one takes note of the exact time when they are not aware that anything hangs on the minute. Well, sir, I think I'll go to bed. Thank you for letting me hear your views about this sad business.'

'We can't get away from the sad things in life,' said Mr Barley bromidically. 'Good-night, Mr Carton.'

CHAPTER XII

MORALLY, the house-party began to break up next day. Mr Barley went to church, taking with him Mrs Minever, a reluctant Ortho Haine, and Mrs Gailey. Nelly Sayers professed to have a headache, but found a cure for it an hour later.

Carton had hoped to get Elaine alone that morning, but he turned up late at breakfast, to find that Elaine and Tollard had breakfasted early, and gone out. He was not in the mood to listen to Nelly's artless comments, so he escaped to his room again, as soon as he could, and sat down to wipe out extensive arrears of correspondence.

At lunch, Tollard was gloomy, and Elaine absent-minded, and their example set the tone for the rest. Carton determined this time to get ahead of the indiscreet Tollard, and managed to monopolise Elaine afterwards for a little time in the garden.

'You ran away this morning,' he rallied her. 'Was that fair or kind?'

She shrugged. 'Ned wanted to talk over things.'

'Very likely. But that was selfish of him. He has seen you lately. I have been away for six years, and have a lot of leeway to make up.'

'We shall have lots of time to talk later, Jim. Ned is heart-broken. He feels it a great deal. Then the scandal and the publicity will be very unpleasant.'

'Short of unfolding a plan for muzzling the reporters, and censoring the papers, I don't see how you could help him. Mr Barley is furious. It appears he was beset by two pressmen on the way to church, and one going back. He had given the

89

lodge-keeper orders to admit no one, without 'phoning the name and business up to the house.'

'I know.'

As she spoke, a little man with a keen, alert face, came up the drive on foot.

'That one of the detectives?' asked Carton, as the new-comer advanced to the porch. 'Looks like it?'

'I never saw him before,' said Elaine, shifting her chair to get a better view. 'He may be.'

The visitor was admitted to the house. Carton resumed: 'Do be pally, old thing. I came all these thousands of miles to enjoy your society, and I want you to play up to me.'

She smiled at him, but faintly. 'Well, here I am.'

'I know you are. But you are developing a habit of am-notting!'

'I'm sorry. I have been worried.'

Grover appeared suddenly from the house, and came over to them.

'Mr Barley's solicitor has just come, sir, and Mr Barley will be glad if you will see him,' he said.

Carton stared, then laughed vexedly. 'All right. I'll come. Just my luck,' he added to Elaine as Grover retired. 'I had looked forward to a little talk with you.'

Mr Barley's lawyer, Mr Greeby, was quite of Barley's mind and Carton's. He agreed that as little as possible should be said about any matter not strictly of fact, and agreed to represent Miss Gurdon as well, if she consented.

'As things stand, she may be involved,' he said, in his mild voice. 'My firm does very little criminal business, as you know, but if any danger threatened, the case could of course be transferred to a firm who specialise in that line.'

'The police don't seem to be doing anything here at present,' said Carton, after a few minutes' discussion.

'I think they have a good many plain-clothes men scouring the country for Mrs Tollard's possible assailant,' replied Mr

Greeby. 'I had lunch at the club with the chief constable yesterday, and he seemed to think they were being very active. Apparently they are also making enquiries in a wide radius for a woman who may have stayed at an hotel or inn, and who was in possession of a red dressing-gown.'

'The chief constable hasn't called yet,' said Mr Barley, 'but certain members of the household have been called on to give evidence tomorrow. Much fewer than I thought.'

'How many?'

'Mr Haine, Mrs Tollard's maid, Mr Tollard, Miss Gurdon, and myself. While Fisher examined some of my other guests, apparently he doesn't need them. Jorkins, the under-keeper, of course, will be there.'

'Well, we had better see what your guest Miss Gurdon thinks,' said Mr Greeby.

'Would you mind asking her to come in?' said Mr Barley to Carton.

'Certainly,' said Carton, and went out in search of Elaine.

He saw very little of her again that day. When the solicitor had gone she was engaged in talk with Mr Barley for an hour, and later he could not separate her from the rest of the party. He went to bed irritated and dissatisfied. Was she purposely avoiding him, or was it simply chance?

Mr Barley's biggest car took them all next morning to Elterham to the inquest. Carton accompanied them, though not to give evidence, and regarded with patient indifference the formalities of swearing the jury, and preparing for the opening of the proceedings.

He glanced at Tollard, who sat stiffly, his mouth grim. Elaine was calm, and studied her surroundings with interest. Mr Barley and Ortho Haine were the most nervous of the party.

Elaine was called on presently to describe what had happened on the morning of the tragedy. She spoke clearly and distinctly, and made a good impression. Asked if she had suspected the presence of a second person in Mrs Tollard's room prior to her own entrance, she replied with a decided negative. She had heard sounds suggestive of a restless sleeper, had gone in and found Mrs Tollard lying on her back on the floor. She was prepared to swear that she was wearing a pale blue dressing-gown at the time. Mrs Tollard wore a green one. Asked if she would call it pale green, she said she would have called it green. It was not emerald in colour, but the adjective pale would not have occurred to her.

A dart was handed up to her. She was prepared to say that it was one of those that had been in a quiver in the hall on the day before the murder. She had handed six in a quiver to Mr Barley, who had had them hung up in their bark receptacle on the wall, together with a blow-pipe, to form a trophy for decoration. Asked if the darts were poisoned, and if so, could she tell the court what was the nature of the poison, she replied that she knew they were poisoned, but that this poison was a native secret. She had shown several guests at Stowe House how to use the blow-pipe. They were Mr Tollard and Mr Haine. She had used it herself at the same time on the lawn, using a dart without any venom on the tip. She did not think that Mr Tollard or Mr Haine had had sufficient practice to hit a mark even at short range, as the weapon was one that required a great deal of expertness to use with effect.

'You have seen animals die after being shot with these things?' the coroner asked.

'Yes, and a man on one occasion, when I was in South America.'

'Was the death sudden?'

'I should describe it as sudden. Of course, in that case the poison was fresh. Stale venom might take longer to kill.'

'You do not believe the dart in this case was tipped with curare?'

'I am sure it was not. These poisons for that purpose are localised to a certain extent.'

'You did not notice the dart in the body when you tried to raise Mrs Tollard?'

'No, I was startled when I thought she must be dead. I let her drop back rather suddenly, I am afraid.'

'You were an acquaintance of hers?'

'I have known her for years, yes.'

'You do not know anyone who would wish her ill?'

Elaine shook her head. 'We all have people who dislike us, but I know of no one who would perpetrate a murder. I have no reason to think she had enemies of that kind.'

Mr Tollard was called next. He swore that he knew no one who bore a grudge against his wife. He identified the body as hers. He told the court that he had left Stowe House on the afternoon preceding the murder, had gone to London, called at his house, then left for Lymington, where he had gone aboard a friend's yacht.

'And you were in the Isle of Wight when the telegram reached you?'

Tollard agreed, and was dismissed. Dr Browne followed him.

The doctor told of his examination of the body, and the conclusion he had formed from certain superficial signs that death was due to the administration of some poison. Taking those observations in conjunction with his finding of the dart in the body, and certain facts already known to him with regard to these darts, he assumed that the poison on the dart was woorali, a vegetable alkaloid, a preparation known to every practitioner under the name of curare. From what Miss Gurdon had said, he was of opinion that he had made a mistake—not in believing poison to be the cause of death, but only that particular poison.

'The Home Office experts are making an analysis,' said the coroner.

'I hear so, sir. That is the usual practice. Until I know their opinions, which may be delayed, I am unable to say definitely the nature of the poison used.'

'Was the dart deeply seated in the wound?'

'Decidedly. But, as I declared when I made the first examination of the body, that may have been due to the fact that Mrs Tollard fell on her back, thus driving in the dart more deeply.'

'Were you in a position to decide the angle at which the dart had entered?'

'That was difficult, on account of the fact I have just mentioned, but I am inclined to think it entered the back while moving in an upward direction.'

'Which would suggest that she had been shot by someone standing some distance away, below?'

'I think so.'

'It seems unfortunate that no witness so far has been able to give the exact hour, or moment, when the murder was discovered. Miss Gurdon thinks it must have been about a quarter-past five, but is not sure.'

'I arrived at the house and went upstairs at five minutes past six. I should say that she had been dead about an hour when I examined her.'

'I think we had better recall Miss Gurdon,' said the coroner, and Elaine took the doctor's place in the box.

'It was only a few minutes from the time when you heard noise, and decided to get up and see if Mrs Tollard was ill?' said the coroner.

'A very few minutes,' replied Elaine.

'She was apparently dead when you entered. Did she seem cold when you touched her? Were you at once aware that she was dead?'

'Her limpness told me that, but somehow I almost had the impression that she had died a few moments before I reached her. But, of course, she cannot have been dead long, for I heard those movements in her room.'

'Might not those have been the movements of a possible intruder?'

'They might,' said Elaine. 'I naturally took them to be made by her.'

She stood down, and was followed in the witness-box by Ortho Haine. He admitted that he occupied a bedroom on the same landing, but swore that he heard no disturbing sounds that morning. He was a friend of Mrs Tollard, and of her husband. He was not able to throw any light on the murder or its motives. He was dismissed, looking very red in the face, and as self-conscious as if he had been the criminal himself.

Mr Barley followed. He had little fresh to say. He declared that so far as he was aware nothing had been stolen from the dead woman's room. Mr Tollard had assured him that his wife's jewels were intact in their case. All his servants had been with him for some years, and he believed them to be strictly honest.

Then came Mrs Tollard's maid. She was as incoherent as most of her class in a similar situation, and her evidence threw no light whatever on the affair.

For some reason or other, the sergeant and Superintendent Fisher gave their evidence last, with the exception of the man Jorkins, who had not yet been called. They spoke to finding the body, and making the requisite examinations, laid stress on the wide open window of the bedroom, and disclosed the fact that they had found nothing in the room or the house that threw any light on the crime.

'But you are of the opinion that this unfortunate lady might have been shot with a blow-pipe from some point of vantage in the grounds?' Fisher was asked.

'That is my present opinion, sir,' said Fisher, and added that as the Home Office experts had not yet presented their evidence with regard to the nature of the poison used, and the police investigations were still incomplete, he would have to ask for a fortnight's adjournment.

'When we have heard the last witness, we shall discuss that,' said the coroner. 'Call Jorkins.'

CHAPTER XIII

who was it?

Jorkins, the under-keeper, gave his evidence with surprising clearness and certainty. Perhaps his occasional appearances in magistrates' courts, when poachers were charged with offences against the game-laws, helped him, but he had also a natural aplomb, which made what he said sound convincing.

He repeated that he had occasion to cross the park at Stowe House on the morning of the murder, and presumed that it would be about a quarter-past five, though he could not be certain of the exact minute. He made no note of the time, because, though he did not often see a woman's figure at a bedroom window so early in the morning, there was nothing in that appearance to suggest a tragedy.

'You were sure it was a woman, not a man in a dressing-gown?' he was asked.

'I seed the head, sir,' he replied. 'Fair hair I think it had, though I can't be sure of that. Anyway, 'twas not short like most of ladies has it nowadays'

'Are you aware that the dead lady had fair hair, which was uncut?'

'No, sir. I never see her to my knowledge.'

Carton listened to this interestedly. Evidently the police had shared his view at first, that a man in a dressing-gown might be mistaken for a woman.

The coroner looked at some notes before him. 'Could you say how the lady was standing when you saw her?'

'Well, sir, if I hadn't had good eyes, I wouldn't have seen that her hair was long, but I was a goodish distance away.'

'But you formed perhaps some impression? Did you think she was facing the window, standing with her back to it, or what?'

'I somehow don't think she stood with her back to it?'

'Or facing it?'

'I should say she was half-ways on, sir,' said Jorkins, very carefully. 'Sidewise like.'

'And wearing a red dressing-gown?'

'A flowing red thing, sir, whatever it was.'

'It might have been a loose coat then?'

'It might, sir. I couldn't say.'

'From where you were, you could see a small shrubbery, which lies twenty or thirty yards from the window?'

'Yes, sir.'

'You did not notice anyone hiding there, crouching among the bushes?'

'No one at all, sir.'

'You might have seen anyone there?'

'If there had been, sir, I think I would. The shrubs is thinner from the side I was, and I'm used to watching movements in cover—have to be, with the poachers to look out for.'

'You did not notice anyone crossing the park prior to that, or moving furtively anywhere in the grounds?'

'No, sir. I went on straight, took up some rabbit-traps, and went down to village to see about some rabbit cartridges. I heard of the murder up at the house, and went with sergeant to tell what I seen.'

He was allowed to stand down then, and Mr Barley was recalled. Asked if any of his household conformed to the description of the woman who had shown herself momentarily at the window, he replied that Mrs Tollard answered to it, except for the fact that she did not wear a red dressing-gown.

That closed the proceedings for the moment. The super-intendent renewed his application for an adjournment, which was granted. As the Stowe House party left the court, the chief constable, who had been present, spoke to Mr Barley briefly. Mr Barley left him, went to Tollard, and asked him if he would go home with the others in the car.

'I must stay for a little,' he explained. 'I may lunch here. You don't mind, do you?'

'Not at all,' said Tollard gloomily, and looked at Elaine. 'We are to go back,' he told her, as Barley returned to the chief constable. 'Isn't that the car over there?'

He signalled, and the chauffeur brought Mr Barley's car up to the kerb. Haine looked discontentedly about him as the others got in.

'If I had known there would have been an adjournment, I should have had my luggage brought down this morning,' he said to Tollard. 'I don't see that there's any use in my hanging about here.'

Tollard was privately of the same opinion. He had found Haine's youthful worship of his dead wife annoying and ill-timed.

'You could get a train after lunch,' he said. 'I don't suppose Mr Barley will be late.'

Elaine sat silent and thoughtful during the drive back, and the others would have done the same had not Ortho Haine started a controversial hare.

'It's a funny thing that the woman at that window should have had fair hair,' he said. 'I can't make it out.'

Carton looked at him. 'That's by no means the strangest feature of the case. After all, there are still a few women who do not shingle, and fair hair is not uncommon in England.'

Tollard grunted. 'If you don't mind, Haine, we won't pursue the subject.'

'Oh, just as you like,' said Haine peevishly. 'But it seems to me very important.'

'Possibly it does to you,' said Tollard savagely.

While the party were driving home to Stowe House, Superintendent Fisher and the inspector were walking slowly back to the station, deeply engaged in talk.

'I'm turning it over to you now, Warren,' said the former. 'You know my views, and have read my notes.'

'What do you think of the evidence of that fellow Jorkins?' asked Warren. 'Clear enough, it seemed to me.'

'In details, yes, but I'm hanged if it's at all clear in any other way, unless we take a big supposition.'

'What is that, sir?'

'Well, if we assume that another woman was actually in the room, wearing a red dressing-gown, or loose coat, she was there for a definite purpose, and that purpose was murder.'

'But if she was in the room, why should she drag a long thing like that blow-pipe with her?'

'I'll come to that later on. Assuming she was there for the purpose of murder, she might wish it to be thought that she was actually Mrs Tollard.'

'In case anyone caught a glimpse of her?'

'Yes. Now, Mrs Tollard had a quantity of fair hair, and wore it long. No one else in the house seems to have had hair both long and fair, but one of them might have put on a fair wig.'

'That might be, sir.'

'And from her position in the room, she might have seen a man—the under-keeper in this case—crossing the park, and shown herself for a moment at the window to make him think it was Mrs Tollard standing there.'

'I see, sir; but, if she was making up as Mrs Tollard, why did she not wear a dressing-gown of the same colour?'

'Well, that point hints that she was an outsider. An outsider might be familiar with Mrs Tollard's appearance in the street, or when dressed for the house, but she would not know what colour of dressing-gown she would wear. The lady might have had two or three, being a wealthy woman.'

Inspector Warren nodded. 'That's true. But, to get back to the blow-pipe. Why should she have it, when she was within hands' reach of Mrs Tollard?'

'We don't know that she had it,' said Fisher slowly. 'Either Jorkins has made a mistake, which is very unlikely, or else we have to suppose the presence of this other woman in the room. Suppose she had the dart in her hand, not the blow-pipe at all, and stuck it into Mrs Tollard, who was lying in bed. The prick may have been slight. You heard what the doctor said about the fall having driven the dart in further.'

'You mean she may have stabbed Mrs Tollard with it, while sleeping, and got away. Then Mrs Tollard began to feel the effects of the poison, and got out of bed, to fall dead near the window?'

'I only say it could have been done that way. There were only the distinct fingerprints of three people on the weapon.'

'Miss Gurdon, Mr Haine, and Mr Tollard.'

'I'm assuming so, since they all confessed to using that blow-pipe once, but you must ask them for their prints today when you go over. What I mean is this, if there was an outsider, and she used the blow-pipe, there would be four fingerprints. Or prints from four hands, I should say.'

'Eight,' corrected Warren. 'It requires one hand to steady the thing and one to aim. But I take your meaning, sir. No outsider either could have cleaned her prints off the weapon, for she couldn't see where the other ones were, and what would have removed one ought to have cleaned off the others.'

'The point is this,' said Fisher. 'This dart could have been used by hand. The sounds Miss Gurdon heard could have been those made by the intruder, and not by the dead lady when in pain before her death.'

They entered the station, and went to the superintendent's room. Fisher sat down, and pointed to a seat.

'What did you think of Mr Tollard's evidence, sir?' Warren asked, after a moment.

'I shouldn't have thought anything of it if it hadn't been for the evidence I took up at the house from those young women. From what they say, and what they were sorry they said, I had a notion that it was not all lavender in Tollard's home. But Mr Tollard certainly looks broken down, and it can't be remorse, for his alibi is good enough. His friend who kept the yacht, is not only prepared to swear he was with him at the time, but took the trouble to get his skipper to write a letter confirming it.'

'I suppose, sir,' said the inspector thoughtfully, 'there isn't a possibility of a poison having been administered for some time secretly. The lady had a bad headache the day before, and didn't come down to some meals.'

'The presence of the dart being a blind to make it appear she was shot from outside?'

'That's what I mean. I don't say it's likely.'

Fisher ruminated. 'Um. We couldn't say if it was even a possibility till the people at the Home Office supply us with their experts' reports. When they analyse the organs, they may find that the only traces of poison were of the same poison with which the arrow point was saturated. Of course they may find something else as well. But that means suspecting the husband, Warren.'

The inspector pursed his lips. 'If he wasn't happy, sir, we can't quite exonerate him yet, can we?'

'Well, you can keep that in mind, but I don't think there is anything in it.'

'No chance of any of the staff being in it?'

'No, and Mr Barley has no motive whatever, apart from not being the kind of man one would suspect.'

'The young fellow, Haine, was on the same landing.'

'He was, but from what I can make out he was more the victim of a silly passion for Mrs Tollard than a man likely to hurt her.'

Warren nodded. 'That leaves us Miss Gurdon. I had a talk with the sergeant.'

'He's an excellent officer in his limits, but not very intelligent.'

'Perhaps not, but it struck him that he had never seen a lady in a like situation, who was so calm and careless.'

'It's the first time he has met a lady explorer, Warren. I've had a look through her first book, and some of the things she did, or says she did, would frighten an ordinary man. Why, somewhere in Paraguay, she helped defend a town against revolting Indians.'

'Allowing for that, didn't it strike you in her evidence today that she skirted round the question of Mrs Tollard having an enemy?'

'It did. I am saving up the real examination for the next sitting of the enquiry. It struck me that she disliked the dead woman.'

'Then there was the husband backing her with money.'

'Not actually her—the expedition to come. I don't think he was doing anything out of the way. But it counts all the same. If his wife was jealous, and unhappy, and he was not happy either in the marriage, we can't rule out the possibility that he was in love with Miss Gurdon. He denied it strongly to me, at least by inference, but that isn't everything. If you can get a quiet talk again with those two young ladies, Mrs Gailey and Miss Sayers, try to pump them. But don't frighten them.'

'From what I could see,' said Warren, 'the old lady would be as good a spec as anyone.'

'You're quite right. Mrs Minever had a lot on the tip of her tongue, and she only swallowed it because she got frightened. Whether it's mere gossip and froth, or truth, I don't know. Find out if you can.'

'Have we had any luck in the matter of searching the hotels and places about for a strange lady?'

'Not yet. It's hard to say if we ever shall. I began this case, Warren, pretty sure that the criminal was outside, but the deeper I get into it the more inclined I am to think that the one who killed Mrs Tollard was in the house, or in touch with someone in the house!'

CHAPTER XIV

AN OPEN MIND

WHEN Jim Carton advised Elaine of the advantages of being logical, and looking at everything with an open mind, he was following the common practice of recommending a course he himself was not following. He was not aware of this, but it was a fact nevertheless.

No human being keeps an open mind in the ultimate sense of the word. Prejudices will creep in, habits give the mind a twist, certain pathways are never explored, and exceptions are made unconsciously.

Had he been able to approach this problem logically, he would not have started with the premise that Elaine Gurdon was necessarily innocent of the crime. But he loved her, and love made it impossible for him to see her in a clear light. He had never doubted his love for her, and now jealousy stepped in to confirm his knowledge.

He did not admit even to himself that he was jealous. But he began actively to dislike Tollard, who seized every opportunity to monopolise Elaine, and did not appear to care that this might lead to gossip, or arouse strange feelings in the man who loved her.

It was possibly this growing hostility to Tollard that made a suspicion creep into Carton's mind; the very suspicion which had been debated between Warren and the superintendent. He did not believe Elaine was at all in love with Tollard, but that did not exclude the possibility of Tollard loving her.

He remembered a case in his African experience, where a native had been poisoned by a witch-doctor, and the skull afterwards fractured with the club of a rival medicine-man, under the impression that this would divert suspicion from the actual cause of death. There were other poisons than those used on the points of darts, poisons that were cumulative in their effect.

He dismissed this suspicion at first with the greatest haste. He was annoyed with Tollard, but he must not allow that feeling to make him unjust. Ned Tollard was hardly the sort of man to use such a cruel means of getting rid of his wife, even if he found the situation intolerable, and was already in love with another woman.

Ortho Haine left by the train after four, and with him went Nelly Sayers. Mr Barley had seen them both, apologised for the trouble and worry that had fallen on them while in his house, and begged them to act as they pleased.

'It was not my fault that this dreadful tragedy happened,' he said, 'but I am sorry all the same. If you wish to go, if any of my guests wish to go, they will please themselves.'

Tollard said that he would remain for a day or two, in case anything turned up. Carton said he would like to stay also, if Mr Barley did not mind. Mrs Gailey, in an access of sympathy for the troubled host, said she thought Mrs Minever might like to have her company for a little while.

'And you, Miss Gurdon?' asked the old man.

'I think I ought to stay. If any point comes up about the blow-pipe and the darts, I may be able to help.'

So, for the moment, only Miss Sayers and Haine deserted the house, and when Inspector Warren turned up in the evening, just before dinner, he was able to record the fingerprints of Elaine Gurdon and Ned Tollard. Haine's address was given to him, so that he could see him if necessary in town.

Dinner was a shorter meal than usual, and Carton announced his intention to Elaine of visiting Jorkins in his cottage before night fell. He asked if she would come with him again, but Mr Barley said he was sure Miss Gurdon was too tired for that field tramp after her anxious day.

So Carton lighted a pipe, after dinner, and hastened towards the fox-cover by the side of which Jorkins had his cottage. Going at a great pace, he reached it in twenty minutes, and found the under-keeper, sitting on a wooden bench outside the front door, cleaning a gun-barrel with great energy.

'Good evening, Jorkins,' said Carton. 'I am staying with Mr Barley, you know, and I thought I would like a word with you.'

'I thought I see you at the inquest, sir,' said the man, touching his cap, and withdrawing a wire brush from the barrel. 'A nasty business it was too.'

He got up, made room for Carton on the seat, and ran a pull-through over his palm. 'Won't you sit down, sir?'

Carton sat down, and produced his tobacco pouch. 'Fill up,' he said. 'I want to ask you a few questions, if you don't mind. I thought you gave your evidence as clearly as anyone today.'

Jorkins smiled, flattered. 'Mebbe I did, sir. Well, anything you wants to ask I'm here to answer.'

'What puzzles me is that red thing the woman at the window was wearing,' said Carton. 'You are sure of that?'

'Of course, sir. I swore it, and would again.'

'I wonder would you recognise the garment again by its shape?' Carton asked. 'I know you were some distance away, but do you think you could?'

Jorkins took up a little bottle of gun-oil from the bench, and began carefully to oil the action of the gun he had been cleaning.

'Doubtful if I could, but I might,' he said. 'But it might look different on the lady when she was wearing it from what it would do in the hand.'

Jim reflected. 'If I could get a lady to wear it, do you think that would be a help?'

'It would, sir, if I could 'dentify the thing at all.'

'With Mr Barley's permission you would be willing to come up and make an experiment?'

'What would that be, sir?'

'Simply to walk past the house as you did that morning, and take a glance at the window from the same distance. I can get someone to show themselves there, and you may be able to tell us if there is any resemblance in the dressing-gown worn.'

'I could do that, sir,' said Jorkins.

'Unless they ask you directly, you need not inform the police of this,' said Carton. 'If you are questioned, of course, you must make no secret of it.'

'I see, sir.'

Carton got up, fished in his pocket for a small note, and handed it over.

'We only want to get at the truth,' he remarked. 'Any information that may be of service to the police will go straight to them.'

Jorkins thanked him, and promised to attend at any time desired. Carton nodded, and turned homewards, arriving just as the dark was beginning to set it. He was fortunate in meeting Elaine in the hall. She had left the others, to fetch something from her bedroom, and turned with him into the billiard-room.

'I've been to see Jorkins,' he told her, 'and now I want you to help me.'

Elaine looked at him curiously. 'In what way, Jim?'

'Well, I want to make sure that he did see a woman's figure, and not a man's, at that window. The police have done with that room.'

'I know. But where do I come in?'

'Well, I thought you might show yourself at the window in a dressing-gown something like Mrs Tollard's, and I would get him to cross the park as he did that morning.'

'But I haven't a red dressing-gown.'

'It's the shape and hang of the thing I want to get at. Do you know what sort of thing she wore?'

'Yes, it was not unlike one Netta Gailey has. I mean the cut.'

'You could borrow hers.'

'But it is maize?'

'Is that a colour?'

'Yes, a sort of yellow.'

'That can't be helped. I want to test Jorkins's observation. Will you do that? Ask Mrs Gailey to lend you hers, and wear it for a few moments at the window?'

Elaine reflected, her face clouding over. 'I don't think I care to, Jim.'

He stared. 'Why not? It may bring out an important point.'

'I think we should leave that sort of thing to the police. Ned thinks the same as I do in that matter.'

'Hang Ned! He hasn't contributed much to the solution of the problem.'

'And you haven't—yet,' she said, smiling faintly.

'And never shall, if everyone keeps on the safe and discreet side. But I wish you would do it. I believe it might tell us something.'

She shook her head.

'I am sorry, but I can't. You forget that very terrible associations are connected with that room in my mind. I found her dead there. I hate the idea of masquerading in that room.'

He frowned. 'It isn't a masquerade. Hang it all! Do you realise what a mess may come of this investigation?'

'I don't believe your scheme will help. I don't see how it could.'

'When someone's safety hangs on the possible presence of another woman in the house?'

'I know, but Jorkins says he saw one, and he will say he saw another after your experiment. What good will that do? Drop it, Jim. I know you want to help, but I think it is a waste of time.'

He wondered why she let herself be swayed so much by Ned Tollard's opinions. He felt sure the fellow had been calling him officious. All Tollard seemed to want to do was to get rid of the publicity in the affair.

'Then I'll ask Mrs Gailey,' he said irritably.

'Well, I can't object to that. I can only say I won't do it.'

He looked down. 'How was she compared with Mrs Tollard, in figure, I mean?'

'They were about the same height. Margery was slimmer, and more graceful.'

'Right. I'll ask her. I wonder could you get her to come here without letting the rest of the crowd know?'

'I'll try,' said Elaine. 'Wait a few moments.'

She slipped away, and left him pondering. She was surprised apparently to find him so keen on investigating the case; he was surprised to find her putting barriers in his way. She had nothing to hide, therefore it must be Ned Tollard who was trying to put on the brake. Had Tollard anything to hide? Carton could not believe that yet.

He told himself irritably that Elaine was indiscreet. It was no good saying that when people gossiped you defied them, and so proved that the gossip had no foundation. That was rubbish. That attitude only added fuel to the fire of calumny. It would have been better for her to see as little as she could of Ned now that his wife was dead. If Tollard knew no better than to follow her about, a word would check it.

Mrs Gailey came in smiling. She had a healthy interest in mysteries, and there was something intriguing to her mind in this secret conference in the billiard-room.

'Elaine told me you wanted to see me,' she said. 'Do tell me if anything exciting has turned up.'

It was such an ingenuous question that she smiled involuntarily. 'Nothing yet,' he said, getting up from the corner of the table, where he had been sitting. 'Have a cigarette, and I'll tell you how you can help me.'

'Can I really?' she cried. 'But how jolly interesting. What do you want me to do?'

'Only to be a ghost for a few minutes.'

She laughed. 'You're pulling my leg, Mr Carton.'

'A live ghost,' he said. 'I have asked Jorkins if he will help me reconstruct the scene, perhaps tomorrow. He'll walk across the park and look up at the window where Mrs Tollard was—I mean the window of her room. All I want you to do is to show at the window for a moment in a dressing-gown.'

'It sounds very improper,' she said, grinning.

'But will really be a most proper action,' said he. 'Elaine tells me you have one rather like Mrs Tollard's in cut. We can't get hers, unfortunately, for the police have it.'

'As if I would wear hers after that, you horrid man!'

'Well, you can't, so that's that! Your own will do quite well. All I ask is that you will go to the window, turn sidewise on to it, then vanish again.'

'It's a jolly good idea,' she said. 'Only I haven't long hair.'

'Nor time to grow it by tomorrow. Agreed! But if you're on, what about eleven in the morning? I can get Jorkins by then. Also, I'll ask Mr Barley to get Tollard away for a drive or something. He may not like my arrangement.'

'So I mustn't tell him?'

'Or anyone. I'll see Barley privately just now. Are you willing?'

'Of course, if it helps. I say, Mr Carton, do you mind if I tell my husband; write him, I mean, that I'm going to do this?'

He grinned. 'No, write him by all means. We must regularise the dressing-gown incident, if you have any qualms about it. Thanks awfully,' he added as she nodded assent. 'You can tell your husband you are going to be a feminine Dr Watson for a little, only with a little more brain than that dull gentleman.'

They returned to the drawing-room together, and it was bedtime before Carton got an opportunity to speak to Mr Barley.

Mr Barley was not averse from the experiment, though he foresaw, as Carton had already done, an objection on the part of Ned Tollard.

'He may hate it, since that was his dead wife's room,' he observed. 'I'll get him out of the house till lunch.'

'Right!' said Carton. 'I'll have Jorkins up here by eleven. If there are any police about at that time, it's off; postponed anyway.'

'At eleven,' said Mr Barley.

CHAPTER XV

THE EYES OF MR JORKINS

FATE assisted Mr Barley to remove Tollard the next morning from the sphere of excitement. A letter came by post from Superintendent Fisher asking Tollard and Miss Gurdon to visit Elterham. A Home Office expert had come down, and was anxious for some details with regard to the darts used.

So they went off together in the car after breakfast, and Carton prepared a note to send Jorkins.

'I'll let you know when you come on view,' he told Netta Gailey, after he had handed the note to one of the servants for transmission to the underkeeper.

She looked very excited. 'All right. I'll go up and get ready about half-past ten.'

Mr Barley took Carton up to the bedroom where Mrs Tollard had died, and went with him to the window.

'Jorkins must have been walking over there,' he said. 'You see, that is the nearest point, and the shrubbery lies between it and us.'

'May I know where Mrs Tollard was lying when you came in?'

'Certainly. Of course you have not been in this room before. She was lying on her back, not quite at right angles to the window, but slanting.'

'Was her head towards the window, or her feet?'

'Certainly not her head.'

'How was it that Miss Gurdon could hear her moving restlessly but not the thud with which she must have fallen?'

'I don't know.'

Carton frowned. 'It seems strange. Of course, if she is ever suspected by the police, it will be a point in her favour.'

'In what way?'

'Well, if I killed someone, and wished to pretend that someone else had killed her, I would say I had heard the fall.'

'Since she had heard the other noises, of course. I hadn't thought of that.'

Carton looked thoughtful, 'Of course, if she was poisoned by the dart, she might have lain down on the floor in her agony. But then one would expect her to cry out and wake the house.'

Mr Barley shook his head. 'I am afraid I have no flair for detective work.'

Jim Carton pursed his lips. 'Very well. When Jorkins comes, I think I shall walk with him across the park, and see for myself how much can actually be observed of a lady at that window. Will you accompany Mrs Gailey into this room, and show her where she ought to stand?'

'Yes.'

Carton took up a position before the window. 'Facing this way and at about this angle,' he said.

'Very well,' said Mr Barley. 'Shall we go down again now?'

Mrs Minever suspected that something was afoot that morning, but was unable to get any satisfactory information. When, however, Jorkins arrived at the house, and Netta Gailey went upstairs to change, the old lady stationed herself in a lower window to see what could be seen. She did not like Tollard, and she had taken a faint dislike to the new guest, who went about so mysteriously, but did not condescend to initiate her into the scope and nature of his investigations.

Carton took Jorkins out again, after they had had a short consultation with Mr Barley, and they walked across the park for three hundred yards, in the direction of the little gate in the surrounding wall, before turning to go back across the front of the house.

'This about right?' Jim asked, as they stopped and faced about.

'Yes, sir, I have a regular path when I come this way. It's a kind of habit with me, and I reckon I could walk him blindfold.'

'Then I'll leave it to you, and simply tail on. Time now. We'll go back.'

They sauntered off, and when they were almost in a line with the shrubbery, Carton saw Mr Barley's face for a moment at the upper window. It was withdrawn again, and Mrs Gailey took his place.

Carton could see the figure in the yellow dressing-gown fairly plainly, and was able to notice that Mrs Gailey's hair was short, though her features were not recognisable at that distance. Jorkins, who understood his job very well, did not stare hard but just glanced up and away again, as he had done on the morning of the murder.

Then they were past, and Carton touched him on the shoulder.

'That'll do, Jorkins. We'll go in now, and see Mr Barley.'

'It looked much the same,' said Jorkins, as they walked towards the house, 'but I could see it was another lady on account of the hair.'

'I saw that too,' said Carton.

Mr Barley met them in the hall. Mrs Minever had realised what was afoot, and hurried upstairs to see what part Netta Gailey was playing in the act. Netta herself was feverishly changing again to get downstairs and join the conference there.

The three men filed into the library, and Jorkins was told to sit down. Mr Barley took up his old position by the mantel-piece, his face eager and interested.

'Well, Jorkins, you saw the lady?'

'Very well, sir. I might a'most have taken her to be the other lady, only for her short hair.'

'And, of course, the colour of her dressing-gown,' said Carton. 'The police have the one that was actually worn by Mrs Tollard on the morning of the murder, so we couldn't get that.'

Jorkins looked at him hard.

'Seemed much the same to me, sir,' he said.

'*What?*' cried Carton, jumping out of the chair into which he had relapsed.

'Seemed much the same to me, sir.'

'I understand, Carton,' said Mr Barley. 'He means it was much the same shape.'

Carton did not appear even to have heard his host's remark. He stood in front of Jorkins, glaring, so that that young man nervously rose.

'Why, you idiot!' he cried. 'At the inquest you swore it was red.'

'So it was, sir,' persisted Jorkins.

Carton looked at Mr Barley. 'He's colour-blind!' he said, sat down limply in his chair, and bit his lip.

'Colour-blind?' repeated Mr Barley. 'Are you, Jorkins? But surely not. Wait a moment! Come to the window, Jorkins. Look out at the grass there, what colour is it?'

'Green, of course, sir,' said the man.

'And the bricks of the house?'

'Red, sir.'

Mr Barley turned again to Carton, who had fallen into a reverie. 'You're mistaken. He knows colours; grass, bricks—'

'Nothing to do with it,' said Carton. 'Colour-blind people know the colours of well-known and familiar objects. They hear grass always spoken of as green grass, and bricks mostly as red. That is well authenticated. If they did not, their visual defect would be discovered early in life. Fellows have lived a good many years without it being known, but when they came to be tested (for signalmen, say), it was found out.'

Jorkins stared. Mr Barley gasped.

'He could mistake yellow for red?'

'He would. If he suffers from red-blindness he would mistake orange, yellow, and green for red. Jorkins, didn't you mean that the colour of the gown worn by that lady today was red?'

Jorkins stammered. 'Yes, sir.'

'Well, it was maize, a kind of yellow.'

'Perhaps; but I suppose blue—' began Mr Barley.

He was thinking of Elaine's dressing-gown, and Carton knew it. 'No, that is not one of the colours in the red-blindness range that are mistaken for red.'

'Then who could have been in the room?'

Carton shrugged. 'It is possible he saw Mrs Tollard only. She wore green, one of the colours Jorkins is liable to confound with red. It is possible she got up, and looked out of the window. There may have been no one else in the room.'

'Then?'

Carton frowned significantly at his host. 'Better leave that over until we are alone. I want to test Jorkins more closely. I wonder if Mrs Minever has skeins of coloured silks.'

'I expect so.'

'Right. Will you ask her to let me have some?'

Mr Barley went out. Carton turned to Jorkins.

'Look here, Jorkins, this won't go any further. But, are you sure you didn't know before that you were colour-blind?'

Jorkins fidgeted. 'I wasn't sure sometimes, sir. I sometimes wondered if there weren't something wrong. But it isn't easy to get a job nowadays if you have some defect, and I'm not one of the learned folk who know these things.'

'No. I think you could not be sure. It's odd how positive some colour-blind fellows are that their sight is as good as anyone else's. I met one in the War. But I'll keep that dark. You needn't volunteer a statement about it to the police just yet. Mr Barley and I'll talk it over.'

'Very well, sir. I don't want to lose my job.'

'I'll see you don't. As a matter of fact, you have been doing what you have to do all right, I hear. But Mr Barley is in the hall. You don't mind my testing your sight in a crude way?'

'Oh no, sir. Only I hope I haven't muddled the police with my evidence.'

'You may have helped to clear up a difficult point, Jorkins.'

Mr Barley came in with many skeins of coloured silk, which he laid out on the table.

'Will that do, Carton?'

'Excellently.'

'Do you mind if I stay to watch?'

'Not at all, sir.'

Mr Barley sat down.

The experiment took some little time, but Carton was patient, and Jorkins willing. It proved, however, beyond question that the latter was affected with red-blindness. He persistently identified the colours of that range with each other, and Mr Barley saw him rise, and prepare to go, with a feeling that was not altogether relief.

'You have done very well, Jorkins,' he said kindly. 'This won't affect your job with me.'

'Thank, you, sir. I hoped it wouldn't,' said the man gratefully.

When he had gone, Mr Barley took a deep breath. 'That disposes of the theory that there was a stranger in the room?'

'I am afraid so,' said Carton, drumming with his fingers on the table. 'Her presence was only assumed on Jorkins's evidence. He said she wore red. Otherwise that hare would never have been started.'

'But where does it leave us? Only the idea that someone with a blow-pipe outside shot Mrs Tollard.'

'Or someone inside.'

'I don't see that.'

'I don't quite either, but we can't say it was not so.'

'Are you going to tell the police now?'

'Not at the moment. I should like to see Dr Browne first. Do you think he would see me?'

'If I gave you a note, no doubt. He's a breezy sort of fellow, and rather curt, but you can try.'

'Will you write a few lines to him?'

Mr Barley nodded, sat down and scribbled a short note, which he handed to Carton. 'He lives in a white house about half a mile the other side of the village. Will you have the car?'

'No thanks,' said Carton, 'I'll walk over at once.'

Mrs Minever had been greatly intrigued by the borrowing of her coloured silks, and when Jorkins emerged from the library, and was going out, she cunningly waylaid him.

'Did it turn out all right?' she asked mildly.

'Yes, mum, it did, in a way,' said Jorkins. 'Seems I'm colour-blind right enough.'

'What a pity,' said the old lady, wise enough to say no more. 'I am sorry, Jorkins.'

It is to be feared that her pity was not very sincere, for she hurried away at once to Mrs Gailey, and plunged into the middle of her disclosure.

'Isn't it odd, my dear! Mr Carton has been making tests and he says Jorkins is colour-blind! Jorkins admits it too. Then, you see, there may have been no woman in red at all.'

'No woman in red?'

'No. That must be Mr Carton's point. It was clever of him, though I am sure Mr Tollard will be furious if he hears that that young man had someone put in his wife's room to represent her.'

'But he didn't. It was in order to appear like the stranger who was supposed to be in the room, Mrs Minever. There was no harm in that. Only, it is odd now. If there was no other woman, perhaps the keeper saw Mrs Tollard herself?'

'Or Miss Gurdon.'

'Good gracious! But how awful! She never said she went to the window, only that she went in, tried to lift Margery, and let her drop again.'

'I didn't say she was there, my dear. I said they might—or Jorkins might, have seen her there.'

'But, if she had been there, she would have said so to the police when they told her what Jorkins said. She would say: "Oh, I went to the window myself for a moment."'

'Not if she was wearing a blue dressing-gown, and Jorkins talked of a woman wearing a red one.'

Here Netta stopped, and her eyes opened wide. 'But if there was no red one at all—'

'The less we say about that the better,' Mrs Minever remarked gloomily.

CHAPTER XVI

THE SCRATCH

THAT curt, blunt man Dr Browne took strange dislikes at times. But, with others of his temperament, he also liked some people at sight, and Carton happened to be one of them.

He had just come in from his round when Carton turned up at the house, and after he had read Mr Barley's note, he offered his visitor a cigarette, and took him into a pleasant sitting room.

'Well, young man,' he began. 'You're a nice character, coming all the way from Africa to upset the police theories, and set us all by the ears. What's this about Jorkins? Is it true?'

'Quite,' said Carton, smiling when he saw that he would have no trouble with the doctor. 'I am sure he suffers from red-blindness.'

'Wait a moment,' said the other, and reached down a book from a shelf. 'I'll look that up, and, later on, I must see the fellow. I haven't come across a case before.'

'At any rate, apart from objects that are very familiar, he mistakes other colours for red,' observed Jim Carton, as the doctor fluttered the leaves of his book. 'And that being so, his evidence about the stranger at the window goes by the board.'

'The stranger, yes,' said Browne, beginning to study a column of close print. 'But not everyone.'

Carton looked out of the window, and kept silence for a few minutes, then Browne closed his book, and looked at him very thoughtfully.

'Done any detective work before?'

'Among the natives; though it was part of my work as Assistant Commissioner, and was not called that.'

'Anyway, you've made a hit here. Jorkins saw a woman. The evidence only speaks to two women in the room that morning—Mrs Tollard and Miss Gurdon.'

'I am sure he saw Mrs Tollard. It's true Miss Gurdon is not shingled, but, whatever Jorkins's shortcomings in the matter of definite colours, he apparently does not mistake dark or brown hair for fair.'

'Then he saw Mrs Tollard. The lady he saw was standing up. When Miss Gurdon saw her, she was lying down. Mr Barley heard a thud. Miss Gurdon did not; except the slight thud made by Mrs Tollard's head falling back when she let her go.'

'That is what puzzles me.'

'The missing thud, in fact! But we will leave that for the moment. You have disposed of a theory, and you must tell the police. But you came to tell me something, or ask me something. Don't be nervous. I bite fools, but not sensible people.'

Jim Carton grinned broadly. 'Thank you.'

Browne smiled. 'What are you doing in this galley? You soared home from Africa for some purpose, eh? It wasn't simply to convict Jorkins of a lacking sense.'

'Not quite,' said Jim.

'I hope you were not one of Mrs Tollard's artistic worshippers, like that fool fellow, Haine?'

'No. I am a friend of Miss Gurdon's.'

Browne pursed his lips, and raised his eyebrows sardonically. 'That it, eh? A masterful woman, and a clever one.'

'I think so, you may be sure.'

'Very well. Now what do you want to know?'

Carton put down his cigarette. 'You examined the body. I don't know if you were quite as explicit in giving evidence as you might have been.'

'You cheeky young rascal! I said all that was necessary.'

'No doubt you did. I don't mean that you kept back anything that seemed really important. But could you tell me if there were any injuries on the body, however slight, that you did not mention?'

Browne reflected. 'There were, besides the slight bruise on the back of the head (caused by the head falling back), the wound made by the dart, a slight scratch on the scalp, obviously made by a sharp comb; and a tiny scratch, dry, not open, on the lower forearm—left side.'

'Near the wrist, or higher up?'

'Just above the wrist.'

'Do you think that bruise on the head came just after death?'

'No, I don't. It's my impression that Mrs Tollard was breathing her last when Miss Gurdon tried to lift her a little. I think she was alarmed, and imagined her dead. But she must have died a few seconds after that at the latest.'

'I see. This scratch was healed?'

Browne twinkled. 'If you think it will prove that Mrs Tollard received the scratch in trying to defend herself against an assailant, you may give up the idea! If it had been so, I should have told the coroner. That scratch was a good many hours old, perhaps a day or two.'

Jim nodded. 'Now that the theory of a stranger in the room is disposed of, I need not consider an inside assailant.'

'Why not?' said Browne sharply.

'Why should I?'

The doctor surveyed him thoughtfully for a few moments. 'When you were clever enough to find out Jorkins, you killed a theory, but gave birth to another, young man! So long as we could assume that an outsider had done it, we had no need to go further.'

'Have we now?'

'Undoubtedly. If they cannot prove there was a man out on the lawn with a blow-pipe, and, or rather, a woman in a red gown inside, how do we account for the dart?'

'I see what you mean,' cried Carton uncomfortably. 'You can dispose of the primary influence imparted by the blow-pipe?'

'Absolutely. Several conditions are necessary—quietness on the part of the victim, of sufficient pain in another part to make a prick unfelt.'

'That's ugly.'

'It is, but there you have it. If you go and upset the old, you must suffer from the new, Mr Carton. Since the dart was made for a blow-pipe, the police cannot get away from the latter. You might as well say that a hat-pin is made to thrust in a hat, so it can't be used to thrust in a human being.'

'That's true. The dart might have been held in the hand.'

'Worse than that is the fact—mind you, I am not going to put it forward yet—that a case might be built up against Miss Gurdon on the strength of that.'

Carton nodded quietly. 'That's why I butted in. I saw that from the first.'

'I'll tell you how,' said Browne, with a grave look. 'It is all supposition, but everything connected with this case is the same. Mrs Tollard has a blinding headache, and keeps to her room the day before. She may be ill in the night, suffer in the early morning from pains, or weakness which makes her dizzy, sick, or incapable of appreciating what is going on about her.'

'I see that.'

'Very well, a second person—we will mention no names— hears the sound of restless tossing, and goes in. We will assume that this second person has a grudge against the sufferer. She finds the latter has got out of bed, in her state of dizziness or pain, and lain down on the floor.'

'Would she do that?'

'Young man!' said Browne, 'do you think I would state it as a possibility if it were impossible? I have had patients do it many times. But to go on: this second person has a dart concealed in her hand. She raises the only half-conscious sufferer, and, while holding her up, inserts that dart under the shoulder-blade, then lets her fall back. Next she goes for assistance, and when she is accompanied into the room, remarks with emphasis that the window is open top and bottom. This is to suggest that the dart was fired from outside.'

As he ended, he looked at Carton, who did not appear so surprised as he had expected to see him.

There was a momentary pause, then Jim Carton spoke. 'That, of course, is the danger I feared. I don't admit either the grudge, or the act. I know Miss Gurdon too well. But I could see that others might take your view—'

'Don't call it my view yet.'

'Well, we may accept the hypothesis you have put forward. I noticed at the inquest that the police let her off lightly, and I inferred from that that they had suspicions. But they might be suspicious of Tollard too.'

'You mean poisoning?'

'Yes. He's as likely to be guilty as she. I don't believe either is, though.'

'We shall know definitely when we hear the Home Office report. But two can play detective, young man. From your jumping so soon to this danger, I gather that you know something definite about the relations of Miss Gurdon and Mrs Tollard that I can only conjecture.'

'Frankly,' said Jim Carton, 'I have only heard gossip, and believe that the two women were antipathetic. I am sure Mrs Tollard was jealous of Miss Gurdon. But that is as far as I will go, I don't think Miss Gurdon cares at all for Mr Tollard, in that way. I am sure she is not in love with him.'

'Passion incites a great many crimes.'

'That is so. But, if you eliminate any passion here, you can find no reason for murder. Women who dislike each other merely do not kill one another.'

'I agree. Look here, Mr Carton, I wish you luck in the job you have undertaken. I am too old a bird to take risks to prove myself clever. No one shall hear a word of this hypothesis of mine, until I have more warrant for believing it.'

'Thank you.'

'But what I may keep to myself the police may light on, independently. It's a pity you found out about Jorkins before you had other evidence to exonerate Miss Gurdon. Could you keep it dark for a little?'

'I might try to,' replied Jim Carton doubtfully.

'Well, try!'

Carton went back to Stowe House looking very grave. Tollard and the others might call him officious or fussy, or what they pleased, because none of them seemed to realise the danger. It seemed to them that they regarded innocence (such of them as were innocent) as its own protection. He knew how false that was. He had just seen how even a doctor, untrained in detective work, was able to build up a case against Elaine.

It was a plausible case too, and one that a jury might accept. The only weak thing in it was the motive, but no motives in the case appeared strong, and jealousy or dislike might, relatively, seem as strong as any. The trouble was that Elaine had found Mrs Tollard. If it could have been proved that she had not been in the room at all, until she entered it in the company of some other member of the household, the hypothetical case against her fell to the ground.

Another thought struck Carton as he pounded back along the hot road. Mrs Tollard's maid had seen her mistress last, the night preceding the murder. Then, to all intents and purposes, there was no one to say that the actual prick with the dart had not been given in the night itself. She might have been asleep then, an intruder might have wounded her, and gone away. That would leave some hours for the poison to work. It would be even possible to say that the action of that poison had a soporific effect, or produced a state of partial coma, in which the victim had struggled out of bed, and lain down on the floor.

Carton shrugged. He had not come home for this. The years of absence had only strengthened his boyish love for Elaine, and he had felt that her refusal of his proposal long ago had not been final. He had been a rather self-conscious and conceited fellow at that time; a cub, he told himself. Perhaps he had been too sure of her. At any rate, he had had hopes when he left Africa.

He still had hopes, but this tragedy had come between them. If it was only that, he would be happy. But unwelcome doubts had crept into his mind the last few days. Was Elaine really as indifferent to Ned Tollard as she professed to be? Of course she was, he said to himself abruptly, but his words were more convinced than his mind.

In any case he could not speak to her now. It would be indecent at this stage of affairs. But he might save her from trouble, and that he intended to do, whatever unpopularity it involved in Mr Barley's overwrought household.

How was he going to counter a new attack? That thought troubled him. He felt sure that he would not be able to cover up that day's discovery. There had been too many in it—Jorkins, Mr Barley, Mrs Gailey. Then the servants might have seen something, and that old busybody Mrs Minever.

Remembering Mrs Gailey, he recollected something she had told him. It was that Elaine had formerly decided to make some investigations herself, and not leave the whole thing to the police. Had this idea dropped out of her mind? He thought it had, since she had told him to leave things to the officers. But it was possible that she was quietly pursuing her enquiries. He might ask her.

The others had finished lunch when he arrived, but he sat down alone, and hurried through a meal mechanically. He went in search of Elaine afterwards, and found her for once alone, sitting in an arbour fronting the rose-garden, writing up her diary.

'I hope two will be company,' he said, as he advanced. 'Do let the proverb rest easy this time!'

She closed the book, put down her pen, and nodded.

'Where have you been, Jim? You weren't in to lunch.'

'Didn't Barley tell you?'

'No.'

'Then perhaps I had better not. But I have been very busy. Your news is more important. What did the police say, if it isn't a rude question?'

She frowned a little. 'I suppose I may tell you. We were not asked to keep it dark. It was simply that the Home Office has sent down the report.'

'They have? Important?'

'I don't know. It depends on the way you look at it. They say—that is, their toxicologist says—that the poison found in the body corresponds to that found on the tip of the dart.'

'There was no other poison?'

'No, none whatever. I didn't expect to hear of any.'

'What was it?'

'They don't know any more than I. I told you the secret was a native one. I repeated it to the superintendent today.'

'Have they any idea what effect would be produced by it?'

'From tests they have made with the minute quantity at their disposal they are inclined to think it would cause death quickly. I believe they talked of a possible lapse of consciousness, followed by a possible delirium, but I did not see the report, and I have a feeling that their conclusions are speculative.'

'In what way?'

'Because of the minute quantity they extracted. But it does not matter much, does it? The point is that the dart caused her death.'

In the light of the new hypothesis Carton thought it might matter a great deal, but he did not say so. 'Perhaps not. Did they ask you and Tollard any further questions?'

'They didn't ask him any, after all. They asked me to explain the symptoms I had seen when a monkey, or bird, and, in one case, a man, was shot with these darts. There was a middle-aged man there, to whom I was not introduced. He may have been an expert of some kind—perhaps a pathologist. He said something at the end about getting back to town.'

'He listened to what you said?'

'Yes, very keenly. I should not be surprised if he was sent by the Home Office.'

Carton pursed his lips. 'Very likely. Anything else?'

'They asked me if I was sure I had not gone in the night to see if Margery wanted anything.'

He repressed an exclamation. It seemed, to him that the police might have jumped to the same conclusion as the doctor. The Home Office experts might have suggested that death had not come quickly after all, but camouflaged their observations from Elaine.

'What did you say?'

'I said that if I had thought she was really ill I would have gone in during the night. In fact I would have seen her before I went to bed. But I had only been told it was a headache, and I had always considered her a healthy woman in spite of her apparent fragility.'

'They accepted that?'

'They had to, of course.'

'Look here,' said Jim Carton, after a pause, 'Barley told me when I first came that Tollard had pleaded urgent business when he left for London on the day before the murder.'

Elaine looked at him quickly. 'Are you sure he said urgent?'

'I am quite sure. Barley said it puzzled him at first, for no one could call going off on a yacht urgent business. Do you know if he got a wire, or was called up on the telephone, that morning?'

'I never heard of it. I don't think so. Unless he called at the post-office in Elterham for a telegram before he left.'

'Even if he had one, I say it is not urgent business. He said nothing about any kind of business in his evidence at the inquest.'

'I know he didn't.'

'At any rate, he went in his car with his wife that morning to get a book for her, I think someone said.'

'Yes, some books. She had ordered them.'

'Did you see them come back?'

A shade suddenly passed over her face, and he saw it and grew alert. He noticed too that she paused perceptibly before she replied.

'Yes.'

Carton studied her face closely, so closely that she flushed a little. 'What had the row been about?' he asked quickly. His experience abroad had shown him the value of assuming knowledge he did not possess, and posing a question abruptly.

'I don't know,' said Elaine, then bit her lip. 'Who told you there had been one?'

'You,' he said, triumphantly. 'I saw it in your face.'

CHAPTER XVII

TOLLARD MAKES A SCENE

ELAINE reddened slowly, and a little flicker of anger showed in her eyes. 'I wish you wouldn't talk like that, Jim,' she said sharply. 'I don't like it. Detectives and people of that kind may trip one up or try to do it, but you are not a detective.'

'No,' he said rather bitterly, 'I am only an ass, who wants to save you from trouble. I am sorry if I annoy you.'

'You won't,' said Elaine, relenting a little, 'if you leave this alone, Jim. I know you are trying to do what you can, but it seems to me quite futile. I had nothing to do with this dreadful business. Little as I liked Margery, I am sorry for her, and would give a great deal to have this undone. But you can't expect an innocent person to go about in fear of the police, and exhibiting all the signs of a conscious criminal.'

'I never said you should, my dear girl. Do you think this is fun for me? Do you think I covet the title of officious ass just for the love of it? Give me credit for a little sense.'

'I give you credit for more intelligence than most people, Jim,' she said softly. 'But it ought to tell you that you are doing no good. You have been trying to discover something for some days now, but I don't see that you have.'

Wounded pride almost prompted him to say that he had discovered an important fact that very morning, but he choked it down.

'I must do what I think best, I am afraid. If you saw me on the edge of a precipice I imagine you would give me a warning. I hope you would anyway. I might be too blind to see it, but I should credit you with good intentions.'

'As I do you,' she said, laying her hand gently on his arm. 'Don't let us quarrel over this. It isn't our *pidgin* anyway, you know.'

As she spoke someone came across the rose-garden, and approached them. It was Ned Tollard, and his face was black as thunder, when he saw who was sitting there with Elaine.

The truth was that Mrs Minever had been unable to contain her store of fresh gossip, and when Tollard and Mrs Gailey went with her into the drawing-room for a few minutes after lunch, the old lady had gradually entered on the topic of colour-blindness, winding up with that morning's discovery of Jorkins's visual defect.

Tollard pricked up his ears at once. 'But how did they find that out?' he demanded, much perturbed.

Mrs Gailey made one desperate attempt to get Mrs Minever away from the topic. But her well-meant pressure of the foot impinged on the old lady's most detested corn, and drew from her an agonised howl.

Mrs Gailey blushed to the eyes, and Tollard turned to her impatiently.

'You were here this morning, Netta. Perhaps you can tell me.'

Netta shook her head, covered with confusion. 'Mrs Minever was going to tell you.'

'If you hadn't trodden on my poor foot,' cried Mrs Minever reprovingly. 'It was Mr Carton did it, Mr Tollard.'

'Oh, Carton?' said Tollard, biting his lip.

Mrs Minever at once began to tell him what had happened, and as she went on her heedless way, his brow grew darker. But he made no explosive comments, though a dozen boiled in his head, merely stopping her once to ask Mrs Gailey a question.

'You helped Carton with this? I suppose it was not your suggestion?'

'Oh, not at all,' she cried. 'He asked me would I help him. I hope you don't mind.'

'It's done now,' he said sternly. 'Please go on, Mrs Minever. I want to hear the rest.'

So she told him how Jorkins had been brought up, had crossed the park, and looked up at the window, where Mrs Gailey had shown herself in a dressing-gown.

'Not my wife's, I trust?' said Tollard bitterly.

'No,' cried Netta. 'Of course not. The police have it anyway, but I shouldn't have thought of wearing this in any case, and I don't believe Mr Carton would have asked me to.'

'It seems difficult to say what he would not ask people to do, Netta. But you stood there, and Jorkins thought the dressing-gown you wore was red. Is that it?'

'Yes. Quite. Yes.'

'What colour was it?'

'Maize—yellow. I do wish I hadn't done it.'

He appeared not to hear her. 'So Carton examined Jorkins and discovered that he was colour-blind.'

'I met Jorkins going out and he told me so.'

'Does Elaine know this?'

'I didn't tell her.'

'Nor I,' said Netta, who was startled by Tollard's black looks.

'Do you know where she is?'

'She said when she came in first that she thought of writing up her diary in the garden after lunch. She may be in the rose arbour.'

'Thank you,' said Tollard drily, and marched to the door.

'Oh, Mrs Minever,' said Netta, when he had gone, 'I do wish you hadn't told him. I can see he is frightfully angry.'

'Is that why you trod on my foot? Don't do that again, please. It was positive agony.'

Mrs Gailey expressed sorrow. 'I hope there won't be a row.'

'If Mr Carton will only mind his own business, there won't be any rows,' said Mrs Minever distinctly. 'Why can't he leave it alone?'

Elaine gathered some of the unpleasantness of what was coming from her first glance at Tollard's face, and she guessed that his anger was directed at her companion.

Her first impulse was to stay, then the thought that she might be asked to go, coupled with the fact that the presence of a third party during a quarrel is often unwelcome, and resented by those more directly concerned, she took up her diary, and turned to Carton.

'I think he wants to speak to you,' she said softly.

'To swear at me, if I am any judge of looks,' he responded, just above his breath. 'Righto! I'll be Ajax, if he is the lightning!'

She did not hear this, but slipped away before Tollard came up.

The angry man walked up to Carton as the latter was lighting a cigarette.

'I have a crow to pick with you, Carton,' he said.

'Well, sit down, and let us see the bird,' said the other, carefully extinguishing his match, and throwing it away. 'Ornithology has always been one of my favourite studies.'

The lightness of his tone made Tollard frown ominously. 'I hear you have been trying experiments this morning,' he observed, sitting down heavily, and staring at Carton.

'One,' said Carton easily. 'Will you smoke?'

Tollard refused the proffered case, with an angry gesture. 'One of that kind is quite enough, Carton! I don't forget that we are old acquaintances, but, in a matter of this kind, one must draw a line somewhere.'

'No doubt. But come to the point. What have I done that annoys you specially?'

'You come here, Carton, as a guest—an uninvited guest, but that is Mr Barley's business, not mine. From the moment you arrived, I hear, you began to poke your nose into this business. No one engaged you to play private detective, even if you can play it, of which we have no proof.'

'Is that your business, Tollard?' asked the other mildly. 'I don't think it is. You are only a guest too, though you were invited before I was. If Mr Barley objects to my activities, I bow to him. He owns the house, you don't.'

'Very well,' said Tollard viciously. 'I'm not going to worry over mere debating points, or whether you have a right or not to do detective work here. But I have serious grounds for quarrel with you when you get someone to dress up to represent my dead wife—'

'Wait a moment,' said Carton hotly. 'I won't have that! I should never have thought of doing such a thing. What happened was this—I got Mrs Gailey to dress up, to see if Jorkins could recognise the garment. No, wait a moment. I want to be correct, and to do you justice. I asked Mrs Gailey if she would wear one cut like your wife's—'

'That is what I said.'

'Yes, but it was on the cards that the intruder in the room might have adopted that rig for camouflage.'

'At all events you sent her into the room where my wife had died.'

'If I had known you objected so strongly, Tollard, I would have asked her to go into one of the other rooms.'

'You had no business to meddle with the affair at all. That is my contention. I won't have it! I'm damned if I let you, or any other man, do it!'

'You're anxious to see the criminal brought to justice, aren't you?'

'Of course; what do you mean, confound you?'

'If I had not done what I did, the police would have gone on searching for a woman in a red dressing-gown, and the real offender might get clear away. None of you has the *nous* to do what I tried to do, and you blame me because I was successful.'

'That's infernal rubbish,' said Tollard, with heat. 'And if it were true, it would only mean that you diverted the attention of the police to Miss Gurdon, who was the one who last saw her alive.'

'That's a question. But, if it comes to that, what has it to do with you? You resent my sending Mrs Gailey into the room that was your wife's. I resent very much your airs of proprietorship with regard to Elaine.'

'I haven't assumed any.'

'Oh yes, you have. It was your silly arrangements that started this muddle,' cried Carton, now as angry as his companion. 'Don't presume to tell me what I must not do with regard to her. If she objects, it is another matter.'

'She does object!'

Carton found himself in a quandary. He could not give up now without laying before Elaine the full extent of the danger. He was not yet prepared to tell her what the doctor had said. That might involve Browne in trouble, for she would very likely take strong exception to an outsider constructing theories, and telling others of them, when those theories suggested that she might be the criminal for whom the police were looking.

'Then she can tell me,' he said slowly.

To his relief, Tollard dropped that point, though his voice was not less angry when he continued. 'I object very much, Carton, to your tone when you speak of Elaine and myself. Are you suggesting that there is anything between us?'

'No, not for a moment; if you mean anything concrete. I think from first to last you have been unwise.'

Tollard's eyes flashed. 'Well, mind your own business from this time on! Don't dare to go into that room again! I shall tell Mr Barley I protest against anyone searching there who is not an officer to whom the duty has been given.'

Carton did not reply. He remembered suddenly that Tollard was, after all, a man who had been recently bereaved under very tragic circumstances. He had forgotten it in the natural heat engendered by the other's dictatorial tone.

'And I shall tell Miss Gurdon my opinion of your ill-timed interference,' Tollard added, when no reply came. 'I am returning to town tomorrow.'

The funeral was to take place in London, and Carton nodded gravely.

'I am sorry we have had this disagreement, Tollard. It was not of my seeking.'

'That is a matter of opinion,' said Tollard coldly, and walked away.

Carton remained deep in thought for a few minutes, then he too went to the house, and spoke to Mr Barley.

'I should like to go into Elterham at once,' he said. 'Could I have a car?'

'Certainly,' said his host. 'I'll send out to—'

'I can drive myself, if you will let me use the two-seater,' Carton told him hurriedly. 'I want to tell the police about my discovery this morning.'

'I was just going to telephone,' said Barley. 'But you can have the little car if you wish.'

'Thank you. I have reasons of my own for telling the police first about Jorkins. I'll go now.'

As he drove off to Elterham ten minutes later, Carton was deciding on his course. With this knowledge of Jorkins's colour-blindness, he had something to go on. The police would welcome this unexpected information, and, if he played his cards well, they might do something for him in exchange.

Now that the whole household knew of it, the thing could not be kept dark any longer.

His interview with Tollard had ruffled him not a little, but he grew calmer during the drive, reflecting that Tollard would be gone next day, and he would have the field to himself. Only, he decided that Tollard's outburst was due to his overwrought state of mind, and threw no light on his relations with Elaine. He had been indiscreet, and now he was stubborn, that was all. Somehow, he thought he remembered those characteristics in him as a boy.

Elaine's reluctance to have him continue his investigation troubled him more. Why the dickens should she be so anxious for him to drop it? If things went wrong she was most likely to suffer for it. On the other hand, if she was innocent, as he, of course, believed, she would laugh at such an unlikely possibility.

He drew up in an hour outside the central police station in Elterham, and asked to see Superintendent Fisher, sending in his card, in the corner of which he had pencilled 'Stowe House.'

The policeman to whom he had given the card returned in a few moments.

'The superintendent is busy at the moment, sir, but if you will wait, he will see you.'

'I'll wait,' said Carton, and sat down in a chair pulled forward for him by the officer.

CHAPTER XVIII

THE DART

WHEN Carton arrived at the police station, Fisher was in consultation with Detective-Inspector Warren. They both looked up with interest when the officer brought in Carton's card, and when the man had gone, Warren smiled slightly.

'That'll be the gentleman who didn't give evidence, but was listening so eagerly at the inquest, sir,' he said. 'I hear from our fellow who is keeping an eye on the maids at the house that he is very busy doing the Holmes business.'

Fisher raised his eyebrows. 'It's an odd thing what a fascination our job has for amateurs! If they were paid to do it, they would soon get sick of it.'

'It's a play to them,' assented Warren. 'But now, sir, we have, I suppose, to pay some attention to the medical theories from London.'

'Of course. Dr Scruttel is a most eminent man. He has been behind the scenes in most of the big cases in recent years.'

'But even a big man can't dispose of the woman in red, sir.'

'No, that is my trouble. Dr Scruttel's theory is a very good one. It fits all the facts, if we can presume malice between those two, as I think we can from what we know. But we can't get away from Jorkins's evidence.'

Warren reflected. 'No one came near her from the time she went to bed until the morning; no one we have evidence of, that is. But what happened during the night we can't say. If the dart could have been used in the hand, and was, it's a pity it was not something with a big enough handle to take prints.'

'Even then they might have been washed off.'

'And this evidence of the expert about the narcotic effects of the poison is great. So far as we have gone into it, sir, we are pretty sure Tollard and his wife quarrelled that morning—the morning before the murder, when they drove into town here. I have seen two people, the assistant at the bookshop where Mrs Tollard had ordered some books, and the man at the garage where they put up their car.'

'Have you any idea what books she bought?'

'I have. The assistant said he had some trouble getting them. One was about music, by some odd American writer, and the other was an art book—at least the assistant said it was; but he told me he had a look at it, and it was the craziest idea he had ever known. It was about pictures not being like the things they are supposed to represent, he said.'

'Oh, that's only modern art,' said the superintendent impatiently. 'But what else did he say?'

'He said the husband looked very impatient, and out of temper. The lady and he didn't exchange a word in the shop, but, when the books were packed up, and the gentleman offered to take them, the lady snatched them away, and carried them herself.'

'Did she look angry, to his thinking?'

'He said not. He told me she was very pretty and pale, but her face was very set and melancholy. She didn't glare at her husband, but looked at him as if she was sorry for herself.'

'Very good. Now the garage.'

'The garage man had the same ideas. He said they did not talk there, but he had an idea the missus, as he called her, was in the sulks.'

'Then it looks like a quarrel, and I'll bet it wasn't the first.'

He rose. 'Well, I think that will do for the moment. Get those reports from our man in London and look into them. A great deal turns on the state of affairs in their place during the last year.'

'Will you see this Mr Carton now?'

'Yes, you might ask him to come in, as you go out.'

Warren left the room, took a good look at Carton, and asked him to step into the superintendent's room.

He would have given a good deal to be present at the interview, but he had had his orders.

'Straight ahead of you, through that door, sir,' he said.

'Thank you,' said Carton, and rose.

Superintendent Fisher looked at his visitor with some curiosity, asked him to sit down, and at once assumed an attentive attitude.

'You are a new guest at Mr Barley's, sir?'

'Yes, I have just come home from Africa, superintendent. Before I go further, I may tell you that I was an Assistant Commissioner among the natives, and had a certain amount of work to do that would be done here by your people.'

Fisher nodded. That explained in part this young man's zeal. 'I see, sir.'

'So, naturally, when I arrived and heard of the state of affairs, and knew that—I mean to say was a friend of Miss Gurdon's, I thought I would help, where and how I could.'

Fisher smiled faintly. 'A not unusual idea, sir.'

'No, but one that you fellows don't like as a rule! However, I don't blame you. You must often be hampered by fellows who know nothing of the job.'

'Cases here are not quite those you meet with among natives,' said Fisher drily.

Carton laughed. 'A mild reproof, but it doesn't happen to hit me on a sore spot. If I was the kind of ass who messed about without producing any results, it might offend me.'

'Have you produced any results, sir?'

'I think so, but you can judge of that later. In this case one of your pieces of evidence is a poisoned dart. Now, in Africa, in one part, there are bushmen; tiny little, ugly fellows, who generally keep to the depths of the forest.'

'I have read of them, sir.'

'And I've seen 'em, superintendent! They use bows and arrows, and are pretty expert. Also they poison the tips as the South American Indians do.'

'I see, sir.'

'So I have some slight knowledge of the subject.'

'The dart wouldn't tell you much, sir.'

'How do you know?' said Carton. I have found out one thing that reverses all your theories, so don't be too sure.'

'You may think so, sir,' said the other sceptically.

'I have. There is no doubt of it. It kills your supposed woman in red, and leaves you without a leg to stand on.'

'If you'll prove it I shall be much obliged.'

'If you will let me see the dart, I'll prove the other thing to you in a minute.'

Fisher reflected. 'I don't think I can, sir. And if you have any evidence that bears on the case, I can subpoena you to attend the inquest when it is resumed.'

'If you do, I shall only swear to what I know,' said Carton with a grin. 'I have heard a good deal of evidence in my time, and I know the rules.'

Fisher looked curiously at him again, then rose and unlocked the office safe, from which he took a small case.

'What do you want to do with the dart?'

'Only to hold it between my fingers for two moments, and have a squint at it through a magnifier.'

Fisher produced a strong lens from a drawer. 'I have one here. If I let you see the dart, will you tell me what you know, or think you have discovered?'

'Every bit of it,' said Carton, smiling to himself as he saw that he would get his own way. 'All.'

'Here you are then, sir,' said Fisher, handing over the small case, and the lens. 'But you must handle it carefully. Wait a moment. I had better get you a forceps. I don't want any fingers on the thing.'

He found a watchmaker's forceps, and handed it over, keeping a steady gaze on Carton as he opened the little case, and picked up the dart with the forceps.

'Did you put it in this case the moment you got it?' Carton asked, looking at the empty case, and seeming interested in it, 'or was it otherwise packed?'

'It was put in this cardboard case at once, sir.'

Carton nodded, and carefully examined the dart under the lens. His face showed no sign of triumph or pleasure as he replaced it in the box, and Fisher was secretly amused at what he thought the amateur's disappointment.

'It doesn't give you much of a clue, sir, does it?'

'Not much,' replied Carton, handing the box back to him. 'But now to my part of the bargain.'

Fisher got out a note-book and pencil, and stared at him eagerly.

'Go on, sir.'

'To be brief, superintendent, the man Jorkins is colour-blind! I tried an experiment yesterday, and he mistook a lady in a yellow dressing-gown for one in red!'

The superintendent exclaimed sharply, and put down his pencil. 'Do you mean to say that is true, sir?'

'I do. I tested him with a lady at that window, and he thought she was wearing red.'

Fisher looked admiration. 'You are very smart, sir. I take back anything I said. If it is true, it reverses the whole case. Who do you think he saw?'

'I think he saw Mrs Tollard herself.'

'Dr Scruttel!' cried Fisher, and then checked himself.

'Is that a man, or an exclamation?'

'I was thinking of something else, sir.'

'I always carry a pinch of salt with me,' said Carton drily. 'But after this, you may not feel that I am so much in the way after all.'

Fisher nodded. 'If you often have ideas like that, I wish you would lend us some. But, if what you are saying is true,

and of course we must have the man examined by an oculist
to make sure, then we have either a criminal outside the
window with the blow-pipe, or one of the guests, or servants, in the house.'

'It might seem so.'

'But we have now compared the fingerprints of the three
persons who used the pipe on the lawn previously with
those that were on the blow-pipe itself, and they correspond
exactly. There were the marks of just three pairs of hands—Mr
Haine's, Mr Tollard's, and Miss Gurdon's. If there was a man
outside, who had stolen the weapon, or borrowed it, and put
it back, there ought to have been the marks of another pair.'

Carton looked seriously about him. The evidence was beginning to close in about Elaine. Ortho Haine might be dismissed
without thought. There remained only Tollard. But what could
Tollard have done when he was away in the Isle of Wight?

Somehow, the superintendent seemed to read his thoughts.
'If you are wondering if Mr Tollard could have had anything
to do with it, you are mistaken, sir. We thought of the possibility of his having administered poison in some other way,
but where could he get a similar poison if it was a secret that
not even the toxicologist of the Home Office knew?'

'I understand.'

'Then, sir, as I knew always, and as Dr Scruttel made clear
to me, some poisons that are deadly on injection, or when
they are introduced into the circulatory system, are harmless
when taken by the mouth.'

'I am aware of that.'

'Very well. Then we can have nothing against Mr Tollard,
unless we infer a conspiracy between him and this lady, Miss
Gurdon—who might possibly have a supply of the stuff, even
if she could not give a name to it.'

'I don't believe it for a moment. Why should she?'

'Well, we know the husband and wife were not on the
best of terms, sir. We know that Miss Gurdon was backed

financially by Mr Tollard, and we know that she disliked Mrs Tollard.'

'She made no secret of that.'

'No, sir, and she made no secret of the fact that she climbed up on a ladder and got the darts, in Mr Barley's presence, instead of leaving it to us to bring them down.'

'What do you infer from that?'

'That she is intelligent enough to be aware that fingerprint research enters a good deal into modern crime detection. Hers were on the quiver, and fresh too!'

'But what about the day she showed them how to use the blow-pipe?'

'That day she used other darts—harmless ones. She took none out of the quiver.'

'May I see the quiver?'

Fisher found it, and showed it to him, holding it up by the point of the forceps.

'That's it.'

'Thank you.'

Fisher returned it, and the dart in its box, to the safe, and locked them up again.

'If she took one out the day before, and happened not to have gloves on, it would be useful to have an explanation.'

'Very,' Carton agreed drily. 'But you are going ahead too fast, superintendent. The motive is insufficient.'

'There was that case of the woman and the young man in London hanged some years ago. That was jealousy and passion, and nothing else. But a great many people didn't think they could be guilty, sir. It doesn't do to think that love for a woman cannot drive a man into crime by itself. Some people lose their heads completely when they get enamoured, and then we hear of ugly murders.'

Carton knew that was very true, but he shook his head. 'I think it is as well that I am having a shot at this case, too, then, superintendent. I know Miss Gurdon better than that.'

'This is quite unofficial, of course,' said the other. 'I won't admit anything I said to you. It is all in the air still.'

'That's right. You may trust me not to let it go any further. It's a help to me, for I see that I must put my best foot forward, if I am to do any good.'

Fisher nodded. 'You'll have to be quick, sir!'

CHAPTER XIX

THE LOCKED DOOR

When he returned to Stowe House, Carton was inclined to believe that he must be the stormy petrel of the household. The waves of controversy blew up when he came along, and the winds of strife whistled in the ears.

Coming into the drawing-room, he found Mr Barley, Mrs Gailey, and Mrs Minever standing about Tollard, who was reading from a letter he held in his hand, in a voice that did not presage good for someone.

'It's disgraceful and intolerable!' he said, thrusting the letter into his pocket; and then he saw Carton, and his face took on a deeper shade of red.

'Has this anything to do with you, Carton?' he demanded loudly, hurriedly fishing for the letter, and flourishing it.

Carton raised his eyebrows, and advanced on the angry man. 'I can't say till I see it,' he said. 'It occurs to me that you imagine I am ubiquitous, Tollard.'

'This is a letter from my secretary,' remarked the other, holding his anger in leash with the utmost difficulty. 'He writes in haste to say he has found a man hanging about the house—my house in town—questioning the servants, and pretending to be a canvasser only.'

Carton glanced at Elaine, and shrugged. 'Will you tell me what Tollard means?' he asked coldly. 'I have not been up to town; merely to the police at Elterham to tell them about Jorkins.'

'Perhaps you have paid someone to spy for you,' said Tollard, with heat. 'You don't answer my question.'

'Oh, come!' said Mr Barley uncomfortably, while the two

women exchanged awkward glances. 'Mr Carton is incapable of that sort of thing, Tollard.'

'He hasn't answered my question,' repeated Tollard obstinately.

'And never shall,' said Carton angrily. 'It answers itself, I think.'

Elaine took Mrs Gailey by the arm, and they went out together. Mr Barley glanced at the two men in turn, hardly knowing what sort of oil to pour on these troubled waters. Carton suddenly turned to him.

'You are in possession of your senses, Mr Barley,' he said. 'I have just seen the police, and I have reason to believe that they have sent a detective to town. I expect he has a roving commission.'

'There!' cried Mr Barley, much relieved. 'I knew there must be some other explanation of the thing. One of their fellows has been making enquiries, not too tactfully, at your house, Tollard.'

Tollard bit his lip, made an apology for his mistake, and left the room. Carton had accepted his *amende* coldly. He was getting tired of Tollard and his moods.

'Mr Tollard is going tomorrow,' he said to his host.

'First train tomorrow,' the older man agreed. 'I am very sorry for him, but really he is rather trying too. I can forgive and excuse it after this tragedy, but it does not make things smooth for my other guests.'

'I should say not,' remarked Carton drily.

'By the way,' said Mr Barley, apology in his voice. 'At a time like this, one has to make excuses, and promises too, I am afraid, one would not make at any other time. I cannot agree that your experiment this morning was inadvised, or without value, but Tollard has taken it rather to heart.'

'It seems a stronger organ than his head.'

'Quite. I had no idea he was so emotional. It proves how much he loved his wife after all.'

Carton shrugged. 'You spoke of making promises?'

'Yes—it was this way. He was angry that you sent someone into his late wife's room for the purpose of testing Jorkins. He said he had spoken to you about it.'

'He did. He rated me as if I were a servant of his. I am beginning to forget that we were ever friends.'

Mr Barley coughed. 'I gathered that you were not prepared to listen to him, and, when he said you would be at it again when he had gone, I told him that I was sure you would do nothing of the sort.'

'What did he reply?'

'He persisted. I was rather in a quandary. He asked me as a favour if I would see that no one entered that room, except the police or someone delegated by them.'

'Did he expect you to keep guard outside the door!'

'No, of course not. But I promised him I would lock the room up. I am sure you don't mind.'

'How can I?' asked Carton, conscious of disappointment all the same. 'I remember—what Tollard seems to forget—that this is your house, and you have the right to do what you please in it.'

'At all events, Carton,' remarked Barley, who wished everyone to be at his ease, 'it can't hamper you much. The police made a very thorough examination of it. The detective-inspector and the superintendent both went through it.'

'They examined Jorkins, sir, and failed to find out the most important thing about him! But let that drop. What puzzles me is—'

He stopped, and stared at Mrs Minever, who had settled herself on a couch to listen, under pretence of reading.

'If you would leave us for a few moments, Jane,' said Mr Barley. 'Mr Carton has something private to say to me.'

'Oh, certainly,' cried the old lady, flouncing up. 'I am sure I don't want to listen to any private talk!'

And she went out with an air of great annoyance.

'I was going to say,' said Carton, when the door closed, 'I can't understand why Tollard is so anxious to close me down. I should have thought he would be keen to get any information he could about the ruffian who killed his wife.'

'It is rather strange,' said the other thoughtfully. 'But the whole thing is strange. Who could have killed her? If there was no one outside to do it, I can think of no one inside who would do such a brutal and savage thing. Have the police no idea?'

Carton looked at him sharply. 'They have, of sorts.'

'What is it?'

'I am sorry I am not at liberty to divulge it. The superintendent let it slip, and I promised it should go no farther.'

'Quite right, if you promised. But did it seem to you at all a likely theory?'

'It was an exceedingly plausible one. It might seem likely to a stranger, but it was most improbable to my mind.'

'I think they ought to have called in Scotland Yard. I suppose they won't now, if they have a theory?'

'I am afraid not. They believe in their notion, and feel they have scored.'

'You intend to carry on, Mr Carton?'

'I do, though my efforts will be limited by Tollard's new regulations.'

'I am sorry, but I gave my promise to him, as you gave yours on the other matter to Fisher.'

Carton nodded. 'Well, I am going to my room. I have letters to write.'

As he went upstairs he was pondering this new move of Tollard's. Before he heard of the promise extracted from Mr Barley, he had intended to ask the latter if he might examine the scene of the tragedy when Tollard had left for London.

Now Mr Barley had locked up the room, and would see that no one entered except the officers from Elterham. It was too bad; it was also rather inexplicable.

At the risk of catching at mere straws, Carton sat down in his room by the window to think of all the possibilities. Tollard had quarrelled with his wife, and gone off to the Isle of Wight in a huff. He had pleaded urgent business, which suggested that he was very anxious to get away.

But, whatever his reasons for that, he had actually been away. It would be foolish to deny the validity of his alibi. Had he done anything, made any arrangements, that would mature during his absence?

Assuming, to take the worst side of it, that he had had a hand in his wife's death, there might be two motives to explain his hurried exit on the day prior to the murder: He would have an alibi. He might dread being near when his plans came to their ugly fruition.

But what plans could he have made? There was only one poison in the body—that which corresponded to the poison on the tip of the dart.

Carton was troubled. It was one thing to feel fiercely certain that Elaine Gurdon had no hand in the murder of Mrs Tollard. But it would have been more reasonable and logical if an alternative criminal had presented himself to his mind. Haine, Mrs Gailey, Mr Barley, Miss Sayers, Elaine, Mrs Minever? It was unthinkable that any of them had done it.

As for the man outside, that was a dead theory. The only man they could prove to have been afoot on the morning of the tragedy at that early hour was Jorkins.

Jorkins? But Jorkins had no motive, and it was most unlikely that he could have used a blow-pipe, in any case. Jorkins had not been altogether disingenuous in the first place. He had suspected that he might be colour-blind, but had made no mention of this when first examined.

Granting that there was someone to whom Mrs Tollard's death was profitable or convenient, the suborning of Jorkins might be considered. Tollard was a rich man. He would not be anxious to kill his wife for her money. But convenience was another matter. If he were actually in love with Elaine, even if she did not return his passion, there was a motive.

This new hypothesis did not cheer Carton very much. He felt that there was a serious flaw in it. At the same time, in fault of better, he determined to work it out.

If Jorkins was a man capable of the deed; if he had learned, in some way, to use that odd weapon the blowpipe, he undoubtedly had facilities for killing Mrs Tollard with a chance of safety. He was afoot at that early hour outside the house, he came forward with a story of seeing a woman in red at that window, a story which would switch attention to some unknown criminal. Had he been bribed by someone to kill the woman? Tollard was a man who had money in abundance, and could make it worth his while.

The flaw was this; Mrs Tollard had gone to bed with a bad headache. How could Jorkins know that she would rise from her bed so soon after dawn, and show herself at the window?

That puzzled him. There seemed to be no getting round it at first. He lit a second cigarette, and gave the matter prolonged thought. Then he imagined he saw a light.

The theory was possible on one condition. Most of us have habits that are not easily broken. Some people look out at the night sky before they go to bed; some get up with the dawn, and look out at the newly illumined world. Did Jorkins know that Mrs Tollard looked out early each morning from her bedroom window? Had he possibly seen her there on other occasions when he crossed the park?

Slight as the possibilities seemed, Carton could not over-look them. A more troublesome snag, after all, was the projec-tion of the dart from a blow-pipe. It argued knowledge and practice on Jorkins's part that he was unlikely to possess. How could he get the blow-pipe from the hall, and return it afterwards, when the house was locked up?

He reflected again. The dart could have been used in the fingers, or blown from the native pipe. Was there any other way in which it could be projected?

As he had told Fisher, Carton was acquainted with some native weapons. He thought of some arrows he had once seen, the head of which fitted loosely in a socket in the shaft, so that the shaft fell from it when the object was struck.

This arrow was shot from a bow, but, in the present case, there were difficulties only too obvious. Mrs Tollard was upstairs. If an arrow tipped with the dart had struck her the shaft ought to have been found in the room.

Carton wrinkled his brows over this. The shaft would certainly carry as far as the object aimed at, unless by chance it hit the window-sill, and bounced back, to be picked up afterwards by Jorkins. But Jorkins would not rely on that slight chance. What then?

Carton resumed his memory-dragging for a more suitable weapon, and one came to his mind almost at once. It was simply the native, socketed arrow again, but, this time, the kind used for shooting fish on the surface, or close to the surface, of the African rivers.

In this kind, the shaft was made of a light kind of reed, so that its loss was of no moment, and a very thin, but strong, line was attached to the arrowhead. When a fish was struck, the reed shaft became detached and carried away, but the fish was in connection with the arrow-head, and that in turn (by the line) with the man on the bank. Attach the cord to the shaft instead, and Jorkins would have a means to recover the shaft after he had fired. There are a thousand men in England who can use a bow and arrow for every one even remotely in possession of knowledge about the South American blow-pipe.

And yet Carton was not satisfied. He wanted to be very sure. The dart of thorn could be inserted in a shaft, but would Jorkins take the risk of missing Mrs Tollard by using an unfamiliar weapon?

Keepers are only familiar with guns nowadays, though, at one time, their forerunners, the verderers and foresters, were experts with the bow. But the dart could not be shot from a gun.

Carton suddenly slapped his knee. Not a gun, where the explosion would smash the woody dart, but an air-gun! What of that?

The thorn dart was very slender, it was used with a little fluff of silk-cotton, which, in an air-gun, would serve to make its butt fit the bore. An air-gun such as boys use might be too small, but the larger air-rifles are not uncommonly used by keepers whose duty it is to shoot rats, stoats, and feathered vermin.

'I wonder if Jorkins has got one?' he asked himself.

CHAPTER XX

SPECULATIONS OF A KIND

Mrs Minever had left the drawing-room with a growing sense of grievance which was part of her life. Grievances were like tides in her mind. A new one was always running up, reaching its high-water mark, and ebbing away to nothing.

She now definitely disliked Mr Carton. He was always, it seemed to her, trying to get her out of the way when anything interesting was on the tapis. What was he, after all? A friend of Elaine's, it is true, but he had been away for years, in one of those desperate places where it was well known that men degenerated, and had even been known to have native wives, in addition to taking to drink, drugs, and brutality.

Where had he come from so suddenly? That was the question. He had appeared from the blue the morning following the tragedy. Elaine had not known he was coming. No one had known. Who was to say that he might not be the man who had waited in the shrubbery, and killed poor Margery Tollard? It was easy to see that he hated Mr Tollard, and Mr Tollard had spoken very sharply about him!

She wondered where Elaine and Mrs Gailey were. They were not in the library, or in the morning-room, but the click of balls from the billiard-room as she went down a passage suggested that they were there. She entered fussily.

But only Mrs Gailey was in the room, bending over the table, practising shots, with a mechanical and absent air. She looked up, and rested her cue against a pocket, as the old lady entered.

'Where's Miss Gurdon?' asked Mrs Minever.

'Gone out,' said Netta. 'Why?'

Mrs Minever closed the door, and sat down on the bank. 'My dear,' she announced cautiously, 'I have had an idea. It has just come to me.'

Netta crossed over to her. 'How did the row end? I could see they were both getting hot. But it does seem a pity they let off steam just now.'

'It hasn't anything to do with that,' said Mrs Minever. 'It is about Mr Carton himself. How do we know that he is what he says he is?'

'Because Elaine knows him, and says he is it, and more,' replied Netta, laughing.

'I know. But Elaine has not seen him for years, and it seems to me that no one has thought of enquiring into his doings on that night.'

Netta stared. 'Of course not.'

'Why not?' cried the old lady tartly. 'Why not?'

'Well, he didn't know Margery, for one thing, and he wouldn't try to kill someone he didn't know.'

'Nonsense! How do you know he thought it was Mrs Tollard? He is supposed to have proposed to Elaine once, and been refused. I shouldn't be at all surprised if he has been brooding over it all these years in Africa, and getting bitter about it. Then he comes home, sees in the paper that Tollard has been backing her, and is in a jealous fury. He thinks that is her window, shoots her with the blow-pipe, and then turns up next morning—no, that very morning, and pretends to be very busy doing detective work!'

Netta smiled. 'But they don't use blow-pipes in Africa. At least, I think not. And why should he try to kill Elaine when he is in love with her?'

'Why did that stable-boy in Elterham kill his sweetheart two months ago?'

'Jealousy. But that was different.'

'No it wasn't. Why, the police seem to think Miss Gurdon may have killed Mrs Tollard out of jealousy. It's the same thing.'

Netta shook her head. 'The police haven't said they suspect Elaine. Besides, Mr Carton isn't a stable-boy with an unregulated mind. He is an intelligent man.'

'And intelligent men lose their intelligence when they fall in love,' declared Mrs Minever. 'You ought to know that—being married.'

'Oh, I think my husband showed high intelligence in marrying me,' said Netta, dimpling. 'But, really, I can't believe this. He is very much in love with Elaine, I am sure, and I believe he will propose to Elaine again.'

'Well, why doesn't he, if he is so much in love with her? Mark my words, my dear: if he doesn't hurry up, Mr Tollard will cut him out.'

Netta gasped. 'Oh, I don't think so. That would be too horrid! Why, it is only a few days since Margery was killed.'

'When you are as old as I am, you won't think anything of that! Widowers often have short memories, when there are pretty women about. Why, my dear, Mr Tollard seems to be about with her half the day.'

'I am sure that is only some business they are discussing.'

'Perhaps the sort of urgent business which took Mr Tollard away from here, though it only landed him on a pleasure yacht!'

Netta protested. 'First you talk as if Mr Carton had something to do with it, and then you talk as if Elaine and Mr Tollard might have.'

Mrs Minever looked owlishly wise. 'I shouldn't be surprised if they all had a hand in it, my dear!'

'Ridiculous! When Ned was quarrelling just now with Mr Carton.'

'Rogues have quarrelled over the loot before now, my dear,' said Mrs Minever; and there is no knowing what she might not have said next, if Carton himself had not appeared in the doorway.

'Coming out for a little, Mrs Gailey?' he asked, as composed as if his interview with Tollard had been all amity.

'If you like,' said Netta; she skipped off the bank, and murmured an apology to Mrs Minever.

When the two had left the room, the old lady followed angrily. 'I knew he would be afraid to leave her with me,' she said to herself. 'He knows I suspect something!'

'Well, here we are,' said Carton, when he and Netta Gailey were strolling in the park. 'I had an idea the old lady was charming your sadness, so I obligingly cut in, like another St George.'

She laughed. 'Thank you so much. She really thinks you are the criminal, Mr Carton. She's frightfully amusing, without knowing it. She thinks you were jealous of Elaine, and came back to revenge yourself!'

He turned to her, reddening, then laughing awkwardly. 'All of you seem to know the worst about me.'

'It might be worse,' said Netta. 'It seems so romantic to me, your coming back so many thousands of miles to—'

'To what?' he demanded.

'Well, you ought to know,' cried Netta, hoping she had not gone too far.

He smiled. 'Perhaps I ought, but, since you seem to suspect something, I ask you if this is a suitable time for romance, or anything of the kind?'

'You've been most unlucky.'

'So I think. Like the linen of the Victorian age, there are some things must be stowed away in lavender to a more suitable season.'

'I wish you luck,' said Netta sentimentally.

'Thank you, Mrs Gailey. I'll need it all. I have to blunder into this affair for someone's sake, but my blundering is likely to lead to strained relations.'

'I think you have been wonderful, making that discovery about Jorkins. No one else ever thought of it. Have you made any discoveries since?'

'One in a day is enough,' he remarked. 'But I must thank you again for your help in that experiment. Tollard may grumble, and feel offended, but it was a valuable find. If no one had objected, I might have asked you to help me again.'

'As I am only responsible to Victor, to my husband,' she smiled, 'I can help you if I like.'

He nodded. 'Good! I am sure your husband wouldn't object to my sending you on a mission to Jorkins.'

'You never know,' said Netta. 'He was a good-looking young man! But I think, on the whole, it would be safe enough.'

Carton reflected. 'Well, it's too late today, but tomorrow, if you cared to help me, and would let it go no further, you might see if you could look up Jorkins.'

'And ask him questions?'

'Not exactly that. I have arranged a little scheme, and it is something like this. You see Jorkins, and tell him prettily that you want to learn to shoot.'

'But I can; after a fashion. Victor took me partridge shooting last September, and I shot two—and a mole!'

He laughed. 'Were you trying to get the nucleus for a fur coat?'

'No, I think the poor mole must have been sitting where the partridge ought to have been.'

'So you shoot sitters!—But never mind. If you haven't shot here, Jorkins won't know, and you can ask him if he would show you how to go about it.'

'But what for?'

'You'll hear later on. The real point is this. You can say the noise of a gun going off might frighten you at first, and wouldn't it be better if you could learn to aim with an air-gun? If he hasn't one, you can thank him, and come away?'

'Couldn't you ask him that?'

'I could, but I want to keep in the background after this last little trouble. When I ask questions now everyone suspects that I have a purpose behind them.'

'While they know I talk at random?' she queried.

He shook his head. 'You are another Solomon! But you will do this for me?'

'Of course I will. But what then? If he has an air-gun, am I to use it?'

'You will have to. But keep your eyes open, and see what sort of air-gun it is. Better, ask Jorkins, and keep a spare pellet, or slug, to show me. If you tip him, you may be sure he'll explain very nicely.'

'Mayn't I know yet what you want with all this?'

'Virtue ought to be its own reward, you know,' he said, his eyes twinkling. 'But you'll be doing a jolly good job, and I shall certainly tell you as soon as I can.'

'All right. I'm on. I'll go out for a walk after breakfast, and say nothing to anybody.'

'Thank you,' said Jim Carton. 'That's being a pal, and if your husband would ever like to see a testimonial to your behaviour here, Mrs Gailey, I'll write a dazzling one. But, having been so good already, will you tell me something honestly?'

'If I can be honest about it.'

'Right. Now, in your heart of hearts, you never thought there was anything in this gossip about Elaine and Tollard, did you?'

He looked at once so eager and so anxious, so much the lover in trouble, that Netta's sympathetic heart warmed to him. Whatever Elaine might feel about him, it was obvious that only the recent tragedy prevented Carton from pursuing an ardent wooing. It was true that he had no luck. He had come back at the wrong time.

'Truly never,' she said. 'I admit I was more on Margery's side than Elaine's, but I never believed there was anything in it of a serious nature.'

'I thought not. But why did they take sides?'

Netta reflected. 'You aren't married, Mr Carton, but I'm not ass enough to think only married people know anything about marriage. Still, a married woman knows what another married woman feels, or can feel.'

'For example. What do you think Margery Tollard felt?'

She shrugged prettily. 'Let us leave her out of it. But suppose Victor (who is really a perfect lamb, and might be left with a harem without the slightest risk), suppose he wasn't in love with, let us say Nelly Sayers.'

'Unthinkable for him, as things stand,' said Jim.

She bowed. 'Thank you so much—but I suppose you meant it the other way—that he couldn't be in love with Nelly? At any rate, if Nelly was making some plans, I should hate it if Victor bothered about them, and was always consulting her.'

'Even if you knew he was not in love with her?'

'Even then. But Margery couldn't know, or wouldn't. In some ways she was backboneless, in other ways she was the most obstinate woman I ever met.'

He nodded. 'So you think it was real jealousy, if baseless?'

'I do. There is only one thing that I could never explain about it. She did not like Elaine. That stuck out a yard whenever they were together; but her maid didn't seem to think that she and Tollard had rows. Would it strike you that Ned was a quiet-tempered man?'

'It wouldn't strike me very hard,' said Jim. 'If I were asked, on the strength of his conduct the last day or two, I should say dragons had mild tempers in comparison. But perhaps I misjudge him. I forget that this tragedy influences him.'

'I don't think he was ever very meek and mild,' she said. 'That makes it all the stranger. It is hard to keep rows out of servants' hearing.'

'It must be,' he observed. 'But you relieve my mind a little. However, Tollard goes to town tomorrow, so I may have a slight hope of seeing Elaine once in a while.'

'You aren't jealous, are you?' she asked ingenuously.

He frowned, then smiled. 'Mrs Gailey has a Peter Pan to look after, that is quite evident,' he said. 'I envy him in that. But what do you expect me to say?'

'Nothing. I can see you are!' she said confidently.

'I am,' he admitted. 'I am in the position of poor Mrs Tollard; jealous without a cause, but can't help myself.'

'Would you like me to fish a bit with Elaine?' she asked helpfully. 'I might find out something.'

This time he laughed out. 'No, Mrs Peter Pan, you mustn't do anything of the kind! It's jolly good of you to suggest it, all the same. But, if you see Jorkins tomorrow, and pump him about the air-gun, you shall have all my thanks.'

CHAPTER XXI

THE LADDER

DINNER that evening was the gloomiest meal of all. The latent hostility of the two men darkened conversation, and reduced the temperature of the atmosphere below zero. Mr Barley did his best, and gave up. Mrs Minever tried to be garrulous, and failed. Mrs Gailey nervously tried to sparkle, or encourage someone else to coruscate, and the spark was promptly quenched by the cold waters of silence.

Jim Carton disappeared after dinner, and was not seen on the lower floor of the house again until the others had carried the clouds of gloom with them into the drawing-room, and settled down to pretend that all was well with the world.

Then he emerged from his bedroom, and descending the stairs, went in search of Grover, the butler.

Fortunately, he found Grover doing something in the library, and buttonholed him confidentially.

'I want to know if there isn't a pair of steps somewhere?' he said. 'A step-ladder, you know.'

'There is, sir.'

"Where are they kept?"

'Usually in a cupboard under the stairs, sir.'

'Why usually? Are they not always kept there?'

'The other day, sir, someone put them in the kitchen. I blamed one of the maids for it, but she said Mr Barley had put them there.'

'Oh, I see, and I think I can explain,' said Carton. 'The day Mrs Tollard was found dead, Mr Barley brought the pair of steps for Miss Gurdon to take down the trophy in the hall.'

'I see, sir.'

'So you can acquit the maids of any carelessness.'

'They denied it, sir.'

Carton felt in his pocket for some emollient, found one, and conveyed it to Grover tactfully. 'Do you think, Grover, that you could convey the step-ladder here without anyone knowing? I want to have a look at it.'

The ingenious Grover looked about him. 'There is a ring in one of the high curtains seems likely to slip over, sir,' he said gravely. 'I could attend to that now.'

'Do,' said Carton. 'The look of it rather worries me!'

'I'll get the ladder, sir, at once,' said the butler, and left the room.

Jim Carton looked round as Grover had done, but with his gaze on a lower level.'

On an occasional table near the window there was a book of photographs, and upon it lay a large magnifying glass, with a handle. He went over, took it up, and satisfied himself that it was fairly powerful.

He put it in his pocket, and returned to stand under the big, hanging, bowl lamp, where the light was good. He had been there no more than a minute, when the door was opened softly, and Grover appeared carrying the step-ladder.

'Put it here, please,' said Carton. 'And I think I had better pretend to be fetching a volume from a high shelf. But, if you will loiter about in the hall outside, and cough loudly if anyone comes out of the drawing-room, it will be a help to me.'

'I will do so, sir,' said Grover, who was growing interested in detective work.

He placed the step-ladder where Carton wanted it, tried a small, preliminary cough, and went out, closing the door behind him.

Carton switched on another light or two, pulled back his cuffs, and slowly ascended the steps, his ears alert for a cough from Grover, which would be the signal to carry the ladder to a bookcase.

Then he came down again, and, with the aid of the magnifying glass, examined every inch of the ladder on both sides of the uprights, finishing with the cross-pieces which formed the steps.

He seemed pleased with his find, for he went over all the surface again with the greatest care, and finally made a mark, a tiny cross, with his fountain-pen, on an upright about eighteen inches from the top.

'This is a brain-wave,' he said to himself. 'I must go into this. I only wonder if Mr Barley is discreet enough to confide in? He could help, and, if he is not too much afraid of Tollard, he will.'

He surveyed the steps from every angle, and was still busy in this absorbing pursuit, when a loud cough from the hall apprised him that someone had left the drawing-room and its ungenial company.

His programme had been to pretend that a high volume attracted him, but on hearing Mr Barley's voice come faintly from the hall, he changed his mind, and went to the door to open it.

'Mr Barley,' he said softly.

Mr Barley saw him and came over. Carton drew him into the room, closed the door behind them, and locked it.

'Sorry to imprison you,' he said, as Barley started and frowned. 'No offence meant, as they say in certain circles. But I don't want anyone else butting in, until I have had your excellent judgment on a very important matter.'

Mr Barley smiled, then stared at the step-ladder, standing in mid-room under the lamp.

'What are you doing with that?'

'Trying to settle a very vexed question. But that will keep. I really wanted to know why you fetched this ladder on the day of Mrs Tollard's death from the kitchen.'

'Miss Gurdon wanted it.'

'I'm afraid I put my question rather clumsily. What I wanted to know was this: why did you fetch it from the kitchen, or look for it there, rather?'

'Because I thought it was usually kept there,' said Mr Barley, with a puzzled air.

'Grover tells me it is usually kept in a cupboard under the stairs.'

'Really? I was not aware of that. I certainly found it in the kitchen. It seemed to me the proper place for it, and I replaced it there when Miss Gurdon had done with it.'

'Don't think me rude asking these questions,' said Jim Carton. 'They are rather important to my mind.'

'In what way, may I ask?' said Mr Barley, looking at sea.

'Well, if a dart comes into this case at all, and it undoubtedly does, sir, it must have been taken from that quiver in the hall. To get it, one would need a ladder. An outsider might not know—' he paused, frowned, and added: 'I must see that cupboard later on.'

'You mean to say that the ladder was used to mount to the trophy before Miss Gurdon used it for that purpose?'

'Exactly. Someone must have got up there, and down again.'

'But, if the ladder was kept in a cupboard, why not replace it there, and not take it to the kitchen, which is farther off?'

'I can't tell till I see the servants.'

'Or the cupboard, you said, though I don't know that it will prove much.'

'Perhaps not. The point I am trying to make about the servants is this: anyone, unless it happened to be one of the servants himself, wishing to return the ladder without being observed, would certainly not take it to the kitchen. You can walk about the hall, or passages, without seeing anyone at certain times, but not the kitchen. The cook would be there, if no one else.'

'That's true; perhaps it was one of the servants.'

'They denied it to Grover, and I don't want to let them know of this in any case. But I said "certain" times, not all times. At night, you could go quietly round the house, and even into the kitchen, without seeing anyone.'

'By Jove, you're right, Carton!' cried Mr Barley. 'You certainly see further into a brick wall than most of us. Go on!'

'I'm going on, to the cupboard,' said Carton. 'Will you show it me? Grover said it was under the stairs.'

'I know it,' said Mr Barley. 'We won't need an extra light. There is a switch, and a small bulb there.'

Carton hurried across the room, unlocked the door, went back to fetch the ladder, and, carrying it horizontally, followed in the wake of his host.

No one was in the hall, Grover had disappeared. Guided by Barley, Carton and the step-ladder proceeded towards the rear of the house into a passage where the secondary staircase to the servants' bedrooms ascended.

'It's in here,' said Mr Barley, turning a small knob on the panelling that shut in the stairs.

Like all cupboards of its kind, this had a ceiling at an angle corresponding to that of the stairs themselves, but it was not high enough at any point to accommodate the step-ladder when standing upright.

Mr Barley switched on a light inside, and Carton examined the interior swiftly, since he knew what he was looking for.

'You see those spikes in the back wall,' he said to Mr Barley. 'Those are to hang the ladder on. It folds up, and ought to be suspended there along the wall.'

'I see that.'

'Yes, but to manœuvre the ladder into the cupboard, and hang it there, is a job that takes a little time, and may make some noise, if the end of the ladder swung round and hit the frame of the door.'

His host assented. 'But Carton, if the person who took it out wanted to hide his work, would he not take some trouble?'

'There was no need, perhaps,' said Carton. 'My point is that the ladder was found by you in the kitchen because the person who took it from here, presumably in the night, thought it would be quicker to leave it in the kitchen.'

'But, if it was originally here, the person who came for it must have been familiar with the house.'

'That's true. That is the ugly part of it. We'll keep this to ourselves for the moment.'

Mr Barley frowned. 'Certainly,' he said. But he remembered that he had shown Miss Gurdon over the house on the day after her arrival, and hoped that she might not be involved after all.

Carton switched off the light, after returning the ladder to the wall spikes, and returned with Mr Barley to the library.

'It's rather mysterious that the police have not returned here lately,' he said. 'I don't like it at all. It shows that they not only have a clue, as I told you, but that they are banking on it strongly. They think they have seen everything that is to be seen above, and now they are turning their attention elsewhere.'

'To London, Carton. I don't like that either. If they have actually sent a man to spy on Tollard's house, they must link him up in some way with the affair. His alibi, I should have thought, would have satisfied them.'

'Well, there are two ways of looking at it. I should say that all their investigations in town are directed to finding that there was bad blood between Tollard and his wife. That involves Miss Gurdon by inference. There's no doubt that their examination of Mrs Gailey and Miss Sayers put them on that track. I don't really blame those two young women so much. They were taken off their guard, they had heard the gossip, and didn't want to tell lies—probably they tried to hedge after, and so made Fisher suspicious.'

'I understand that they did hedge.'

'Fatal,' said Carton, 'If you have anything to say, say it, and be done! Withdrawals are dangerous.'

'I quite agree with you. Still I don't think I saw enough to make me believe Tollard and his wife were really—'

'On such bad terms,' Carton interrupted. 'But that we cannot decide. The thing now is to get busy with this new point. Someone wanted to get one of those poisoned darts. He had to climb up to the trophy on the wall to secure one. From what I saw of the quiver, a dart might be drawn out by the fingers without the hand touching or grasping the quiver itself.'

'Very likely.'

'This person was sufficiently familiar with the house to know where the ladder was kept, but knew that it would be dangerous to go to that cupboard by day. He went at night.'

'That rules out Tollard.'

'Unless the dart was taken the night before Tollard left. I think not, since the butler would have noticed it in the kitchen, on the day preceding the murder. But I am using the word "he" as one does use it at times, to signify a human being, not to specify the sex.'

'I understand.'

'He went by night, removed the steps, and carried them into the hall, mounted them, and removed a dart. Perhaps he had found it difficult enough to take the steps out of the cupboard, and decided not to attempt to replace them. He carried them to the kitchen, which was easy of access, and left them there. I am going to assume that the blow-pipe was not used.'

'It would not be necessary indoors.'

'No. But we must now concentrate on the people in this house. We must go over them again without fear or favour. Haine we cannot get at just now, but I am inclined to rule him out anyway. An imaginative person might conclude that he had let his harmless passion for Mrs Tollard get the better of him, and killed her when she had refused to countenance it, but personally I look on Haine as a decent young ass, without sufficient temperament to run into any passionate danger.'

'I am sure of that.'

Carton nodded. 'Well, will you undertake, sir, to question your servants, severally, and secretly, about the moving of the ladder from the cupboard? Put the fear of death in them, if they gossip about it, but see if any of them knows anything.'

'I shall certainly do what you say,' replied Mr Barley.

CHAPTER XXII

THE ARROW THAT FLYETH BY NIGHT

MRS GAILEY came down next morning in tweeds and a pair of brogue shoes, ready for her tramp over to Jorkins's cottage. She said good-bye to Tollard, who was leaving immediately after breakfast, and then sat down next Mrs Minever.

'Going out, my dear?' the old lady enquired.

'To get the cobwebs blown away,' said Netta.

'Mr Tollard looks a wreck,' whispered her neighbour.

'Yes, poor old thing,' said Netta softly, and began her breakfast.

Carton had bade her good-morning when she came down, but did not speak to her now. He seemed more concerned with his food than with any less material matter, and ate on steadily without looking at anyone. Even when Netta got up and pushed back her chair he did not make any remark.

Netta thrilled secretly. She was engaged on very important business—a mission, no less. It was strictly between the two of them.

She was not aware that Carton had been down half an hour before anyone else, and had telephoned to the police at Elterham.

He had lain awake a long time after going to bed, worrying at his problem from every angle. Something, it might be a recollection of the expression on Fisher's face when he had last parted from him, it might be a premonition he could not explain; but something told him that the police had made up their minds to pounce on Elaine Gurdon during the next day or two.

If they arrested her, she would have an unpleasant time thereafter; for, even if a prisoner is proved innocent, there are always those who will not give credence to the verdict, but go about remarking that the acquitted person was very lucky.

He had decided before he slept, to put his new clue in the hands of the police. They could not afford to disregard it, whether it was right or wrong, and it might give him a day's respite in which to conduct further operations.

He did not believe in this clue so much as he had done before the ladder incident attracted his attention. If the removal of the ladder had taken place in the night, but had been done by someone inside, it was unlikely that Jorkins was implicated. But the police knew nothing of the ladder. Let them carry on!

Netta set out rapidly for the under-keeper's cottage, and found that it was as well she had made such an early start. Jorkins had been out on some job, returned for breakfast to his cottage, and was leaving it when she came in sight. Netta called to him, and he stopped still and waited for her to come up.

'Oh, Jorkins,' she said breathlessly, as she hurried across, 'are you very busy just now?'

'Not very, miss, if there is anything I can do for you,' he replied.

'You see, I thought I should like to learn to shoot.'

He smiled. 'Some ladies does, now, miss,' he replied. 'This gun, being what they call a keeper's gun, is not so light as some, but perhaps you wouldn't mind that.'

'It looks so big,' said she, flattering herself on her acting. 'I suppose it makes rather a nasty noise?'

His grin was respectful, but wide. 'Reckon it does, miss, but you got to get used to that, if you shoot. It don't sound so bad after the first few times.'

He offered the gun he had held under his arm, butt first to her, but Netta laughed and refused.

'I wonder if I couldn't learn to aim with something smaller, Jorkins? You see, if I got used to handling it, I might not mind the noise later on.'

To her annoyance, he threw open the breech of the gun, and extracted the cartridges. 'Well, miss, there isn't any need to fire her. You could just do the motions of loading and aiming, but keep your finger off the trigger.'

She reflected. 'No, it is too heavy. Haven't you an—what do they call it? Oh, an air-gun?'

Jorkins smiled and nodded. 'I have, miss. At least Mr Barley bought me one of those B.S.A. ones; .22 bore, for killing rats and vermin.'

Netta could hardly contain her delight and excitement. Mr Carton was really wonderful. He had thought Jorkins might have an air-gun, and the man really had one. She beamed on Jorkins, and went on.

'May I use that?'

Jorkins considered. 'Well, miss, if you was to come down tomorrow, or this afternoon, say, you might. But it's rare rusty. I never could get the hang of those things, and I find I can do all I want with my old twelve-bore here.'

He patted his gun affectionately.

'You mean you could clean it up?'

'Yes, miss, but please don't tell Mr Barley I let it get that way. He was very keen on me buying one, along of some advert he saw. But, though he's a very generous and kind gentleman, he don't know much about my job.'

'May I see it, and the kind of thing it shoots?' she asked. 'Of course, I won't tell anyone you let it get rusty.'

Jorkins turned back, unlocked the door of his cottage, invited her in, and took down a powerful air-gun from the wall, giving the rather rusty barrel a brush with his coat-sleeve before he handed it to Netta.

She examined it carefully. 'What does it fire, Jorkins?'

'Slugs or shot, miss. Anything that will fit the bore. It is good enough for a man who aims by sights, but I always was a snap-shot, more by hand than eye, and I can't make good shooting with it.'

'I thought a slug was a kind of worm, or snail, or some-thing!' she said innocently.

'This sort is a kind of small bullet of a peculiar shape, miss. If you wait a moment, I'll get one for you. I keep them in a tin box over the fire there. I reckon I haven't used many.'

'Oh, thank you. I should so much like to see one,' she said.

He brought down the tin, and handed her three slugs.

'Them's the sort, miss.'

'And what did you say the air-gun was; what size, I mean?'

'A twenty-two bore, miss. There's a smaller size that boys uses. This can kill a rook, or a rabbit, at near range—perhaps better than that.'

She memorised this detail, and looked for a tip. She had just compensated Jorkins for his trouble, and was going to make a suggestion about coming again that afternoon, when a figure darkened the door of the cottage, and Inspector Warren came in.

Jorkins started, Netta looked guilty. The inspector touched his hat to the lady, nodded to Jorkins, and fastened his eyes with curious significance on the gun in the under-keeper's hand.

'Don't keep your tools very bright, do you?' he asked the latter, in a conversational tone. 'It wouldn't do if our police folk let their handcuffs get into a state like that!'

Netta's first impulse was to say good-bye to Jorkins and vanish with expedition, but she decided now to stay and hear what was in the wind. Mr Carton might be glad to get information.

Jorkins seemed more at his ease now. 'You might, and they might, if it was a tool you didn't expect to use much.'

'What do you keep it for then?'

''Twas bought for me, inspector, same as your boss might buy you a note-book you didn't need, believing your memory was good enough,' said Jorkins, and almost winked at Netta.

The inspector smiled drily. 'So you are just having a look at it, to see if it needs cleaning.'

Here Netta thought it was her duty to come to Jorkins's assistance.

'I asked Jorkins to teach me to shoot, and I thought he might have this air-gun cleaned, so that I could use it, inspector.'

'I see, miss. Aren't you one of the ladies I saw up at the house the other day?'

'Yes, I am Mrs Gailey.'

'Mr Carton still up there?' said Warren casually, appearing to forget Jorkins for the moment.

'Oh yes, he is still there. Mr Tollard was leaving today though.'

'Very sad for the poor gentleman,' said Warren gravely. 'I suppose he's gone up to the funeral?'

'Yes.'

'I suppose the dead lady's friend, Miss Gurdon, has gone too?'

Netta had been once bitten, and now she was shy. She heard the creak of the pump in his voice, and replied demurely.

'I don't think so.'

Jorkins had seized the opportunity to put the air-gun away again, but Warren saw the action and turned swiftly.

'Let's have a look at that Jorkins.'

The under-keeper obediently handed it down, and Netta saw that this was the moment for a retreat.

'If I come back for a lesson after lunch, will you have it ready?'

'Yes, miss,' said Jorkins, who was looking uneasily at the detective. 'I'll try to.'

When Netta Gailey had gone, the inspector opened the breech of the air-gun, and glanced through the barrel, which he held up to the sky, as seen through the window of the cottage.

'Looks rusty inside and out.'

'Not only looks. It *is*!'

'.22 I should say?'

'Just that.'

'Powerful weapon of its kind?'

'Good as they make them. But I'm no shot with them, or a rifle, either.'

'But you're a keeper.'

'I reckon I am a pretty good one too. You folk who aren't used to guns don't know that a gent, for instance, may be a clinking game shot, and not able to hit a door with a rifle.'

'I don't see. Why is it?'

'Rifleman looks along the sights; a game shot often flings up his gun, keeps his eyes on the bird, (same as you do with t'other ball at billiards), and lets go. It's the hand does it with a snap.'

'You win,' said Warren easily. 'But now this lady—did she come down so early to learn shooting?'

'So she said.'

'Why didn't you lend her your other gun?'

'"Cause she said she didn't like the bang, and if I had an air-gun she might learn to aim first.'

'But she could learn with the other gun unloaded.'

'I'm only telling you what she said.'

Warren nodded. 'Did she know you had an air-gun?'

'No. She said *if* I had an air-gun she might try it. She wanted to know what it shot, and I gave her some slugs.'

Warren gave up that line of questioning. He knew now that Carton had not only telephoned his theory to them, but had sent Mrs Gailey privately down to get information.

'I think I had better have this, to show the inspector,' he said. 'I mean the superintendent.'

Jorkins looked alarmed. 'Why, what have I to do with him? You aren't kidding yourself that I shot the lady, are you?'

'Not for a moment,' said Warren, and put on an air of great confidence. 'But we have to make enquiries, for this cottage of yours is not always lived in, you being away for hours at a time, and we never know but someone might have sneaked in, and taken this gun.'

'Rusty?'

'What's rust, Jorkins? Why, I had a case where a knife was used. It was rusty too. Water, my son! You can put a bit of rust on most metal in a short time, if you want to. No, you let me have this, and we'll return it to you as soon as we can. Since you say you don't use it, it won't hamper you much.'

'What about the lady what's coming back this afternoon?'

Warren shrugged. 'I have an idea she won't be back today. If she is, you tell her I had to take the thing away.'

'Are you going with it now?'

'I am. I have to get back with it.'

'Well, don't go and try to mess me up in it,' said Jorkins gloomily. 'You fellows are never happy but meddling with folk you ought to let alone.'

'That is what the poachers say about you keepers,' replied the inspector, with a grin. 'I expect it is about as true!'

Meanwhile, Netta Gailey had fled home, and found Carton lying back in a deck-chair in the sun. She took out the slugs she had got at the cottage, and put them in his hands.

'The slugs.'

'Good.'

'I had to hurry away. The inspector came.'

He whistled and looked blank.

'What for?'

'The air-gun.'

'Oh, that?'

He seemed to understand now, though she did not.

'He seemed interested in it. I think he was going to get it from Jorkins.'

'But you left before that?'

'Oh yes. But I saw the air-gun before the inspector came. It was quite rusty.'

'It would be, even if he did use it,' said Carton, cryptically to her mind. 'That is not hard to do. But it seems to be a .22 bore, and that is the calibre I thought it might be.'

'If he had one.'

'Quite. You see he had. However, I can leave that part of the business in Warren's hands. Do sit down, and rest. It was jolly good of you to go for me, and you have done all I wanted.'

'I must go in,' she said, smiling, and shaking her head. 'But I am glad I was able to help.'

Carton thanked her again, as she turned away to go into the house, and then he reflected on something else.

'Now I think of it, that cupboard had a key,' he said to himself. 'I had better have a look at that.'

CHAPTER XXIII

A BIT OF FLUFF

WHEN Carton went privately to the cupboard under the stairs, it was apparent that he wanted to do something more than look at the key to it. He turned the key in the lock, put it in his pocket, and hurried up to his bedroom.

'They can get another ladder, if they want one,' he said under his breath. 'I wish I could have a look at the key of Mrs Tollard's bedroom next.'

But here his reflections were broken into by a knock at the door, and a voice that informed him Superintendent Fisher was below, and wished to speak with him. He hurried down at once, heard that Fisher had been shown into the library, and joined him there immediately.

'Congratulations, sir,' said the superintendent softly. 'It is really a most important point you have brought out about the air-gun, and does you credit.'

'Thank you,' said Jim Carton, pleased to find that the fish had bitten. 'I thought it might be.'

Fisher beamed. 'Of course, it is too early to say what may be the result of our investigations, but I have sent Warren down to get the air-gun, if there is one—'

'There is,' said Carton, smiling. 'Mrs Gailey wanted shooting lessons, so I suggested an air-gun, and sent her to Jorkins. She has just come back. It is a .22 bore, and rusty.'

Fisher frowned, then relaxed. 'You seem to keep busy on your own account, sir! Anyway, you guessed right, if the lady has seen the weapon. I dare say Warren has gone back with it to Elterham.'

Carton did not dwell on its rustiness. He wanted time: 'You remember what Miss Gurdon said about a bit of fluff, of silk-cotton, that went on the butt of those darts to make the bore of the blow-pipe air-tight? That is what gave me the idea. The impulsion with the blow-pipe is of the same nature; compressed air. But a gun would send a dart with greater velocity, with much greater accuracy, and could be used by a native of this country to far better purpose.'

'That's true. I saw what you meant the moment we got your message. The only difficulty will be to prove what motive Jorkins could have. We will put a man on to watch him, and make enquiries to see if he has been spending money.'

'If there is anything in it, it was a bribe, of course.'

Fisher nodded absently. 'For the present this does seem to clear Miss Gurdon. She wasn't well-to-do, or she wouldn't have had to go to Tollard for money for an expedition. But I may tell you, Mr Carton, that I had half a mind yesterday to get a warrant for her.'

Jim Carton breathed relief, though he made no comment on this last remark. Fisher went on, after a pause.

'So far we have been hampered in our theory of an outside assailant by Jorkins's evidence. He was out there, he said he saw no one. Naturally, if he did it, that is what he would say. Undoubtedly he is colour-blind, but his talk of a woman in red looks like a plan after all. To clear himself, he would have to pretend that someone, other than Mrs Tollard, was in the room.'

'Quite,' said Jim, who, in spite of his later find, was unable to decide definitely that Jorkins was outside the radius of suspicion.

Fisher looked down. 'So I think we'll hold up the matter of getting a warrant, for a day or two, and concentrate on this. If Jorkins did it, he may have been concealed in the shrubbery. If he used an air-gun, as you say, he would have that bit of fluff on it to fill the bore. Even bits of fluff don't vanish, though they can get blown about in winds.'

'I should say that the compression between the expanding air in the breech, and the back of the dart in front, and also the rapid passage of the missile through the barrel, would tend to harden and solidify the fluff of silk-cotton.'

'That's true, sir. A wad in a gun does get like that between powder and shot charge when a gun is fired. It might make it into a softish pellet; just as paper gets, when you crumple it up in your fingers.'

'I think so.'

Fisher pondered the matter with growing excitement. 'It was Warren who looked over that bit of ground immediately between the shrubbery and the window. But I expect he was looking for a white fluff, not anything harder or smaller. An intensive search over an area of a hundred square yards or more ought to bring us on the thing. But it will have to be really thorough.'

'Couldn't you put several men on it?'

'I'll give instructions when I get back. I am sorry now I didn't tell Warren to bring the gun up to me here. But there is the lady you speak of, Mrs Gailey.'

'Yes, she saw it. She spoke to Jorkins, and brought me some of the slugs.' He put his hand in his pocket, and passed the little missiles to Fisher. 'Shall I go to fetch her?'

'If you would, sir,' said Fisher.

Carton soon found Mrs Gailey, and told her what was wanted. 'Don't make a secret of anything,' he said. 'You can tell him all you know, for I said I had sent you.'

'All right,' she said, with some trepidation however. 'I'll come.'

Fisher received her courteously. 'Mr Carton tells me you have seen Jorkins and his air-gun, Mrs Gailey. I hear it was rusty.'

'Oh, it was. I had it in my hand.'

'Did he say why it was rusty? Keepers as a rule are very careful about fire-arms of any kind.'

'He said he couldn't shoot well with it, that Mr Barley bought it for him, but he preferred his keeper's gun.'

'Seems an odd excuse. In ordinary circumstances, I should say a keeper who had a rusty gun was one who wanted people to see it was rusty! I have been in their places before now, and I noticed that even old fire-arms, of a kind unused nowadays, were kept clean and bright, even if they only hung on the wall.'

'I don't know anything about that.'

'You couldn't, madam. But the rust in itself need not worry us, unless it is so extensive and deep as to pit the barrel, or lock. I think, Mr Carton, that a close examination of the gun when taken to pieces, or of the rifling in the barrel, might show a fibre of the silk-cotton stuff.'

Netta listened eagerly. Here she was not even a messenger now, but a member of a crime conference, listening to the superintendent's views!

Carton shook his head. 'If the gun was used—which is all that concerns us—but is now rusty, it was probably left in water for some time. In that case, the silk-cotton fibres might be washed out.'

'Possible. But the expert will see to that. I think we had better send it to the makers in Birmingham.'

Jim Carton agreed. 'Well, we have had some wonderful summer days lately, but you never can tell when the weather may not change. A shower of rain, or a high wind, may wash out any traces.'

'I will telephone from here,' Fisher decided. 'I'll have three men over at once to search the ground.'

'You don't want me in the meantime?'

'No, sir, nor this lady. I have to thank you both for your help. I shouldn't be surprised if this doesn't put us on the right track.'

'I hope it will,' said Carton, and withdrew with Mrs Gailey.

'I think you're wonderful,' she said naïvely, when they were in the hall. 'The superintendent actually consulted you.'

'Actually,' he agreed, grinning a little. 'But don't make any mistake, Mrs Gailey. Fisher is no fool. I have had a bit of luck that did not come his way. On the other hand, he is careful and thorough.'

'Then you don't think the police are as stupid as some people make out?

'No, I don't. I think they're a very high average lot, even if they don't always work miracles.'

He left her at the foot of the stairs, and went back to his bedroom. He was thinking of Tollard, and swearing mildly at the author of the new regulations.

Here he was, the matter sufficiently urgent (if the case against Jorkins broke down), and there was Mrs Tollard's room that positively called for a more intensive search than even the garden below the window. That day he had seen it with Barley was not enough. He had not known then what he knew, or imagined he knew, now.

But Barley had given his promise, and would stick to it. He could not in honour ask the man to break it.

It might have been a sophistical reflection, but he did reflect now that, while he had heard Barley say that no one was to go into the room, he had not himself promised to keep out of it.

To get into it, however, was the problem. To be found there would look very ugly, and might result in his being turned out by his host. But he would have chanced that if he could have been certain of making an easy entry. The windows had been closed since the room was locked, and he could not climb up that way.

'The worst of it is,' he murmured, 'that I could do no good by night; the only safe time otherwise. I want all the light I can get.'

Mr Barley had locked the room himself, so, presumably, he was now in possession of the key. He might keep his keys in some place together. It would be dangerous to touch them.

Otherwise, he did not think it would be wrong. His motive was sound. Though he appeared cheerful enough, he was really more than anxious about Elaine. The idea that she might be arrested and charged with the crime was beastly, but it was a decided possibility. Suppose Jorkins's story proved true, and the rust on the air-gun was sufficiently deep-seated to prove its long standing, then his theory went by the board, and Fisher would be back on the old trail with a sharper eye for Elaine than ever before.

'He'll nab her, if I'm not careful,' he said to himself. 'I wonder if she is keeping anything back? Could I frighten her into letting it out? But, on the other hand, what could she know?'

Of course, up to the last moment, he should call in the police, and give them details of his latest discovery. But that had its dangers. A twist to the evidence, and what he had noted might seem as convincing evidence against Elaine as anyone else. It all depended on the way one looked at it.

At lunch Elaine appeared. It was the first time he had seen her since breakfast, and it appeared that she had driven down to the station with Tollard, afterwards visiting the village, and indulging in a short walk. Fisher was still in the house somewhere, but he had not called for her.

'I shall be glad when this melancholy business is over,' said Mr Barley. 'It is over, in a sense, but the thought of the funeral today brings it back. I wonder now if I ought to have gone.'

Elaine shook her head. 'He did not wish anyone to go from here,' she remarked quietly. 'But he was full of your kindness, Mr Barley, and most grateful to you.'

'Nothing! Nothing at all!' said old Barley, flushing.

Mrs Minever looked at Elaine. 'Do you know the policeman is here again?'

'It's Superintendent Fisher,' said Mrs Gailey, 'and he is going to have some men back to search the garden.'

'Is this true?' asked Barley, looking at Carton.

'So he says, sir. It appears he thinks he may find a clue there. It wasn't thoroughly done last time, but now he is going to comb it out to the last inch.'

'I don't see that he need look for the criminal out there,' muttered the old lady.

'He must look for him everywhere,' said Barley. 'You ought to know that, Jane.'

She sniffed sceptically, and went on with her lunch.

Jim Carton was sitting next to Elaine, and now turned to speak to her. 'Are you too tired with your morning's excursion to give me a look-in this afternoon?' he asked softly.

She smiled. 'In what way, Jim?'

'Say a walk. I was prophesying to Fisher a possible change in the weather, and it is a pity to mug about in the house on a beautiful day like this. Where's a good place to go, Mr Barley?'

'For a walk? Well, you can't beat the road to Kirkley—at least that's my opinion. You turn left after you leave the lodge, go past the beech avenue on Sir David's estate, and strike a lane. It rises all the time till you get to the top of Wale Hill, and the view is splendid.'

'Ortho Haine took me once in his car,' said Mrs Gailey. 'It really is lovely.'

'All right,' said Elaine composedly. 'That will do. Ought we to tea out, or can we do it, and come back for tea here?'

'That depends,' said Mr Barley, 'on how fast you go.'

For the first time since the tragedy he almost achieved archness. Mrs Gailey laughed, and even Elaine smiled.

Jim Carton was, curiously enough, the most embarrassed person there, but he managed to turn it off by saying that an explorer like Elaine ought to be able to put up a walking record.

'I'll be ready any time after lunch,' he added.

'At two,' said Elaine. 'I have one or two things to do first.'

He nodded acquiescence.

But he felt nervous and disturbed in his mind when he stood in the porch later, waiting for Elaine to come out. How would she take it? Would she resent his meddling, forgetting how he felt about her? Would she refuse to take the menace seriously, and so hamper him at the last when there was most need for haste?

He made up his mind that it would be better to tell her frankly what Fisher had hinted to him—that, if the case against Jorkins fell through, she might be arrested on that most serious charge at any minute. Fisher would have Mrs Gailey and Nelly Sayers on the gridiron again, and this time he would not mince matters. He felt sure that neither of those young women would stand a searching examination, pushed to conclusions.

'I won't let Elaine put me off this time,' he said to himself, as he heard her step in the hall.

CHAPTER XXIV

ELAINE IS STUBBORN

JIM CARTON managed to sustain a conversation that was chiefly confined to banalities as they went down the drive, and during their walk to the lane leading to Wale Hill. His nervousness waned a little when he discovered that Elaine was herself not as composed as usual.

'This is more like old times,' he ventured, as they turned into the leafy lane, and found themselves shut in on either side by hedges that were colourful with the blossoms of the wild rose. 'I wish we could get back to them, and cut out the last few weeks, don't you?'

She looked sidewise at him. 'Look here, Jim,' she said seriously. 'I have a feeling that you didn't get me out here to talk of old times.'

'You're quite right.'

'I felt it. But is it worth while? Are you going over what you said before?'

He frowned. 'Elaine, I wonder if you know what I think about you at all? Do you think I don't care what happens to you?'

'I'm sure you do, Jim,' she replied warmly. 'I know you do. It isn't that. But what could happen to me? I think you exaggerate. I know it is because you do care, but just that makes you see little events out of proportion.'

'That is how I feel about you,' he returned bluntly. 'You are quick to see most things, but not this. I know you are in a most dangerous position, and I want to help. But I can't help, so long as you refuse to confide in me.'

'I have,' she said earnestly. 'As much as I can confide.'

'As much? What does that mean?'

'Well, what can I say?'

He shrugged. 'You may think I have Ned Tollard on the brain. Perhaps I have. But I would bet a good deal that he asked you not to talk about him and his wife.'

'And if he did, Jim, can you blame him?'

'I'm not allotting blame. But all these things ought to go by the board, when it is a matter of life and death.'

'No doubt, but I can't see it like that. The superintendent is sending men to search the garden again. That means he thinks he has a new clue, and if so it must refer to someone outside.'

'He has a clue. I gave it to him.'

She started. 'Did you? May I know?'

He told her briefly of Jorkins and the air-gun, and her face hardened as she listened. 'But that is unthinkable, Jim. You can only implicate Jorkins by supposing he was bribed by Ned.'

He stared down at the ground irritably. 'Well, if I do? But I had another motive. That was to delay Fisher for a day or two while I try another line. Even if Jorkins is not guilty, I have gained a day or two.'

Surprise was now visible on her face, and in her eyes. 'My dear boy, what do you mean? Why should you try to hold up the police in their work?'

He stopped in his walk, and laid a hand on her arm.

'Because I heard from Fisher today, what I suspected before, that he was on the point of getting a warrant for your arrest, Elaine! He admitted, too, today that, if Jorkins proved a wash-out, he would carry out his first plan.'

She turned white, and bit her lip. He saw that this was a blow over the heart, and watched her anxiously, though he did not move closer to her.

After a few moments, her colour returned, her mouth was firm. She pulled herself up, and answered in a clear voice that did not tremble.

'So that's it. You are very good, Jim. I understand you better now, and I understand too why you have been so anxious.'

'Or officious, as Tollard would say,' he replied gruffly, touched by the change in her tone. 'You see how it is now. Innocent as you are, a jury might not see it. Mrs Gailey and Miss Sayers were bad witnesses for our side, and I imagine they will give the impression that Margery Tollard was jealous of you, if Fisher gets them in the witness-box.'

'I know they rather muddled it before.'

'Absolutely. They meant well, but they were not sure what he was after, and he did not give them a chance to compare notes. Next time, he won't be so easy with them. He will be out for blood, and determined to get at the exact facts.'

She walked on, and when he caught up with her again, she shook her head. 'I see that. But what can we do?'

'Tell me all you know.'

A vexed look crossed her face. 'You will insist that I have some special knowledge.'

'You know more about them both than I do,' he said obstinately.

'A little perhaps. But I can't see, Jim, what it means to you. Suppose Margery was jealous, what can you make of it? All that it may lead us to is a suggestion that Ned committed a crime.'

'I don't care what it may lead to,' he said fiercely, 'so long as I prevent the police from charging you with having committed one.'

'Be frank,' said Elaine; pale again, and with a frown on her brow. 'If you go along that line, where do you end? If Margery was jealous, she was jealous of me.'

'Well?'

'And if she was jealous of me, and this crime can be fastened on Ned—as we know it cannot—'

'I don't know anything of the sort.'

'Then the inference is obvious, and it is an insult to me,' she went on.

'You know I want to protect you, not to insult you. Apart from that, what you say simply isn't true. I could never believe you had anything to do with it.'

'Ned was away, I was not.'

'I know that. But what is the clue the police are working on now, do you think?'

'I can't understand it.'

'I can; it is one that may involve him—mind you, I only say "may"—but has nothing to do with you at all.'

She looked at him, with a sort of desperation in her eyes. 'I am as far from it as ever. But never mind. What do you want me to tell you? If Margery was jealous? I believe she was.'

'Of you and Ned?'

'I suppose so.'

'Thank you. Now I would like to know if Ned said anything about it. He must have done. Why, he has been with you a dozen times since she died.'

'It has nothing to do with that.'

'Well, tell me, and I shall know where I am.'

'I have told you all I know.'

Carton shrugged and looked angry. 'I thought I had told you enough to let you see how serious the case was from your point of view.'

'I do see that.'

'Well, then—what I mean is this. Tollard must have been angry with her. I don't know if he differed in any way from the normal husband, but most of them would be furious if their wives were like that when they had given them no cause. Was there a real breach between them lately?'

'I believe Ned loved her.'

'Then he took a strange way of showing it.'

'You mustn't say that! You don't know him as well as I do.'

Carton took a pull on himself. He was losing his temper, and she saw it and resented it. 'Sorry. The fact is that she was jealous, and we can assume jealous because you and

he were so busy together over the details of this projected
expedition. Very well. A man in love with his wife, would, I
think, take some trouble to soothe her down, even if he did
not give up communicating with his friend.'

Elaine shook her head, and set her lips firmly. She was
not going to be examined any more in this way, and her face
showed it. It was unfortunate that Jim Carton took her this
way. But the matter was so urgent, the time so short, that he
knew of no other.

'You mean to say he never told you how he felt about it,
or allowed you to see that it was making a breach?'

'No.'

'You mean he didn't tell you, or you didn't see?'

'He didn't tell me.'

'But you saw it might be doing that?'

She tried to be patient, to understand his point of view.

'Jim, you don't understand what my position was. A person
who is treated as if he were ready to do some kind of nasty
trick at any time (even hears a chance suggestion that he, or
she, had already done it), is apt to resent it. If you are going
on your ordinary way, and a woman suggests that you are
following her to pick her pocket, you don't turn back, and
give up. If you did, she would be sure you were a criminal
detected just in time.'

'I see that,' he murmured.

'So you keep on your way, which happens to be parallel
with hers, Jim. It may seem to outsiders that you are
provoking her unnecessarily by going on; but why should
you back out? If we had to step out of the way of all the
fools in the world, we should never get anywhere! I am
sorry for Margery now, but I can't feel that I had anything
to be ashamed of.'

'You won't tell me any more?'

'No, I won't. I should like you to believe in me, Jim, but I
do absolutely refuse to be treated as if I were a hostile witness

in a court of law. Anything Ned said to me in confidence I can't tell you. It would not be fair, or decent.'

'My heavens!' he cried savagely. 'Are we to talk about fairness and decency when the police may try to arrest you? Will the counsel in a case, if one comes on, say that he knows you promised not to tell something Ned Tollard told you, and won't hurt your feelings by asking it? Not much! He'll have it out of you one way or another.'

'It's different,' she protested. 'If I have to give evidence under duress, it's different. I have a duty to the law, and to the oath I should have taken. But that hasn't come yet.'

'Would you tell me privately what he said, if he had not asked you to keep it secret?'

'Yes, I think I would, now things have come to this point.'

'Why not anticipate events?'

'No. If this clue that you talk about proves false, I might have to reconsider it. But I must wait.'

He walked on quicker. 'Look here. Can you tell me this—does the thing you heard from Tollard, what he told you, throw any blame on him?'

'In what way?'

'With regard to his wife's death.'

'I don't think so. No, I should say not.'

'Are you sure it doesn't?'

She reflected for a moment or two. 'No, I don't think it does. But I can't tell you all the same.'

He laughed bitterly. 'It's a pity Mr Barley didn't come forward earlier with his offer.'

'I didn't know him then. This is my first visit to his house. I should never have met him if he had not recently been the chairman at my Elterham lecture.'

'He—that is, Tollard—had a row with his wife the morning he drove to Elterham. Did he see that you had overlooked them when the row was in progress?'

'I saw no row. If I guessed that there had been one, at least Ned did not know it.'

'How was that?'

'They did not see me.'

Carton smiled triumphantly. 'Then, if he didn't know, he did not make you promise not to tell what you saw. It wasn't a row, but the aftermath of a row. Didn't you think so?'

She shut her lips tightly. It was unfortunate to the last degree that the man who loved her, and had come so far to tell her so, should have to figure in this rôle. It presented him in an unamiable light, in spite of the fact that she knew he was trying to do his best for her. And it presented her, by reaction, in an ungracious part.

'You won't tell me even that?' he asked.

She turned about. 'Jim, I think we had better go back. This is only worrying us both, and doing no good. I don't want to talk to you as I have to talk. I remember the old days too. But things were different then.'

He shrugged. 'Confound Tollard and all his restrictions! He gets that bedroom locked up so that no one can examine it, and he locks up your tongue.'

'The police can get into the bedroom at any time.'

He did not reply to that, but trudged back by her side. 'Very well,' he said, after a long silence. 'I'm going to be damned unpopular, but I don't care about that. I'll go up to town and put Tollard through it.'

She opened startled eyes. 'Don't do that!'

He scowled at the dusty roadway. 'If oysters won't open by themselves, you have to use a knife,' he growled. 'I shall go.'

'I shall dislike it very much if you do.'

'I'm sorry for that. But I can't help myself.'

'It's not fair to distress him after this business.'

'It won't be fair to arrest you for it.'

They said no more, but walked steadily on, side by side, each engaged with thoughts that the other could not read.

When they entered the park, and were nearing the house, they saw three or four men quartering the ground under a window, bent double, evidently searching for something with the greatest assiduity.

CHAPTER XXV

CARTON V. TOLLARD

As Elaine and Jim Carton neared the porch, Superintendent Fisher came out. He bowed to Elaine, who returned his bow and went in, but detained Carton.

'Excuse me, sir, might I have a word with you?'

'Certainly. You are not long getting your men on the job.'

'No, they rushed them down by car.'

'Have they found anything yet?'

'Not a sign, but we aren't half through. When it's a case of looking for a pellet of fluff it takes time.'

'Quite. Well, what is it?'

'It's about this air-gun. It won't work!'

Carton started. Had he not gained more than a few hours after all, too little to effect anything?

'I thought you were sending it to Birmingham?'

'We are. But Warren tried the pump, when he got back to the station, and it would not work.'

'Jorkins might have put it out of action on purpose.'

'Otherwise I would have called off the men here. It is not at all unlikely, what you say, but it does bring in a doubt.'

'Granted, my dear fellow, but you can't afford to leave the matter uninvestigated for all that. Birmingham, where the makers are, is the place where they can decide the point.'

'I telephoned Warren to that effect, and asked him to take it down at once by train.'

Less time saved! Carton had counted on their sending by post. But he must make the best of it.

'Thank you for telling me. I intend to go up to town at once. I hope you won't need me for twelve hours?'

Fisher looked at him closely. 'May I ask why, sir?'

'In this case, you may. I am going to see Mr Tollard. I want to ask him some questions. Any objection?'

'As you are not concerned with us, I don't see that I can object. In any case, we shan't be able to decide the point about the air-gun until we hear from the makers.'

'That might be tomorrow morning?'

'Or late tonight,' said Fisher grimly. 'It's just two-and-a-half hours, fast train, and Warren has instructions not to let the grass grow under his feet.'

'All right. I hope you get something to go on. Oh, here is Miss Gurdon again.'

Elaine had gone up to her bedroom deep in thought. She had hardly reached it, and shut the door, when she came to a hasty decision. Then she thought of Superintendent Fisher, and decided that she ought to speak to him. She went out at once.

Carton wondered if she were going to tell Fisher what she had refused to tell him. Fisher himself seemed to think there might be a revelation coming, for he looked very alert and eager as she came up.

'I wondered, superintendent, if there was any objection to my going up to town for a few days,' she said, without looking at Jim Carton. 'I know I am one of the witnesses, but the inquest won't be resumed for some time yet.'

Carton held his breath. The superintendent looked as amiable and bland as he could, but shook his head slightly. 'If you don't mind postponing your visit to London for a day or two,' he murmured. 'A day or two.'

'Which is it—one day, or two?' she asked, forcing a smile.

'I think I may say that, after tomorrow, you could do what you pleased—if all goes well,' he replied slowly.

Her colour ebbed a little. She knew now as well as Jim Carton what that last qualifying clause meant. If Jorkins was implicated, if the latest clue proved a good one, she was out of the affair. If it fell through, Fisher was going to move.

'I could give you my address in town.'

'I should prefer you to stay here for another day at least, miss.'

'A day isn't much,' said Carton.

She nodded to them, turned, and went back into the house.

'I am not going to miss a point if I can help it,' said Fisher apologetically. 'I should have liked to oblige the lady, but I can't let her go.'

'Do, you know why she wants to go?' Carton asked bitterly.

'No, sir. Do you?'

'I think so. She is finding me very trying. Like the rest of them, she thinks that I am being officious.'

Fisher smiled. He had thought that at first, but, after all, this man was not exactly an amateur, and he had brought some grist to the mill.

'I'll know where I am tomorrow.'

Carton turned. 'Well, I must tell my host, and get ready to go. If you really want me, telegraph to the Colonial Club. I shall leave my address there.'

'Very well, sir,' said Fisher, and went on to the men who were still persistently searching the lawn and the shrubbery.

Carton went at once to Mr Barley. The latter heard with surprise that his guest was making a hurried trip to London, but did not attempt to detain him. Perhaps he felt that Carton had not, in spite of his good intentions, put the other guests quite at their ease.

'But I'll come back by the earliest train tomorrow, if I may,' he said.

'Do,' said Barley hospitably. 'I hope it isn't a falling out with Miss Gurdon, Carton?'

'No, it has nothing to do with that,' said Jim. 'I'll get the 4.50 comfortably. I'll run up and pack a bag now.'

Tea was waiting for him when he came down again, and he ate it rapidly, and went out to the car which Mr Barley had ordered. In twenty minutes he was on the station platform, and caught the London train comfortably.

As he sat solitary in the corner of a carriage, he was musing on Warren's discovery. It seemed to him, in spite of what he had told Fisher, that the break in the air-gun coupled with the rustiness of the weapon was a strong point against that weapon having been used. Time pressed more than ever. He was banking on a theory now, and, if that went, he did not see what there was to prevent the police from arresting Elaine.

The jury might refuse to be convinced, but he could not afford to risk that. The key to the whole thing might rest in Tollard's hands. What if Tollard proved obdurate?

It was possible. More than possible. He had annoyed Tollard, and the man would be showing his roughest side. It was no pleasant interview that he faced now. But he had one lever, and he would use it—Elaine's danger.

If Tollard loved her, even if he were only the poorest kind of friend, he could not stand by and see that injustice done. If he did, Carton felt ready to believe in his guilt.

He took a taxi-cab to Eaton Place, where Tollard had his house. The butler there informed him that Tollard was not home yet.

'Would he be at his bank?'

'Unlikely, sir, but you might try his club—the Bankers'. He takes his dinner there sometimes, if he is going out in the evening.'

Carton was going away to try his luck at the club when he saw another car drive up. He waited, and saw Tollard get out.

Tollard bowed to him stiffly. 'Did you want to see me?'

'For half an hour.'

'I am afraid I cannot spare you the time.'

He was angry. Carton repressed an impulse to reply as sharply, and said in a low voice: 'This is most important. I must see you.'

'Come in,' said Tollard, and led the way into the hall, his head high, his colour rising.

They were relieved of their hats and sticks, and Tollard went into a snuggery off the hall, inviting Carton to follow him. There he closed the door.

'We did not part on very good terms, Carton,' he said, when the other had sat down. 'I shall expect you to justify your remark that this matter was important.'

'I shall,' said Carton shortly. 'I want to know something too.'

'If your questions are as injudicious and impertinent as before, I am afraid I shall refuse to reply to them.'

'Do, and be damned!' cried Carton. 'Look here, Tollard, I am not working for myself, but for Elaine, and I won't stand your attitude!'

'I don't admit that you have any right to speak for her.'

'Will you then? It seems not. You stand there, being infernally high and mighty, but you don't move a hand to save Elaine.'

'Don't be melodramatic! Save her from what?'

'Arrest!'

'Absurd!' said Tollard; but he turned white nevertheless, and sat down abruptly, to stare with angry eyes at Carton. 'Do you suggest that they could arrest her on such flimsy evidence; mere supposition?'

Carton got up. 'I have no time to waste. I am not here to explain what circumstantial evidence is, or how weighty a thing it can be. I have told you. Are you prepared to answer a question or two, or would you prefer me to go back?'

That startled Tollard. 'I am sorry if I seemed to throw doubt on your sincerity. But what leads you to think this terrible thing possible?'

'Superintendent Fisher himself. I knew directly from him that he intends to apply for a warrant against her.'

'I must go down at once.'

Carton shrugged scornfully. 'A lot of good you did before! I have given the police a new clue to work on, that will keep them busy till tomorrow. I don't know if there is anything in it. If not, things will happen. But I gained time. I have another clue on hand I have not given them. It depends on you if it can be worked out or not. If it is, I don't say that you will care for the result, but you will save Elaine from arrest, and a jury from a possible miscarriage of justice.'

Tollard looked at him eagerly. 'I don't care for myself. Let me hear your question, Carton.'

Carton looked at him straightly. 'Were you on bad terms with your wife?'

Tollard flushed, glared, and burst out. 'This is intolerable!'

Carton played his last card; he moved towards the door. 'I thought you were not very much in earnest about saving Elaine,' he sneered. 'Very well. I need not detain you any longer.'

Tollard bit his lip, and restrained himself with an obvious effort. 'Stay! Wait a moment, Carton. Was that the only question you wanted to ask?'

'There might be a few more.'

Tollard pondered, his frown marked, but his eyes turned away from his visitor. Gloom settled on his face.

'I think I may say I was not on bad terms with my wife,' he said at last.

Carton nodded. 'Put it another way; was your wife on bad terms with you?'

Tollard did not reply, but his eyes sought Carton's face again, and remained there with transparent dislike.

'I refuse to answer questions of that kind.'

Jim Carton shrugged. 'Very well. You refuse. You have done nothing all along, but try to hamper me; and, incidentally, the police, for some reason of your own.'

'I told the police what I knew.'

'With reservations, Tollard. You can't deny that! You didn't tell them all, you won't tell me.'

'Naturally, I refuse to discuss my dead wife with a mere acquaintance.'

'Let it drop. You did more than that. Out of jealousy, or some other motive, you persuaded Barley to lock up the room where the tragedy took place.'

'I had a feeling about it.'

'No doubt, but feelings have to give place to common-sense at times.'

'The police could go in and out.'

'But you were determined that I should not. Didn't you give me any credit for common decency? Did you think I was going there out of vulgar curiosity? I discovered something from my first visit. I was trying from the first to do my best for Elaine.'

'I was not jealous of you and Elaine. I loved my wife.'

'Then what the devil was your real motive, Tollard? But I needn't ask. You were always an obstinate fellow, and so long as you can preserve your petty little pride, you don't care what happens to anyone.'

Tollard was stung now. His face was very red, and his mouth worked a little. 'That's not true.'

'Then time presses. I thought I made that clear. The trouble is that I may have not sufficient time left to do anything. The clue I gave Fisher is being investigated by Inspector Warren. He went to Birmingham by fast train today. Fisher says he may be back late tonight. If the clue is no good, then they will apply for a warrant.'

'What can I do?'

'Answer my questions.'

'No!'

Carton moved to the door. 'I have had enough of you, Tollard! Good-bye. I promise to see that counsel puts you through it, if the trial comes on.'

'Wait!'

Tollard seemed broken up. He stared at Carton in silence for a few moments, when the latter came towards him. He hunched his shoulders, and clenched his hands tightly together.

'I'll let you have a note—to Barley, telling him that you may examine the room. Will that do?'

'Better than nothing,' said Jim. 'Let me have it now. I can get back the sooner.'

Tollard reflected. 'No. I'll go down with you. My car is very fast, and the trains are bad.'

'You will only be in my way,' said Carton bluntly. 'I would sooner have the note.'

Tollard shook his head. 'I promise not to interfere in any way. You shall have a free hand.'

Carton thought for a moment. 'Right!' he said. 'Hurry like blazes, and get your car!'

CARTON had counted on the police waiting until Warren had returned with his report from Birmingham. He had even assumed that the test of the air-gun might take some time. He had not allowed for a hasty decision, and a telegram.

Both came. Inspector Warren had not been three hours in the city when he left the gun-works, and went to a post-office to wire his superior. Fisher got the telegram, and started for Stowe House at seven. He went in a fast car, and turned up while the dinner was on.

When a message from him was sent in that he wished to see Mr Barley at once, the host was rather pale and disquieted. Elaine too looked disturbed.

'What can he want now?' cried Mrs Gailey.

'I shall go to see him at once, Grover,' said Mr Barley, rising.

Fisher was in the library. He had a telegram in his hand, and passed it to Mr Barley.

'This has just come from Inspector Warren, who has been in Birmingham, sir.'

'But what does it mean?' Mr Barley asked, after he had looked at it. 'I don't understand this at all. It simply says, "Gun rust old. Spring break not recent. Firm quite sure of this." But what gun does he mean, Fisher? I have not heard of any guns in connection with this case.'

Fisher explained briefly. 'Mr Carton thought that dart could be fired from an air-gun. Jorkins had one, it seemed. We examined it, found it rusty, and with a broken spring. We had it taken to the makers for an opinion. The wire gives it clearly.

They are of opinion that the gun must have been defective before the tragedy. So Mr Carton's clue proves useless.'

'I see. I see,' mused Mr Barley, rather helplessly. 'I see. But where are we now? What comes after this?'

'We may have to take a rather unpleasant step,' said Fisher grimly. 'Will you ask Miss Gurdon to see me here, sir?'

'Good heavens, Fisher! Do you really suggest—'

'I am suggesting nothing, sir. I merely ask you if you will tell Miss Gurdon I want to see her.'

'Of course, of course,' said Mr Barley, 'I'll go at once.'

Fisher read the wire again as he sat waiting for Elaine's appearance. Carton had been too ingenious after all. He had raked up a very plausible thing, but on examination it proved no more than a mare's nest.

Elaine had had time to compose herself before she went in to see the superintendent. He asked her to sit down, and then told her quietly what he had told Mr Barley.

'That leaves us where we were,' he added, 'and I shall have to ask you some questions which may be of a painful, and are certainly of a personal, nature.'

'I am not afraid of them. I hope you will not hesitate,' she said proudly.

'No,' he remarked drily. 'I shall not warn you in advance, as it is necessary to do in certain cases, or at a more advanced stage of the enquiry. You will appreciate that point.'

'I know what you mean.'

'Well, we come to the late Mrs Tollard. Prior to her death (which may have altered your feelings), you disliked her?'

'Yes.'

'Thank you. On what grounds?'

'Because she seemed to me to be making her husband unhappy.'

'Did he tell you so?'

'No. I saw it.'

'What business was it of yours?'

'I had known him since boyhood.'

'He was a friend then?'

'A great friend.'

'Had you any reason to believe that he disliked his wife?'

'I am sure he did not. I believe he loved her.'

'You say she made him unhappy.'

'People you love may make you very unhappy,' she said.

'True,' he said, and looked at her closely. 'Having said that he was in love with his wife, you do away with the possibility of his having been in love with anyone else?'

'With me, you mean?'

'Since you put it so, yes. But the fact, even if proven, that he did not love you does not eliminate another possibility.'

'Be frank,' she said quickly. 'Say you mean that I may have been, may still be in love with him?

'Your frankness helps me considerably, Miss Gurdon,' he said quietly. 'That is what I do mean.'

She nodded. 'You have only my word for it, but I assure you as solemnly as I can that I don't love Mr Tollard. I never did love him. We were on terms of friendship, nothing more than that.'

'But he was going to back you financially?'

'Mr Barley made the same offer lately, but that does not prove I was in love with Mr Barley.'

'No. That is a point. But to get on. As a result of this scheme to back you in a projected expedition, Mr Tollard and you had frequent, and, in some cases, private, consultations. At first they took place in his house; his wife objected. They afterwards took place elsewhere.'

'Yes, I have said so before.'

He nodded. 'On the day before the tragedy Mr Tollard took his wife to shop at Elterham. There is evidence that an assistant in a book-shop, and a man at the garage where they put up the car, noticed that there were strained relations between Mr Tollard and his wife.'

Elaine shrugged. 'That may be so.'

'It was so. Then when they returned here, Mrs Gailey and her friend seemed to have noticed the same thing. Mr Tollard was here on a visit, and had said nothing of leaving. Almost immediately after his return, he went to his host, and told him urgent business called him away. That urgent business was nothing more than a trip on a friend's yacht.'

Elaine interrupted. 'I can understand that. If he had had a quarrel with his wife, he might wish to get away for a little, to let matters calm down.'

'Well, he made an excuse, and went away. Mrs Tollard had a bedroom between two bedrooms formerly occupied by you and her husband. His was empty that night. You heard sounds, and went in. You say you found Mrs Tollard lying on the floor, either dead or dying. You believed she was dead, but the doctor thinks she must have been just on the point of death then. That is immaterial. The fact is that she had been ill, that you went in to her room before anyone else in the house. You raised her up, almost to a sitting position?'

'Yes, I did.'

'Are you prepared to deny having visited her, or having entered her bedroom in the night, or at any time between the hour when you retired and the moment when you found her?'

'Absolutely; on oath when necessary. I had no occasion to go there, and did not go there.'

'Very well. To go further back: you brought some darts to Mr Barley; poisoned darts, which he bought with the blow-pipe for a trophy. You had also some other unpoisoned darts which you once used to demonstrate the blow-pipe on the lawn?'

'I sold six in the quiver to Mr Barley. I handed the quiver to you, pointing out that only five were left. I had already pointed it out to Mr Barley.'

'You knew, of course, that the quiver would be examined by us, once it was established that Mrs Tollard had been killed by a poisoned dart of the kind Mr Barley bought.'

'I assumed that, of course. I am merely explaining that I didn't dispute the fact that the dart found in the body came from the quiver, but actually was the first to point it out.'

He admired her lucidity as much as her courage. 'Thank you. Now I am going to put a very pertinent question indeed; so pertinent that I shall not try to force an answer. I may put what construction I please on your refusal to reply, but—'

'Let me hear it. I understand,' she said impatiently.

'Are you prepared to declare that when you entered Mrs Tollard's room that morning, you had nothing in your hand?'

'I am. My hands were empty. If you mean that my raising her up into a sitting position, or nearly, gave me an opportunity to wound her with a dart concealed in my hand, I deny it absolutely! I had nothing in my hand. I simply did what I have told you.'

'She is a cool one!' thought Fisher, studying her closely. She knew what he was after all the time, and did not refuse to meet his tacit challenge.

'Thank you. You are aware, of course, that you will be asked the same or similar questions at the adjourned inquest's resumption, and that you will then be on oath?'

'Of course. I can only repeat what I have said—the truth.'

He nodded. 'Do you know that I have certain powers that I can exercise at once, or in a very short space of time?'

'That does not affect me, superintendent. No powers can make any difference. If you arrest me tomorrow, I shall still say what I have said today.'

'Who said I might arrest you tomorrow?' he demanded sharply.

She shrugged. 'I am aware that you may.'

He saw that he could not shake her. 'Miss Gurdon,' he observed, 'don't assume too much. I have put all the questions that are most likely to pain you. I need not tell you that anything I may ask after this is as likely to prove your innocence of any hand in this matter as—'

'As my guilt?' she said scornfully.

He shrugged. 'So I am going back to the darts, but impersonally, if you know what I mean. The quiver hung in the hall. I am of opinion that taking out one dart from that quiver could be effected easily enough.'

'Yes. A native has his weapons placed so that he can use them quickly. A slip, or a bungle, to him means a lost dinner, perhaps a lost life.'

'But however easily the dart was withdrawn, a ladder was needed to mount to the height of the wall-trophy?'

'I got one. Mr Barley found a step-ladder in the kitchen. He told me before dinner today that the ladder was usually kept in a cupboard under the stairs.'

'But he found it in the kitchen?'

'Yes.'

'Then the person who took the dart from the quiver may have used that very ladder?'

'It is quite possible.'

'You are sure you never used that ladder, before you used it that morning in Mr Barley's presence?'

'Certainly not. I can assure you of that.'

Fisher mused. 'And it is kept under the stairs in a cupboard? I may tell now that we did not worry about that ladder because of the nature of our theory. We were working on an assumption—'

'That I did it?'

He did not answer that question, but went on: 'But we have still plenty of time. Your fingerprints may be on it, of course, as they were on the blow-pipe. But that proves nothing. Unless we find them *duplicated* at about the same height.'

'You won't find that.'

'If we don't, we may find others. Wood is a rather tell-tale material, Miss Gurdon!'

He watched her, to see if she flinched; but she shrugged.

'Then it seems to me the sooner you get the ladder, and forget your erroneous assumption about me, the better,' she observed sarcastically.

He rose. As he got to his feet, it flashed on his mind that she might have sold Mr Barley six darts for curios, but only put five in the quiver before it was hung up. But he did not mention that possibility, reserving it for consideration later, if the step-ladder proved a barren clue.

'Let us get on to Mr Barley at once, and have it out,' he said. 'I suppose dinner will be over by now?'

'I should think so,' she replied calmly. 'I'll go to the drawing-room and get him.'

'I'll wait in the hall,' said the superintendent.

CHAPTER XXVII

THE LUCK OF THE LADDER

Mr Barley and Elaine joined Fisher in the hall a few moments later. Mr Barley was calmer again. He had feared that the superintendent had come so hurriedly that evening to make an arrest, and was much relieved when Elaine came into the drawing-room without any appearance of agitation.

'What is it now, Fisher?' he asked.

'I want to see the step-ladder that usually is put in a cupboard, sir.'

'It must be there now, superintendent. Mr Carton put it there while I was watching.'

Fisher's brow clouded. 'Why; was he examining it?'

'Yes.'

'Most irregular!' said Fisher. 'He had no business to do that, and I shall tell him so pretty sharply.'

'I'm sorry,' said Barley nervously. 'Do you want to see it now? I'll go and get the key. Miss Gurdon, I think, knows where the back staircase is. If she will take you there, I'll join you in a minute.'

Elaine took Fisher away, and through the swing-door that separated the servants' quarters from the main building. Neither of them heard a car draw up at the front of the house, nor knew that Tollard and Carton had arrived from town.

But Mr Barley met them as he came downstairs from his bedroom, where he had searched in vain for the key of the cupboard, until he had recollected that it was not that key, but the one from Mrs Tollard's room that he had put away.

He greeted the appearance of the two hot men with surprise, told them hastily that Superintendent Fisher was in the house, and anxious to see a step-ladder that was kept under the stairs.

'He is much annoyed with you, Mr Carton, for examining it,' he added.

Carton started. 'Good heavens! I had the key of that cupboard in my pocket all the time. Here it is. But don't tell Fisher.'

'I'll take it to him at once,' said Mr Barley. 'You should not have done that, Mr Carton.'

'I want another key now, Mr Barley,' said Jim. 'The key of Mrs Tollard's room. I must see that room at once.'

'I have agreed to his making an examination of it,' said Ned Tollard.

Mr Barley hesitated. 'My dear fellow, Fisher may not like it. He is waiting for me now.'

Carton frowned. 'A lot turns on this. Let me have the key, sir. I want to look round before Fisher has time to get up.'

'Please,' said Tollard.

Mr Barley made a nervous gesture, then ran upstairs again, and was coming down with the key, when he met Carton and Tollard ascending.

'You must take the responsibility,' he said.

'Willingly,' said Jim Carton. 'Come on, Tollard.'

Barley went down to Fisher. In the passage on the first floor Carton saw Mrs Gailey suddenly emerge from her room.

'I should like to have her, too. Do you mind?' he asked.

Tollard shrugged. 'If it is necessary.'

Netta exclaimed on seeing Tollard there, but Carton spoke a few words to her, and she accompanied them to the door of the room where Mrs Tollard had died, and followed them in, when the door was unlocked and the light turned on.

Tollard remained near the door, his shoulders leaned against the wall, his head bent. He did not appear to wish to follow Carton's movements very closely.

Carton turned on another light over the dressing-table, and quickly went to the spot where Mrs Tollard had been found lying. He looked to every side, and presently asked Mrs Gailey if she would mind standing with her back to one wall of the bayed window. She assented, with some hesitation, and stood at a point he indicated, while he remained in the room in a line with the wall of the bay, and appeared to be studying her in profile.

'Now a yard further on,' he said.

'Is this necessary?' said Tollard, looking up.

'Very,' said Carton. 'Right, Mrs Gailey!'

She could not move any further along that side, for she was already beside the straight front of the window.

Carton took a sight along the wall, and placed his hand at a certain point.

'Now you can move away,' he said, and she obeyed him eagerly. 'Would you mind coming over here, Tollard, and telling me something?—Fisher may be here at any minute.'

Tollard walked over. 'What is it?'

'You must have been fairly familiar with this room when your wife slept here.'

'In a sense, I suppose I was.'

'Did anything hang just here, or near here?' He indicated a point on the wall.

Tollard stared. 'No. Wait a moment. I imagine a little wall-calendar hung there. My wife always carried it about with her.'

'You do not see it now?'

'No.'

Mrs Gailey gave a little cry. 'I hear them coming up the stairs. Shall I go?

'No, please stay! I shall want you again,' said Carton.

He went over to the door, and threw it open. Mr Barley and the superintendent were coming along the passage. Fisher carried the step-ladder, a handkerchief round his hand.

'Now, sir,' said Fisher, as he stood in the doorway, and glared at Carton. 'What do you mean by this? It's tampering with evidence, and obstructing the police! I'll make you smart for this!'

Carton bowed. 'I gave the key to Mr Barley the moment I knew you were in the house. I intended to show the ladder to you later.'

'You had no business to move it, or examine it, at all.'

'You can hold me responsible.'

'You have no right to be in this room either!'

'I have the right of common-sense, but I'll waive that.'

Fisher was heated. 'You'll explain at once what you are doing, or have been doing in this room; and for what purpose.'

'Willingly,' said Carton, very gravely. 'I have been examining this room to find who killed Mrs Tollard. That was my only purpose.'

'And I suppose you have found another fine clue like that air-gun?' said Fisher.

His annoyance was natural, and Carton did not blame him.

'No. I have, I think, found who killed Mrs Tollard.'

Tollard gave a cry, and went up to him. 'If you're making a joke of this I'll give you a damned good thrashing.'

'It is no joke,' said Carton quietly. 'Have you examined the ladder, superintendent?'

'No. When I heard you were here interfering again, I came up at once.'

Carton nodded. 'Very well; then perhaps you will follow the details of my little investigation before you think of taking any action against me.'

'If you're quick about it,' said Fisher harshly.

'I'll try to be,' said Carton. 'Tollard, didn't you tell me just now—'

'I said there was a little calendar hanging on the wall, but what has that to do with it?' cried Tollard fiercely.

'Where do you think it was?'

Tollard walked across to the wall where Mrs Gailey had stood. 'Here, I think. Yes, there is a small nail-hole.'

'But no nail?' said Carton.

Fisher propped the ladder against the wall, and hurried over. 'What's this? Oh, I see. There had been a small nail here. It has fallen out.'

'Or been taken out,' said Carton.

The others murmured surprise and perplexity, except Fisher, who looked more grim than ever.

'Well, sir, if it has?'

'If it has, superintendent, will you please examine that ladder thoroughly? Under peril of your displeasure, I took the risk of examining it myself, and you will find a small cross made in ink near the top of one of the uprights.'

For a moment Fisher seemed about to make some hot reply, but he calmed himself, brought the ladder, set it up under a lamp, and drew a lens from his pocket.

'This you mean, sir?' he said presently, breaking a silence which had grown more intense each moment.

'That,' said Carton. 'You will see, I think, that there is a tiny splinter on the edge of the wood.'

'And dried blood on it,' said Fisher. He drew a deep breath, and again turned to the ladder to examine that tiny clue more closely.

'Someone went in the night to that cupboard, and got the ladder,' Carton went on, 'took it into the hall, and got a dart out of the quiver hung on the wall. Either in ascending or descending, that tiny splinter made a scratch, and drew blood. That person afterwards found it difficult to put the ladder back in the cupboard without making a noise, so simply removed it to the kitchen. It was found there by Mr Barley, when Miss Gurdon asked him to get her one.'

'That's true,' cried Mr Barley excitedly.

Fisher had now turned, and was listening attentively. 'Go on, sir.'

'If you will look also on the same upright, but nearer the bottom, superintendent, you will see that there are several very fine splinters; attached to one of them is a silky fibre or two, that I should like you to examine, and afterwards send to a textile expert.'

Tollard moved closer, his eyes wide. Fisher bent quickly, and then straightened himself, with something held between the tips of forceps he had taken from his pocket.

'You are right, sir,' he said wonderingly. 'This is a fibre of silk.'

'Put it away carefully, and I shall try to hurry on,' Carton said. 'I come to this room now. I was looking for something, and I found it.'

'What was that, sir?'

'A pure speculation, but it has come out all right. I wanted to find a hole in the wall, and I found it. That calendar Mr Tollard admits seeing there formerly is gone. So is the tiny nail on which it hung. You see that for yourselves.'

'Of course,' said Tollard.

'But I don't see the point,' remarked Fisher.

'I am coming to that. Mrs Gailey, you were kind enough to help me before, will you help me again?'

Netta Gailey was trembling with nervous excitement, but she nodded, and stammered that she would do what she could.

Carton thanked her, took a matchbox from his pocket, and sharpened one end of a match hurriedly with his penknife.

'Watch this carefully, superintendent,' he said. 'I am going to insert one end of this in the hole left by the withdrawal of that nail.'

'Very well, sir. I am watching.'

Carton inserted the wooden match in the hole where the calendar had hung, and motioned to Netta Gailey, who came forward slowly.

'Will you please stand a little away from the wall, and lean back against it gently? Opposite that match. No, a little more to the left. Right! Don't move any more. Lean back. Stop!'

Poor Netta was flushed and self-conscious, but she held that pose very well, and Carton turned to Fisher.

'Will you put your hand flat, and very carefully behind Mrs Gailey's shoulder?'

Tollard put a hand over his eyes, and went blindly towards the door. Elaine followed him, her face tragic. They left the room together, as Fisher obeyed Carton, and slid his hand along the wall behind Netta Gailey's back.

No one attempted to stop them. The door closed. Carton did not even look round, and though Netta's eyes turned to follow Tollard's retreating figure, she kept her position bravely.

Fisher drew a deep breath. 'I can feel it, sir. It is just under the left shoulder-blade.'

Carton nodded, his face intent. 'The two ladies were about the same height. That is why I asked Mrs Gailey to help me.'

Netta shuddered a little. 'Please may I go now?'

'Yes, you have been very good,' said Carton. 'I don't know what we would have done without you. I know you didn't like it, but it is over now, and you may know that it was a great help.'

She left her place, and stood near the middle of the bedroom. Fisher looked at Carton, and shrugged.

'I don't care if you did, in a way, forestall us, sir,' he said generously. 'You got on this when we hadn't a notion of it.'

'A bit of luck, superintendent,' said Carton. 'That was all. I can assure you that, if I had been at all certain of my ground, I would have put this clue in your hands at once. But I hated the idea of interfering again, only to find that I had not effected anything.'

Superintendent Fisher nodded. 'We aren't out for glory, sir. We want to clear up the case, that is all. If I am not much mistaken, this does clear it up finally.'

'We shall have to hear Tollard's story,' said Carton.

Netta had been listening, turning to look first at one and then the other of the speakers. She burst out now.

'But what does it mean? What do you know? Have you really found who killed Mrs Tollard?'

Fisher nodded. 'I think so, Mrs Gailey. I shall have to have the fibres of silk compared with those in the dressing-gown of course, but I think there is no doubt where they came from.'

'But I don't see it even then?'

'It is really quite simple, now that we have these clues in our hands,' said Fisher. 'The two fibres of silk I found on the splinter on the ladder just now are green, so far as I can see. They came from the garment of someone who climbed up that ladder to get a dart from the quiver on the wall. Mrs Tollard was wearing a green silk dressing-gown when found dead. I have no doubt that the fibres came from that; which proves that she was the person who took the dart.'

'But why?'

'I am coming to that. There was also, as Mr Carton here discovered, a splinter higher up which had caught the arm of the person climbing.'

'And Dr Browne told me there was a slight scratch on Mrs Tollard's forearm,' interrupted Carton.

'I saw that,' said Fisher. 'But, as it was dry, I assumed that it had been inflicted some time before, and therefore had no bearing on the case. As it turns out, it partly proves that Mrs Tollard climbed that ladder, either when your party were away on the picnic at Heber Castle, the afternoon prior to the tragedy, or in the night. I am inclined to the latter theory, as she would then be undisturbed.'

Netta gasped. 'It is unbelievable!'

Fisher continued. 'What followed, as nearly as I can recon-struct it, with the valuable demonstration just given us by Mr Carton, is this: She returned to her room with the dart, and possibly went to bed. She rose after dawn, her mind made up, and removed the wall-calendar, which we found—though we attached no importance to it—in the wastepaper basket when we searched the room. A small nail was twisted in the ribbon that held it up when in position.'

Carton raised his eyebrows. 'You never told me that.'

'I saw no need to. I could not think it had any meaning. But, to go on: Mrs Tollard removed the nail from the wall, and inserted the butt of the thorn-like dart in the hole it left. Then she stood with her back to it, the point almost, but not quite, on a level with the lower edge of her shoulder-blade, and leaned gently back. That leaning movement gave to the dart the appearance of having been driven in from a position slightly below. Is that your theory, Mr Carton?'

'You have interpreted it exactly, superintendent.'

'Then, as I see it, she lay down on the floor near the window. I should say that death followed within an hour, perhaps much less.'

'But she cried out?' said Netta, white as a sheet.

Fisher and Carton exchanged glances. Carton shook his head almost imperceptibly. He thought it unnecessary for Netta to hear all. Fisher understood him, and continued hurriedly. 'We may take it that even suicides are not immune from pain. But I have no doubt now that Mrs Tollard committed suicide.'

Netta burst suddenly into tears. Fisher signed to Carton, who took her gently by the arm, and led her out of the room, and down a further corridor which led to her bedroom. He left her there, and returned to Fisher, who was gently scraping with the point of a fine penknife at the hole in the wall, and removing from it, with the points of his forceps, some fine vegetable fibres.

'By Jove! That's some of the silk-cotton!' he cried, when he saw what Fisher was doing.

'And I think it clinches the case,' replied Fisher. 'We'll go below now, sir, and hear Mr Tollard's story.'

CHAPTER XXVIII

THE BROODING SILENCE

THE sound of voices came from the library as the three men descended the stairs. From the moment when Carton had completed his demonstration until they left the room which had been the scene of the tragedy, Mr Barley had not said a single word. He had remained stupefied, and silent. The whole thing had been so unexpected by him that he was stunned by it.

Now, as they paused outside the door of the library, he shook his head mournfully.

'She meant more than that,' he said, as if to himself. 'Surely she must have been out of her mind?'

Fisher, his hand on the handle of the door, replied softly: 'Jealousy is a frequent cause of madness, sir. But quietly now. We shall hear more in a few minutes.'

As they went in, they saw Tollard sitting by the table, his head bent on his hands. Elaine was in a chair near the window. She was staring out blankly when they entered, and did not look round.

The mixture of misery and horror on Tollard's face for a moment immobilised the three men on the threshold. Then Fisher quietly closed the door behind him, and spoke.

'May we have a word with you, sir?'

Tollard nodded mechanically. 'You think it was suicide?'

'I am afraid so, sir.'

Elaine rose from her chair. 'I had better go.'

Fisher made no objection. He let her out, and went to stand near Tollard. Barley and Carton moved over to the window embrasure, and stood there together.

The superintendent's voice was sympathetic as he began. 'There is hardly a doubt, sir, that your wife took her own life. But a more difficult question arises from that. It will be for you to decide if the coroner's jury is to know that their verdict is *felo-de-se*, or if these other and more painful things are to be gone into in court.'

'If you are satisfied, that it is suicide, I am prepared to take your view,' said Tollard, in a stifled voice.

'I think you are wise, sir. That silk fibre came, I am sure, from your wife's dressing-gown. She obtained the dart, and used it in the way Mr Carton demonstrated. I have since found some minute traces of silk-cotton in the hole into which the dart had been thrust.'

'I am prepared to accept that,' Tollard murmured bitterly.

'Then, sir, we come to the motive; but, to understand that, we shall have to ask you for the story of your relations with your wife since Miss Gurdon's return to England. If you prefer to tell that story to me alone, I shall ask Mr Carton and Mr Barley to withdraw.'

Tollard shook his head. 'God knows I did it for her sake,' he said. 'I was afraid of this, and yet I couldn't think it. I hated the idea of the publicity; not for my sake, but for hers. I loved her, Fisher! I have never faltered in that. I meant to say nothing of our difficulties. I thought the case would fall through, and be forgotten.'

'It was nearly sending Miss Gurdon into the dock,' said Fisher.

Tollard bit his lip. 'I know that now. Because that is so, I would rather Mr Barley stayed, and Carton too. I owe it to them to explain. I have already told Miss Gurdon.'

Fisher bowed. 'Thank you, sir. Take your time. This is a painful thing for you, and we'll make every allowance.'

For a few moments there was silence. Tollard looked straight before him, his eyes reminiscent, tragically lacklustre.

'There was never anything stranger than our married life,' he began at last. 'I loved her, and she loved me. I have no doubt that she loved me. But we had different tastes, sympathies; we were as different as man and wife can be. Until Miss Gurdon came back to England we were very happy. But even then I discovered a temperament in my wife that I could hardly understand. A man of my sanguine temperament can understand a temper that flares up, and is gone. My wife was not like that. I see now that the brooding, introspective temperament is more dangerous to peace of mind than the other. I got a glimpse of her when little differences cropped up, as they do in all married lives. But it was only when Miss Gurdon visited me, and I undertook to finance an expedition, that I realised to what a pass jealous love can drive a woman.'

He paused a moment, wiped his forehead, and went on: 'From the first, I want you to understand that Miss Gurdon was not responsible. It was she who insisted that we should discuss matters at my house. To the very end she thought it was unwise to let Margery even appear to stand outside the circle of our interests. It is due to me that she has been so reticent since the tragedy. I insisted that as little publicity as possible should be given to my differences with my wife. I knew that they were the result of my wife's love for me, and the, perhaps mistaken, attitude I had taken up.'

'I understand that,' said Fisher gravely.

Tollard nodded. 'They were antipathetic from the first. My wife disliked, and finally hated her. She never made a scene with me. She was not a woman to reproach one in words. But, strange as it may seem, I can assure you that after I had arranged to finance this expedition, and she had declared that she would not allow Miss Gurdon to come to the house, she hardly said a word to me when we were alone. She took refuge in a silence that I felt more deeply than any reproaches. For months, except in public, she rarely spoke. I was cut to the heart, but I did not know what to do.'

He drummed with his fingers on the table as he continued: 'I decided at last to ask Miss Gurdon to let me withdraw my promise. She agreed readily. Then it occurred to me that I might consult Margery's doctor. She had suffered once from neurasthenia, and I knew that he was an expert in that kind of case. I went to him, put the case before him, and asked his advice. He told me categorically that I would make a great mistake if I took the line I proposed taking. He assured me that people of Margery's temperament would not be convinced by my action. It would seem to them a confession of guilt. "Be firm, but very kind," he told me. "Let her see that you are unconscious of any wrongdoing. This Miss Gurdon will set off on her expedition. It will take a year or two, and your wife will come round. She takes after her father. He is a curious man, and has been spoiled by people giving way to him. Neurasthenics are like hysterical people. Too much coddling and sympathy does harm, not good." I believe he gave me the best advice he could. At least, he convinced me. I determined to go on as I had been doing.'

'I don't see that you could have acted otherwise, after what the doctor told you,' said Fisher.

'Perhaps not. Perhaps not.' Tollard wiped his brow again, and bowed his head. 'I told Miss Gurdon, and she reluctantly agreed. We discussed the matter for some time, until she bowed to the specialist's superior knowledge. I blame myself very deeply for overruling her. It has subjected her to a great deal of gossip and pain. But I can't go back on that now.

'We came here on Mr Barley's invitation. I knew Miss Gurdon was to be here, and I welcomed the opportunity of demonstrating to my wife that my relations with that lady were only those of friendship, and common interests in exploration, I discovered, in a day or two, how mistaken I was. I could see that Margery was in a silent fury all day. When I took her to Elterham, on the morning of the day before her death, I knew that it was a mistake. I could read her face by then, and I determined at all costs to leave the house; where, if I had remained, I would have had to meet Miss Gurdon daily, under my wife's eye. So I made the excuse of urgent business, and left that same afternoon for London, going on from there to Lymington, where I joined my friend on his yacht. The next thing I knew was the telegram which told me that she was dead.'

He bit his lip, and stopped. Silence fell again. When he had recovered himself a little, Fisher put a question.

'You see, sir, what the circumstances surrounding this tragedy imply? You could not be aware before, but you are aware now that this was not planned only as a suicide, but as a suicide that would have the appearance of murder; the guilt of which would most probably seem to attach to Miss Gurdon?'

Tollard suppressed a groan. 'I can only think she was not responsible for her actions.'

Fisher nodded. 'Nothing seems more certain. Come, sir! We won't harass you any more. If I can arrange it so, there will be no mention of this extraneous matter at the inquest. We had better subpoena this London specialist, to give evidence to the effect that your wife was neurasthenic. On the strength of that, the jury will bring it in as "suicide while of unsound mind"—Do you agree to that finally?'

'I do,' said Tollard. 'Thank you, superintendent. And you, Carton, and Mr Barley. Now, if you don't mind, I'll leave you. This has shaken me badly.'

The superintendent stood aside, and Tollard rose and went out. No one followed him. The three men stood silent and grave. From the hall they could hear Tollard's heavy footfalls going slowly away.

CHAPTER XXIX

A JOINT EXPEDITION

AUGUST had come when Jim Carton and Elaine again went down to Stowe House to stay with Mr Barley. Elaine was going out to South America on the expedition she had formerly planned, so was glad to snatch a respite from her preparations, and the thousand and one things that needed to be seen to before she could set out.

Tollard had gone abroad for a long trip, after the adjourned inquest had resulted in a verdict of the kind Superintendent Fisher had foreshadowed, and his guarantee to Elaine had been withdrawn at her request.

Mr Barley stood in now. He had his wish, and it had been agreed that he was to finance the Matta Grosso expedition. The Gurdon-Barley expedition, the newspapers called it, and the old man was already anticipating, and gloating innocently over, his vicarious triumphs-to-be.

What Jim Carton thought of it, is another matter, and it was from a benevolent anxiety to get his views that Mr Barley asked him down to Stowe the week that Elaine was to be there. There were no other guests.

It seemed to Mr Barley that Elaine was very different from the composed, rather assured, young woman who had stayed with him in the early summer. She was softer, brighter. He wondered if the call of the wild had worked this metamorphosis, or the fact that her long-planned expedition had now every prospect of a successful start.

Carton, too, noticed the change, and was happier, but he did not make the mistake his host made in attributing Elaine's new attractiveness to such a material cause. He knew now that the early summer had seen her under the cloud caused by the Tollards' troubles, in which she had been involved against her will, and her better judgment. The shadow had lifted; that was all.

'I wonder, Elaine, if you want a man to join your expedition?' he asked her, twinkling, on the third day of their stay. 'I know of one, who is out of work, and might consider it. He's a hard worker, knows something of the wilds, and would go without pay.'

'I might think of it,' said Elaine smiling. 'Who is he?'

Jim came closer. 'Not very far away, my dear,' he said softly. 'Though nothing would make him happier than to be still nearer! Darling, if you go off on this jaunt. I'll follow you! That's as true a thing as I ever said. But I would sooner you took me? Have I a bare chance, dear?'

Elaine flushed, and was no more the composed young woman of whom the world knew most.

'I hate the idea of going,' she said rapidly, but softly. 'I was so keen on it when I came here before. But I'll love it if you come, old boy.'

'Will you?' he cried, and his eyes glowed now. 'Do you mean it—really? As I mean it?'

She did not reply, and he needed none. She went into his arms, and then, suddenly, Paradise was lost for a while. Mr Barley, full of the most sudden and benevolent intentions, entered the room.

They jumped apart guiltily, and he stared at them; a smile taking the place of the startled look that had come to his face when he realised things.

'I believe you have forestalled us again, Carton!' he cried gaily. 'I had a splendid idea, and was just coming in to put it to you both—'

'It's not too late to tell it, sir,' said Carton, smiling.

'It was only to suggest that it might be a good plan if you

two joined forces in this expedition. But you seem to have settled that already.'

'On mutual terms!' said Jim.

THE END

THE DETECTIVE STORY CLUB

FOR DETECTIVE CONNOISSEURS

recommends

"The Man with the Gun."

THE BLACKMAILERS

By THE MASTER OF THE FRENCH CRIME STORY—EMILE GABORIAU

EMILE GABORIAU is France's greatest detective writer. *The Blackmailers* is one of his most thrilling novels, and is full of exciting surprises. The story opens with a sensational bank robbery in Paris, suspicion falling immediately upon Prosper Bertomy, the young cashier whose extravagant living has been the subject of talk among his friends. Further investigation, however, reveals a network of blackmail and villainy which seems as if it would inevitably close round Prosper and the beautiful Madeleine, who is deeply in love with him. Can he prove his innocence in the face of such damning evidence?

THE REAL THING *from* SCOTLAND YARD!

THE CRIME CLUB

By FRANK FRÖEST, Ex-Supt. C.I.D., Scotland Yard, and George Dilnot

YOU will seek in vain in any book of reference for the name of The Crime Club. Its watchword is secrecy. Its members wear the mask of mystery, but they form the most powerful organisation against master criminals ever known. The Crime Club is an international club composed of men who spend their lives studying crime and criminals. In its headquarters are to be found experts from Scotland Yard, many foreign detectives and secret service agents. This book tells of their greatest victories over crime, and is written in association with George Dilnot by a former member of the Criminal Investigation Department of Scotland Yard.

LOOK FOR THE MAN WITH THE GUN

THE DETECTIVE STORY CLUB

FOR DETECTIVE CONNOISSEURS

recommends

" The Man with the Gun."

MR. BALDWIN'S FAVOURITE

THE LEAVENWORTH CASE
By ANNA K. GREEN

THIS exciting detective story, published towards the end of last century, enjoyed an enormous success both in England and America. It seems to have been forgotten for nearly fifty years until Mr. Baldwin, speaking at a dinner of the American Society in London, remarked : " An American woman, a successor of Poe, Anna K. Green, gave us *The Leavenworth Case*, which I still think one of the best detective stories ever written." It is a remarkably clever story, a masterpiece of its kind, and in addition to an exciting murder mystery and the subsequent tracking down of the criminal, the writing and characterisation are excellent. *The Leavenworth Case* will not only grip the attention of the reader from beginning to end but will also be read again and again with increasing pleasure.

CALLED BACK

By HUGH CONWAY

BY the purest of accidents a man who is blind accidentally comes on the scene of a murder. He cannot see what is happening, but he can hear. He is seen by the assassin who, on discovering him to be blind, allows him to go without harming him. Soon afterwards he recovers his sight and falls in love with a mysterious woman who is in some way involved in the crime. . . . The mystery deepens, and only after a series of memorable thrills is the tangled skein unravelled.

LOOK FOR THE MAN WITH THE GUN